Bleeding Hearts

To Dana,
Love always!

Josh 11/9/01

To Dana,

for always,

Joy

1/9/11

Bleeding Hearts

Josh Aterovis

Renaissance Alliance Publishing, Inc.
Nederland, Texas

ISBN 1-930928-68-8

First Printing 2001

9 8 7 6 5 4 3 2 1

Cover art by Josh Aterovis
Cover design by Linda Callaghan

Published by:

Renaissance Alliance Publishing, Inc.
PMB 238, 8691 9th Avenue
Port Arthur, Texas 77642-8025

Find us on the World Wide Web at
http://www.rapbooks.com

Printed in the United States of America

Acknowledgements:

I'd like to thank Luke, without whom I would have never begun to write, Jon for being my constant source of strength, encouragement and love, Auntie Blacksheep (us Black Sheep have to stick together!) for all her support and acceptance, and last but not least, everyone who has read *Bleeding Hearts* as a work in progress and encouraged me to continue writing, offered critiques or provided me with assistance. This has been a labor of love and you have all made it possible. Thank you.

This book is dedicated to...

...my little brother, Luke.
...the love of my life, Jon.
...Auntie Blacksheep.
...all the Lost Boys.

Chapter
1

There is a flower native to North America called bleeding hearts. It's a delicate looking plant with long arching branches that, when in bloom, are covered with tiny heart-shaped blossoms. Each blossom has what looks like a drop of blood coming out of the bottom of it—hence the name. It likes shade and doesn't much care for wind. Unfortunately, we were getting a lot of wind that day.

I was sitting at the window overlooking the garden watching the wind blow furiously through the brightly colored flowers. Many of the plants had already lost their petals, but so far the bleeding hearts were holding their own. Which is more than I could say for myself. I was feeling more and more lost by the second.

Suddenly, it seemed that I had to do something for the plants. I couldn't do much for myself, but maybe I could save them. I stood up and went outside into the storm; no one said anything to me and I wasn't surprised. Once I was outside, the wind buffeted my body and the driving rain almost instantly soaked me, my tears mixing with the raindrops. I didn't care. I was half hoping the raging storm would blow me away—or at least blow away the storm raging inside me.

But wait, I should back up. I've probably lost you already. I'm not even sure where to start, but I'm pretty sure the middle isn't the best place. I was never very good at language arts; my teacher said I lacked imagination. But I guess maybe like Lewis Carroll said in Alice in Wonderland, "Start at the beginning and when you come to an end...stop."

My name is Killian—Killian Travers Kendall. I'm sixteen years old and a junior in high school. It's only two weeks into the school year, but I've already learned a lot, mostly about myself. I'm not the same person I was on the first day of school. But we'll get to that.

My father is the District Attorney for the county we live in on the Eastern Shore of Maryland. The Eastern Shore is a peninsula bordered by the Chesapeake Bay on one side and the Atlantic Ocean on the other. It's mostly a rural area, filled with sprawling flat farms with small towns interspersed at random. My family lives in an old-fashioned town and my father is an old-fashioned kind of man. Over all I would say I've been a disappointment to him. He was the star of his football team, had every girl in the school drooling over him, handsome, charismatic: he had everything going for him. I, on the other hand, couldn't catch a ball if you held a gun to my head, have never dated a girl, and I'm very shy. I took after him in looks though, that's something at least. I have the same piercing blue eyes (which I hide behind glasses), wavy blonde hair and strong, even features. I weigh in at about 135 lbs and 5'7". My father's been trying to get me to try contacts for years, but the idea of sticking my finger in my eye is repulsive to me so I've stuck with my wire frames.

I guess I get my shyness from my mother. We're a lot alike in personality. She has a way of melting into the background, almost chameleon-like. No one ever remembers meeting her. The only time she ever seems animated is when my father is around. It's almost like she worships the ground he walks on. And that's where the similarity between us ends.

I don't have any real close friends, but I hang out with Asher Davis, Jesse O'Donnell and Zachary Phillips. We are the same age, but that's about all we have in common. They all three play soccer like it's the way to salvation, so they are all in shape and very built. Asher has curly dark brown hair, light gray eyes that seem almost silver at times, eternally rosy cheeks, and is a few inches taller than me. Jesse is a little over six feet tall, but thin, with reddish-blonde hair, freckles, and bright green eyes. Zachary, or Zack, has brown hair, bluish-gray eyes, and is about the same size as Asher.

I'm usually the odd man out since I don't play sports and I'm smaller than the rest of them. I'm the last one to get called when someone wants to do something, almost like an afterthought. I don't even remember how I ended up in their little group; we'd grown up in the same neighborhood and our parents knew each other. Everyone just always assumed we were friends and it had just always have been easier to go along with it than make an effort to find someone that I'd have more in common with. Making new friends was a terrifying concept to someone as shy as I was.

But this is all just background. The story really starts with the first day back to school. I wasn't looking forward to it. I do well enough in school, but even with my very popular friends I don't fit in and I know it. The only thing I like about school is theater. There I excel. There I can lose myself in a part. There I am actually looked up to. And that is where everything changed.

Theater was my last class of the day. My first day back had been fairly uneventful up to this point and I didn't really expect this period to be any different. The drama teacher, Mrs. Tatum, gave us her usual speech about this being a "play" class but not to expect any playing. "This is a serious class," she intoned imperiously.

Just then the door opened and a head popped in.

"Yes?" Mrs. Tatum asked.

The rest of the body came into view. And a nice body it was. I'd never seen him before so he must have been new. He stood about my height, maybe a little taller and slightly more built. He had red-gold hair that seemed to stick up in every direction and elfin features. In fact, he looked amazingly like an elf. Even to his incredibly green eyes. I wondered if they were colored contacts. Then I wondered why I cared. Why was I so intrigued by this guy?

"My name is Seth," he said, "Seth Connelly. I'm transferring into this class. Here's the paperwork."

He handed her some papers and looked around the room. He carried himself with an air of confidence. Not arrogance exactly, but not far from it. After Mrs. Tatum had looked over the paperwork she looked up at him, staring for a second.

"Looks like it's all in order. Why don't you find a seat, Mr. Connelly, and we can continue with the class," she said finally.

He looked around the room again and locked eyes with me. I

hadn't looked away since he'd walked in. Maybe he'd sensed me staring. I quickly looked away. Next thing I knew, he was sitting down right beside me.

"Hi," he said extending his hand, "I'm Seth."

"Killian," I said shaking his hand. He held on a second longer than seemed necessary then smiled at me before turning back toward Mrs. Tatum. My head seemed to be swimming and I felt warm. I wondered if I was coming down with something. I mean I couldn't be attracted to Seth. He was a guy! But I'd never felt like this before.

I tore my eyes away from him and tried to pay attention to Mrs. Tatum, but my eyes seemed to have developed a mind of their own. They kept finding their way back to Seth. I hoped like crazy that no one in the class noticed my sudden obsession.

Finally the bell rang. I scooped up my books and headed for the door with my head down.

"Killian! Wait!" I heard Seth call.

I stopped just outside the door and waited for him to catch up, but didn't turn around.

"Hey," he said when he came alongside me.

"Hey," I said back as I started walking again. What can I say? I'm a brilliant conversationalist.

"I'm new here," he said, pointing out the obvious, "I'm still getting lost. Think you could show me how to find my locker?"

"Yeah, sure," I mumbled, still not looking at him, "Where is it?"

He told me and we went on in silence. I felt Seth studying me as we walked. Finally he spoke up again,

"Killian, that's a different name. I don't think I've ever heard it before."

"It's Irish, I think," I explained. "My grandfather was from Ireland. He named me."

"Are you close to your grandfather?" he asked. There was a strange note to his voice that made me look up at him for the first time since we had left the classroom. There was a look of sadness in his eyes that made me wonder where the question came from.

"No," I answered, "He died when I was 4. I don't really remember him."

I saw disappointment in his eyes. He had very expressive eyes, like you were looking into his soul.

"Why? Why did you ask if we were close?" I asked him.

"No reason. Just wondering," he said, his eyes shifting away. Then he looked back at me again. "I'm not close to either of my grandfathers. They disowned me."

I looked at him curiously, but I had been brought up with too many manners to ask why they had disowned him. He read the question in my eyes anyway and answered.

"Killian," he said softly, "I'm gay."

I stopped dead in my tracks.

"I think I can find it from here," Seth said after an awkward pause. "Thanks, man. See ya around." And he was gone.

I'm not sure how long I stood there, maybe just a few seconds, maybe minutes. I was lost in thought and I didn't care. The stream of people flowed around me and I didn't notice any of them.

Suddenly someone grabbed me around the neck and got me in a headlock.

"What are you doing, Space Boy?" they yelled. "Waiting for your people to come back and get you?" It was Asher.

"Get off me, Asher," I said sharply.

"Whoa, dude," he said letting go, "what's wrong?"

"Nothing, I just gotta get home."

"Well, if you're in such a rush why were you just standing there?"

"It's nothing. I've got to go."

I started off quickly down the hall and Asher rushed to keep up with me. "Dude, Kill, man, what's up?" he asked again. When I didn't answer he said, "The gangs getting together tonight to hang out, maybe catch a movie. You wanna go?"

"No thanks," I said. By now we were at the door to the student parking lot. My dad had given me a car for my 16th birthday, one of the new Volkswagen Bugs. Maybe he thought it would make me popular. If so, he was destined to be disappointed yet again. I headed for my car with Asher still on my heels. Just then, Zachary intercepted us.

"Hey Zack," Asher called out.

"Hey Asher. Hey Killian," Zack said as I started to unlock my car. "Didn't I see you with that new kid right after the bell?"

I looked up, dropping my keys in the process. As I bent down to pick them up I answered, "Yeah, his name's Seth."

"I know," Zack said. "He's in my second-period class. We all had to share 5 things about ourselves. You know what his were?"

I had the door open by now, but I didn't get in. I felt frozen where I stood.

"What?" Asher asked.

"#1, he just moved here from Baltimore. #2, he swam on a team at the school he came from. #3, he likes acting. #4, he lives with just his dad. #5," Zack paused dramatically, "#5...he's a faggot."

"*What?*" Asher yelled. "He said that?"

"Yeah, man. A real live fairy," Zack laughed. "Well, he said gay, but you know."

"Who's a fairy?" Jesse asked as he walked up to us. "Killian?"

Everybody laughed, except me, then Zack said, "No, at least I don't think so. You're being awful quiet there, man."

I shrugged and started getting in my car.

"So who's a fairy?" Jesse asked again.

"That new kid, Seth," Zack told him.

"No way! How do you know? Did he hit on you?"

"No! He better not, unless he wants to end up a dead fairy," Zack said and they all laughed again.

"He seemed nice to me," I said before I had time to think.

As one they all turned to stare at me.

"Man," Asher said, "don't tell us you're a fag too, Killian."

"I didn't say I was gay," I said quietly but firmly. "I just said that I thought he seemed nice. Why does that make me gay?"

"Because he is, Kill," Zack said. "You don't hang out with fags unless you are a fag."

"Bullshit," I said angrily. "Hanging out with you guys doesn't make me an idiot." I slammed the door, started the car and drove off, leaving them staring after me with their mouths gaping. I have no clue where that came from. I never ever reacted like that.

I thought about it all the way home. Thoughts were flying through my mind like bullets and they seemed just as hard to grasp. When I came to my house, at the last minute I decided to keep driving. I wasn't ready to face any one at home. I was still tense and confused from the strange scene in the parking lot. I decided to drive to the beach.

We were having unseasonably cool weather for September in Maryland, so I didn't expect too many people to be there and I was right. I parked the car, fed the meter, and started out on the beach.

I had been walking for about 15 or so minutes when I was surprised to hear someone call my name. I turned and caught my breath. It was Seth and he was jogging towards me. He had changed out of the jeans and polo shirt he'd worn to school and now he wore Adidas jogging pants and a T-shirt.

"Hi, Killian," he said when he got to me, only slightly out of breath.

"Hi," I said looking at my feet.

"What are you doing here?" he asked.

"I just needed to get out so I decided to take a walk. The beach always calms me," I told him.

"I live here," he told me as if I'd asked. "I like to jog on the beach. Like you said, it calms me, too."

When I didn't say anything he continued, "Look, if you don't want to talk to me, I'll understand. I mean I know I probably freaked you out when I said I was gay, but I hate lying. I did that long enough. It's better to get things out in the open right away. That's why I told you." Still I didn't say anything and he seemed to have a real need to fill in the silence so he continued on. "I mean I'm used to everybody hating me. My own family hates me so why shouldn't you—"

"I don't hate you," I interrupted.

He stood looking at me with surprise for a few seconds.

"You don't?"

"No," I said, "I don't even know you, why would I hate you?"

"Because I'm gay."

"That's not a reason to hate somebody."

"Everyone else seems to think so."

"I've never been one to go with the crowd," I said a little bitterly.

"I sensed that about you. That's why I sat next to you." We stood there for a minute not talking, then he said, "Want to go grab a bite to eat and we can talk?"

I thought for a few seconds then shrugged. "Sure, why not?" I said.

We headed up to the boardwalk and found a pizza joint, placed our order and sat down at a table to wait for our number to be called.

We talked until the pizza was ready, telling each other general information about ourselves. The kind of stuff you tell people when you're just getting to know them. When we had finished eating I asked the question that had been plaguing me from the beginning. "So how long have you known you were gay and how did you know?"

He paused for a moment, looking me in the eyes for so long that I had to look away. "I guess I knew for a long time before I admitted it to myself. But I've known for sure for about a year," he began. "I lived with my mom since my parents split when I was eight. I never really knew what happened until I was 15. I just knew I hardly ever saw my dad. But when I was 15, I realized I was gay and decided to come out to my mom. She hit the roof. Then she hit me. I hit the floor. Long story short, my dad was gay and that's why they split up. So she kicked me out and I moved in with my dad."

I sat staring at him with my chin, I'm sure, somewhere around my ankles. I'd never realized how sheltered I was in my little Eastern Shore town.

"So anyway," he went on, "how did I know? Hmmmm. I just knew. I can't explain it really. I mean, beyond the obvious, my attraction to guys over girls. I can tell with other people too, you know. It's called gay-dar." A big grin started spreading across his face.

"Oh really?" I asked, suddenly feeling a little nervous. I wasn't sure why. I mean I wasn't gay, so what did I have to worry about? Sure, I'd never dated girls, never even been interested in them if I was honest with myself, but I'd never been interested in guys either. Had I? Doesn't everybody take peeks in the locker room? And all I felt towards Asher, Jesse, and Zack was friendship. Right? Thoughts of wrestling with Asher flashed through my mind. Enjoying the closeness of his body, trying to hide a hard-on. I shook my head to clear the images and hoped I wasn't blushing.

He was still smiling.

"Why are you smiling?" I asked testily.

Seth laughed. "I dunno. It's better than crying."

I glanced down at my watch and gasped. "Whoa, I'm late. I gotta go or I'm gonna be dog meat." I pulled out my wallet and threw some money on the table, enough to cover my part of the bill. "Bye, dude. See ya in school tomorrow."

"Okay," he called after me, "see ya, Killer!"

I stopped in the doorway and smiled back at him. Killer...I liked it!

Chapter
2

I drove home as quickly as I dared without risking a speeding ticket. That was the last thing I needed at this point.

As soon as I walked through the door, Dad was waiting.

"Thanks for the call," he said tightly, "Always nice to know where my only son is."

"I'm sorry, Dad," I said quickly. "It was stupid of me. I had a fight with Asher, Jesse, and Zack, and I needed some time by myself so I went to the beach. I lost track of time."

"Your mother was worried," he said in that same carefully controlled voice. My father almost never raised his voice.

I looked over at her; she didn't look all that worried. The only thing that ever worries her is when Dad is late for dinner.

"Well, don't just stand there, hurry up and wash up for dinner. It's going to get cold," he snapped.

I rushed upstairs and threw my backpack on the bed, then hurriedly washed my hands before rushing back down. My parents were already at the table. Dinner conversation was strained as it was more often than not. But if I thought it was bad before, it was about to get worse.

"Buck Phillips called me this afternoon," he started. Buck was Zack's father. That caught my attention. I looked up from my spaghetti. "He said there's a homosexual at your school now." He pronounced it Ho Mo Sex You Al, over enunciating each syllable.

Mom's eyes flickered over to me for a second before fixing back on her object of worship. I wondered what that meant.

"You know anything about it, son?" he continued.

"I met him, if that's what you're asking," I said softly.

"You met *it?*" he seemed almost incredulous, as if I had said I ate lunch with the Pope.

"No, I met *him*. He's a human being. His name is Seth," I said fighting hard to maintain my temper. It wouldn't be good to lose my temper at the dinner table. Then again, it was never good to lose my temper with my father.

"He's not a human being," he sneered. "It's unnatural. Don't you even tell me you're a fairy lover, boy. You stay away from him."

I stared hard at my spaghetti, "Yes, sir."

I managed to gag down the rest of my dinner somehow, although it was almost more than I could take even to sit at the same table with him; I was so angry. He continued to expand on his theory that gays and lesbians were the downfall of modern society. As soon as I had eaten enough to politely be excused I headed straight for my room. I had my own phone line and I immediately called Asher. I hoped they hadn't left yet. Even though I wasn't real close to any of the guys, I was closest to Asher and I needed to talk to someone.

"Hello?" he answered on the third ring.

"Asher," I started. "I'm sorry about today in the parking lot."

"Man, what happened?" he said.

"I don't know. I just get so tired of hearing that kind of crap from my dad...I just didn't want to hear it from you guys, I guess."

"But dude, he's gay."

"So what? Why does that make him a lesser human being?" I was starting to get angry again.

"Whoa, man, calm down. I dunno. I'm not saying he's like a lesser human being or anything. I just don't want him to make any moves on me, you know? Or you either. I gotta protect my buds, you know?"

"I spent all afternoon with him and he didn't make any moves on me," I said surprising myself. I hadn't planned to tell him.

"You what?" Asher yelled.

"Shhh," I hissed. "I said I spent all afternoon with him."

"Is that why you didn't want to go with the guys?"

"No, I didn't plan it. I was upset after the scene in the parking lot and I just needed some time alone, so I went to the beach. I ran into Seth there. We started talking and we ended up getting some pizza."

"Whoa. You went on adate with him."

"*I did not go on a date with him*," I screeched.

"Shhhh," it was his turn to warn me. "Sorry, dude. I was kidding. So what's he like? Is he, like, all feminine?"

"No, not at all. He's really nice. I actually had fun."

"Man, I wouldn't talk about this in front of Zack or Jesse. You know how they are."

"Yeah," I mumbled. "I wasn't even gonna tell you. It just kinda slipped out."

"Well, make sure it don't slip out in front of the wrong people," he warned me.

"Yeah, I know."

"So did he say why he decided to be gay?" he asked.

"It's not like that, Ash. You don't decide to be gay, either you are or you aren't. Trust me, after hearing what all he's been through I definitely don't think he chose it."

"What do you mean?"

"Well, I don't want to talk about stuff he told me, you know?"

"Oh yeah, that's cool."

"It was just some really bad stuff that happened to him because he came out."

"Came out? Now you're starting to sound like 'em," he chuckled. I laughed, too. "Look, man, I'm still not comfortable with this by a long shot, but whatever you do, don't hang out with him at school too much. I know you like to be different and challenge the status quo, but this could get you hurt."

"What do you mean?"

"Look, Zack just pulled up so I gotta go. We'll talk about this later, okay?"

"Yeah, okay."

"Great, see ya later." And he was gone.

I lay back on the bed, more confused than ever. Everybody seemed to think that I should avoid Seth. I thought about how I felt, always getting left out, always being ignored. That was bad enough. How would it feel to be actively discriminated against?

I didn't even want to think about it. I made up my mind to be friendly towards Seth, but not too friendly.

The rest of the week was pretty much an average first week back to school—assessing the new teachers to see how much we could get away with, figuring out homework loads, etc. I talked to Seth in class even though almost no one else did. By now, the word was all over the school that Seth was gay. People gave me funny looks, but for the most part no one said anything. I didn't go out of my way to talk to him outside of class, but I didn't avoid him either. It seemed like with each day that went by, Seth got a little lower, a little less animated.

The weekend passed, or maybe I should say it passed away. It was a slow, boring death and I was actually glad to see Monday roll around. I wondered if Zack, Jesse, and Asher were avoiding me. They didn't call me the whole weekend.

It was raining hard when school let out on Tuesday. I waited for a while by the door until it became obvious that it wasn't going to let up, then I made a dash for my car. I jumped in, turned up the defrost and put the windshield wipers on high. I'd had to stay after to talk to one of my teachers about a project that was due Friday (geez, the second week of school and I had projects due already), so I was one of the last people to leave.

As I was leaving there was one car ahead of me. While I was pulling out I noticed someone walking on the side of the road. The car ahead of me swerved suddenly towards the person. I yelled but they swerved back away, splashing the person in the process, which was probably their goal all along, I realized belatedly. I stopped next to the now thoroughly soaked person, then saw it was Seth.

"Seth," I yelled. "Are you ok?"

He turned towards my car and nodded. "Hey Killian. Yeah I think so. A little wet, but I'm ok."

"A little wet?" I laughed. "Why are you walking?"

"My Dad forgot to pick me up," he said in a matter-of-fact voice.

"Well hop in, I'll drive you home."

He grinned at me, then ran around to the other door and jumped in.

"You'll have to tell me how to get there, dude," I said once he was settled and we'd started up again. "All I know is that you live by the beach."

He gave me directions and then we talked while I drove.

When I pulled up to his apartment building he said, "My dad isn't home. His car's gone. You wanna come up for a few minutes?"

I thought for a minute then turned the car off. I looked over at him and smiled. "Sure!"

We ran into the house and Seth slammed the door then slumped against it. I looked over at him and couldn't help but laugh. He was completely soaked from head to toe. Water dripped off of him, forming a puddle around his feet. His hair was slicked down and his clothes drooped, soggy with the rain.

"What's so funny?" he asked me.

"You look like a drowned rat," I said in between laughing.

"What exactly does a drowned rat look like anyway?"

"I dunno," I gasped. "But you sure look like one."

"Very funny," he said even though he was smiling, too. "I wonder where my dad is?"

He went off down the hall, leaving a trail of water on the hardwood floor for me to follow—which I did, feeling a bit like Hansel and Gretel—into the kitchen. Seth was reading a note and dripping all over the table and floor.

"He got an emergency call from Steve, that's his friend. He said he'll call later tonight, but he probably won't get home till tomorrow."

He opened the refrigerator and pulled out a couple of root beers, the kind that comes in the brown glass bottles. "You like root beer?" he asked me.

"I love it," I said.

"Well, here ya go." He handed me a bottle and started for the door. He called over his shoulder, "The living room is across the hall, dude, make yourself at home. I'm gonna go change and be right back down."

I went into the living room. It was furnished with worn, but comfortable, looking furniture, a nice entertainment system, and pictures of Seth everywhere. Books were strewn about liberally. It was a very comfortable room.

I walked around the room looking at the pictures and Seth seemed to grow up before my eyes. There was a woman in some of them, I assumed his mother, and a man in others, his father. I went over to the entertainment center and looked over their video selection—*Sleepless in Seattle, Armageddon, Ghost, Air Force One, The Object of My Affection, Beaches, You've Got Mail,* all the *Naked Gun* movies. I liked their taste.

"See anything you wanna watch?" Seth said suddenly, making me jump. He started laughing.

"Geez, sneak up on me why don't you?" I laughed, too. He had changed into black running shorts and a plain white T-shirt. He'd dried his hair but he apparently hadn't brushed it. It was standing up in every direction, as it usually did.

"Sorry, I didn't put my wet shoes back on, so I guess you didn't hear me coming in just my socks."

"Obviously, I don't usually jump and breathe heavy just because you enter the room," I joked.

"My loss," he said with a shy grin.

I blinked in surprise for a minute, not sure what to say. Was he hitting on me?

"Killian, I was kidding," he said after an awkward pause.

"Oh, sorry," I mumbled. "Maybe I better go."

"No, please stay for awhile. We can play a game or something. I have N64. Do you like Zelda?"

"Yeah," I said slowly. I thought for a few seconds while Seth stood there looking miserable.

"Ok," I said finally. "But let me call my parents so they won't freak out."

I crossed my fingers and dialed, then waited while holding my breath. Thankfully mom answered. She accepted the fact that I wouldn't be home till later without any questions. They would come later from dad, but I would think of something before then.

"It's cool," I told him.

"*Yes!*" he shouted. "Killer's the man!"

We played Zelda and talked about nothing for a few hours. Then suddenly Seth announced that he was hungry, so we ended up back in the kitchen. He made us both lunchmeat sandwiches and we sat at the table while we ate.

"Well I don't seem to have made many friends in my first week of school," he said as I took a huge bite.

We sat in silence while I chewed, which gave me a chance to think of what to say.

"No, not many," I said, "but you made one at least—me."

He smiled and almost looked like he was going to cry for a few seconds. I hoped like crazy he wouldn't. I hate it when people cry. It always makes me want to cry, too. My dad always yells at me for being a sissy and crying too much.

"Thanks, Killian," he said with a slightly husky voice. "That means a lot. Probably more than you know."

"I think I have an idea."

We ate the rest of our sandwiches in silence.

"I don't get it," he said suddenly.

"Get what?"

"I don't get why you grew up in the same town as all these other kids, but you're the only one who doesn't treat me like some kind of pariah."

I shrugged. I didn't understand it myself. I was risking a lot just by being Seth's friend. For some reason, the risk seemed worth it to me.

"Do you know what your name means?" he asked me out of nowhere.

"No, I think it's the name of a beer, but I don't know what it means. Why?"

"Cuz I do," he said.

"What? What does it mean? And how do you know?" I asked. This was taking a very weird turn.

"I looked it up; there's a site on the Internet where you can look up names and find out what they mean. Killian means 'blind.'"

"Blind? What kind of a name is that?"

"What's your middle name?"

"Travers, but I still don't get blind." I was struck by the utter weirdness of having a name that means "blind."

"Maybe it's symbolic," he said softly.

"Symbolic? Symbolic of what? My glasses?" I scoffed.

"No, of your inability to see yourself."

Whoa, now we had gone from weird to bizarre. If I wasn't careful, before long he'd be calling me Grasshopper and telling me I need to have patience.

"You're weirding me out, dude," I said. "I can see myself just fine, thank you."

"Not really," he said. "Not the way I see you."

"What do you mean?"

"I see you differently than I think you see yourself. Look, I haven't known you for that long, but I can tell that you don't think very much of yourself; and yet you're smart, funny, kind, and not to mention drop-dead gorgeous. But you hide behind those glasses and your friends, and no one ever gets to know you. And besides all that, you don't even let yourself see the real you. You've buried it beneath so many layers you've forgotten it's there."

My head was reeling. I think I was on overload. My mind had heard everything but certain phrases kept echoing through my brain. Drop-dead gorgeous. Me? Ha! Hide behind your friends. How do I hide? You don't even let yourself see the real you. What the hell was that supposed to mean? I latched onto the last one.

"What the hell do you mean by I don't let myself see the real me?" I demanded. "If I don't see the real me, then who does? You?"

"Maybe."

"Then why don't you introduce me? I'd like to meet myself."

"Ok, I will," he said in a strange voice. It was kind of sad, but almost like he had known what would happen. "Killian Travers Kendall," he started, "I'd like you to meet yourself."

Then he stood up, came around the table, leaned over me, and quickly pressed his lips against mine. For a second I was so shocked I didn't move, then suddenly my reflexes kicked in and I shoved back so violently that my chair flipped over backwards and I sprawled across the floor.

"What the hell was that?" I yelled.

Seth looked like he was about to cry again but I didn't care anymore.

"I thought you were gay, Killian," he said so quietly that I barely heard him. In fact, maybe I didn't hear him right.

"What did you say?" I asked him in a deadly calm voice. I had learned that from my father.

"I said, I thought maybe you were gay," tears started rolling down his cheeks. "I'm sorry, Killian, I was wrong. I'm so sorry. Please don't hate me. You're my only friend." With that he sank down to the floor and began to sob.

I sat across the kitchen from him and just watched him cry. I felt like I should do something but I had no clue as to what. It felt like my mind had shut down. Everything just went blank. I couldn't even think clearly enough to leave, so I just sat there. Occasionally, Seth would choke out another "I'm sorry" in between sobs. After a few minutes I reached up to wipe my face and I was surprised to find it was wet. I was crying, too.

Slowly my mind began to wake up. The first question that

went through my mind was, "Am I gay?" I wasn't so sure any-more. I really hadn't minded the kiss so much; it was just the shock of it that I reacted to. Even in my addled state I knew that much. I thought about the way I had been almost obsessed with Seth from day one. Asher suddenly popped into my mind and that really shook me up. I needed to get out of here. I needed to think.

I struggled to my feet and started out of the kitchen. I paused at the door long enough to mumble, "I don't hate you. I need to think," and then I was gone, leaving him crumpled in a heap on the kitchen floor.

Luckily, Dad was at a meeting when I got home and I was able to go right to my room, calling out to Mom that I was going to do my homework and I'd already eaten.

I fell backwards onto my bed and began to cry all over again. I was so confused. Had I been blind to the real me all this time? Was that why I always felt so empty, so incomplete? I sat up and looked in the mirror. My face was a little blotchy from all the crying and my eyes were red, but other than that, I knew I wasn't bad looking. There had been lots of girls who had asked me out persistently over the years, but I'd never been interested. Why? Every time I wrestled with Asher I got aroused. Why? The one and only erotic dream I'd ever had had featured none other than Asher. The clues were pretty obvious all of a sudden.

I had been blind.

Chapter
3

I was gay.

The realization was almost overwhelming.

I was gay.

I kept repeating it over and over to myself. It didn't seem real. It couldn't be real. I couldn't be gay. And yet, now that I'd faced it and said it to myself, I knew I was.

I was gay.

But I didn't want to be gay. My parents would hate me. My friends would hate me. I mean, look how everyone's treated Seth. Oh my God! What would Zack, Jesse, and Asher say? Or more importantly, what would they do?

I was gay.

Did that mean I would be kicked out of my church? Only my mom and I ever went. Dad said church was for women, and that's half the reason I continued to go week after week. It was one of the few things that Mom did without Dad's approval. For some reason I always felt a sense of peace there. Did God hate me? I was fuzzy on the whole religion thing. I guess I hadn't paid enough attention.

I was...

The phone rang, startling me out of my thoughts. It was Asher.

"Hey, Killian, dude," he started as soon as I said hello. "I called you earlier and you weren't there? Where were you?"

"I was at Seth's house," I said. My voice was still somewhat shaky.

"You were where? Are you ok? You sound funny."

"I was at Seth's house and I'm..." My voice trailed off. I was going to say I was fine but suddenly it seemed pointless to lie.

"You're what, dude?" Asher asked me. "You want me to come over?"

I couldn't face that right now. I looked like a mess and I didn't know how well I would be able to lie my way through it. Why was Asher showing such an interest in me anyway, especially now of all times? He'd never really shown that much interest in me before these last few days.

"I don't think so, Ash," I said quickly.

"No, man, you're upset, I can tell. I'll be right over." And with that he hung up.

Great, just what I needed. Since when did Asher become a nurturer? I rubbed my face to try to get rid of the tear tracks. There wasn't much I could do about the red eyes. I turned off the overhead lights and turned on my computer. Maybe if the lights were dim he wouldn't notice, and the computer would give me something to do so I wouldn't have to look him in the face.

Asher only lives a few houses down from mine so he was at my house in a very short time. My mom let him in and he was at my door before I was even signed on to the Internet. He was wearing jeans and a long-sleeved shirt and his curly hair had been carefully brushed, as always. It struck me how different he was from Seth; then I wondered why I was comparing them. Asher had a concerned look on his face.

"Hey, Killian," he said. "Why's it so dark in here?" And he flipped on the light. So much for my dim lighting plan.

"Hey, Ash," I said. I was glad I had control of my voice again. "You didn't have to come over. As you can see I'm fine." I was hoping he'd take the hint and leave. Not Asher.

"I know I didn't have to. I wanted to. You're my bud." He came closer to me and peered intently at me. I looked away, but not quick enough. "You've been crying," he accused me.

"No I haven't," I lied. "I think I have allergies."

"I've known you forever, Kill, you don't have any allergies." Asher shot back. I'm very bad at lying.

"Look, Asher, I'm fine."

"What did he do to you?" Asher's voice had changed, taken on a harder tone.

"Who?" I stalled; he was making me even more nervous than I already was.

"Kermit the Frog. Who do you think? What did Seth do to you?"

"Seth didn't do anything to me," I said. My eyes shifted away. I hated lying more than anything in the world. That's why I was so bad at it. I had been known to get myself in trouble simply because I wouldn't lie.

"Did he hurt you?" Asher said as he took a step closer to me. His voice was as hard as steel now. I could feel his tension. I looked up at him, surprised by his reaction. "If he hurt you, I'll kill him." At that moment I believed him.

I couldn't take any more confusion today. It took all the self-control I could find just to keep from bursting into tears again. I took a deep breath, then another. Finally I was ready to speak. I made my voice go steely to match his.

"First of all, Seth did not hurt me. Second, why would it matter so much to you if he did? You've never paid any attention to me before. Why start now?"

Asher blinked at me, his mouth slightly open in surprise. "You're my friend, Killian. You've always been there. Whenever I've needed to talk, I always knew I could talk to you. I could never talk to Zack and Jesse like I talk to you. I know I haven't been the best friend in the world. I guess I kinda took you for granted. You were just always there. But now, Seth comes along and you're suddenly hanging out with him. And he's gay. I don't get it. I...I guess I'm kinda jealous."

Now it was my turn to stare open mouthed. "Jealous? Of what?"

"I don't want to lose you as a friend. Especially not to—"

"Don't say it," I interrupted, an unspoken warning clear in my voice.

We stood there staring at each other for a minute. We both jumped when a loud, deep voice shattered the silence. "Welcome." I had made it online. Almost immediately the Instant Messenger chime sounded. I glanced at the screen. The IM was from SethCon123 and the message read, *this is seth...please talk to me.*

I quickly turned back to Asher, "Look, you're not losing me as a friend. Why can't I just be friends with both of you? Why does it have to be one or the other?" Then before he could answer I rushed on, "Ash, I need some time alone right now. I'll call you later, ok?"

Asher nodded and left without saying anything else. I quickly turned back to the computer.

how did u find me? I typed.

membership directory search, he answered. *look, i'm really sorry...i can't believe I was that stupid*

you weren't stupid...you were right

WHAT?

you were right...i think i'm gay There was no response for several seconds, so I typed some more, *i'm still trying to figure everything out...i'm very confused*

can i help?

i don't think so...it's something I have to figure out for myself

can we get together to talk later this week? i'll give u some time to think first...how about friday?

i dunno

look killian, u need to talk to somebody...if not me then find someone else

ok, i'll think about it...i'm gonna go now

ok...bye Killer

I signed off and shut down the computer, but stayed in front of my computer for several minutes just staring at my reflection on the blank screen.

I, Killian Travers Kendall, was gay. I was a homosexual. I was attracted to my own sex. The more I said it the easier it became. But I couldn't tell anyone. I knew Seth wouldn't tell anybody; besides, whom would he tell? I was his only friend. And even if he did tell, no one would take his word over mine. He was too new to the town; I'd lived here all my life. I was starting to feel a little calmer about the whole thing.

I heard Dad come in downstairs and all the fear from earlier came flooding back. What if he took one look at me and knew? Seth had known. Could other people tell?

I scrambled for my book bag and dumped out the contents all over the bed. I grabbed a book at random (I think it was my history book) and opened it, pretending to read. At that moment, there was a knock at my door and it swung open. It was Dad. The knock was simply a formality and we both knew it.

"Doing your homework?" he said.

"Yup," I answered, looking up from my book.

"Good. Get it finished before you go to sleep." And he was gone, shutting the door behind him.

He hadn't noticed. He hadn't suddenly screamed at me and ordered me out of the house. I let out a shaky breath that I didn't even realize I'd been holding. What was I going to do? I felt like I had narrowly escaped this time, but what about next time? What about my friends? What was I going to do about Seth? A feeling of despair and confusion suddenly overwhelmed me. I realized how emotionally drained I was. I pushed everything off the bed and onto the floor and lay down without even taking my clothes off. I was asleep in minutes.

Surprisingly enough, I slept very well. The next day, however, went by in a blur. I couldn't tell you one thing that happened in school, except that I spent most of the day dodging Seth and Asher in the halls. I didn't have any classes with Asher, so he wasn't too hard, but I had theater with Seth. We spent the whole period trying hard not to look at each other. The word "torture" springs to mind.

I took off as soon as the last bell rang. I had my destination in mind. I drove straight to our church. There was one car in the parking lot, but I had no idea whose it was. I parked next to it and knocked on the office door. Pastor Mike opened it. Mike, as he liked to be called, was the associate pastor, but more importantly, he was also the youth pastor. I was relieved that it was Mike since he was pretty young, I think only in his mid-20's. He had curly brown hair and friendly brown eyes and was even shorter than me. He always reminded me of an overgrown kid. He looked at me for a minute as if trying to remember my name.

"Killian? Right?" he said. I nodded and he continued, "What can I do for you?"

"Can I talk to you?" I asked him somewhat timidly. I don't think I had ever even spoken to him before. I was surprised he even knew my name.

"Sure," he said warmly, "come on in."

I followed him into his office and he pointed me to a couch. He took the chair next to it.

"So what's up?" he asked me once we were seated.

"I need to talk to you about some stuff," I started. He nodded as if to say go on, "But if I do, do you promise not to tell anybody? I mean can I trust you?"

"Well, look Killian, it's like this. If you trust me enough to tell me, then you have to trust me enough to do what's best with what you tell me. What I mean is, if you tell me you are really depressed and you're going to kill yourself, then I'd have to tell someone to protect you. But if you just need some advice or clarification on something, then I think we should be able to keep it confidential."

I sat and looked at him for a minute, weighing my options. If I talked to him, he might go to my parents. I really needed to talk to someone, though, and I felt like I could trust him. He sat across from me now, leaning forward with his elbows on his knees, waiting to see what I decided.

Finally I made up my mind, "Well, maybe you can answer some questions first," I started.

"I don't pretend to know all the answers, but I'll do the best I can," he said very seriously.

I nodded, "Does God hate gay people?"

Mike sat back in his chair and let out a little breath, not a gasp, almost like a hiss. "Yowzers," he said. "You sure like to start with the touchy issues, don't you?"

I tried to smile but couldn't quite pull it off. He saw this and quickly moved on.

"Actually, the topic is touchy, but the answer to that one is quite simple. No. God loves gay people just as much as He loves the pastor or Mother Theresa or anybody else. But I have a feeling that's not really what you're here to ask."

"What if...what if someone in the church was gay? Would they be kicked out?"

"No, I don't know of anyone ever getting kicked out of our church. You come fairly often, Killian, think about what you see when you are here on Sunday mornings. We have a very open church. Everyone is welcome. It doesn't matter what color your skin is or what color your hair is or what you are wearing."

He was right; we had inter-racial couples, people with more metal pierced through their skin than a Volvo, people with bright fire engine-red hair—and they were all accepted.

He continued, "We believe that God's love is for everyone, not just a select few. And you don't have to be 'good enough' to meet His standards. He meets you where you are. Am I making any sense here?"

"I think so," I said. "So does that mean it's ok to be gay? Doesn't the Bible say it's wrong?"

"Killian, that's a question I don't think I can answer for you. I've not studied it. As far as I know, yes, the Bible lists it as a sin. Jesus himself never actually mentioned it, but Paul does a couple times. But then again Paul also said women shouldn't speak in church and should never cut their hair and never wear jewelry." He shrugged. "We seem to have decided that those don't count. Who gets to decide? I don't know anymore. I'm not speaking for the church as a whole at this point, but personally I think that we need to focus more on sharing God's love than condemning people. You talk to God about that one, see what He tells you."

I sat for a minute thinking about all that had been said.

"Killian?" Mike said, interrupting my thoughts. "Do you think you might be gay?"

For a minute I froze, then slowly I nodded my head, my eyes never leaving his face. I didn't want to miss his reaction. His eyes never changed, never wavered as he looked back at me. He nodded once, then reached out a hand and rested it on my knee.

"If you ever need to talk to someone, you can come to me. And you don't have to worry, I'll keep this confidential until you are ready to tell people yourself."

I felt my whole body relax. He didn't hate me. He wasn't going to tell my parents. He wasn't going to announce it to the whole church and have me kicked out. He was going to be my friend. And that's what I really needed right now. I hadn't realized how tense I had been until it was all over.

Mike patted my knee and then sat back. "Do you have any other questions for me? I don't know, something easy maybe, like why do bad things happen to good people?" Then he grinned to let me know he was kidding.

I grinned back and shook my head. "I think I have enough to think about for now, but if I think of something else, it's okay if I come back?" I asked.

"Of course it's okay," he said. "In fact, I really hope you do. You're a good kid, Killian. I'm glad you felt like you could talk to me."

We both stood up and he walked me to the door. He waved as I pulled out of the parking lot.

Well that was one set of questions settled in my mind. Now I only had a million more to take care of.

I e-mailed Seth later that night asking him if I could talk to him sometime in private. I had decided that he would probably be able to answer some of my questions and it would help to talk to someone else who was gay. Mike had been a big help on the religious issue, but he wouldn't be able to shed much light on what it was actually like to be a gay teenager.

Seth had answered when I checked my account in the morning. He again suggested that we meet Friday evening at the park by the pond around 7:00. I replied saying that was fine with me and I would see him there. Now I only had to make it till Friday.

The week seemed to drag by. I was so distracted. I knew my grades were probably plummeting. Oh well, it was still only the second week. I would catch up.

Finally Friday arrived, but by the time the day was over I wished it never had. It was bad day from the beginning, when my alarm clock failed to go off and I had to run around like a chicken with its head cut off to avoid being late. Then all the teachers seemed to be in a bad mood, and I got yelled at several times for not paying attention. Geez, were they just noticing now? I mean, I hadn't been paying attention all week. Why was today so important?

A girl who had been after me since last year cornered me in the hall and demanded to know why I wouldn't go out with her. I came so close to telling her it was because she didn't have the right equipment. Instead, I bit my tongue and managed to slip away when a friend of hers who was running down the hall calling her name distracted her.

And then, as if my day hadn't already been crappy enough, I got into a huge fight with Zack, Asher, and Jesse, once again in the parking lot. This time they were waiting by my car when I came out. I eyed them suspiciously as I approached. This didn't look like it would be something I would enjoy. I was starting to dread getting my car from the lot. Maybe I would start riding the bus.

"What's with the welcome wagon?" I asked when I got close enough. "Did our dear old school elect you guys to the parking lot hospitality committee?"

"Funny, Killian," Zack said. "We need to talk to you."

"About what?" I asked.

"About Seth," Zack answered.

My eyes immediately went to Asher and he looked away, obviously uncomfortable.

"What about Seth?" I asked warily.

"We think you are spending too much time with him."

"Too much time? I haven't spent any time with him."

"Asher told us about the other day." Jesse threw in smugly, as if that proved my guiltiness of some gross crime.

"Oh, did he?" I once again looked at Asher and he still wasn't looking at me. He seemed to have suddenly found his Air-walks quite fascinating.

"Yeah, he did," Zack confirmed. "And we're worried that Seth is messing with your mind, turning you against us. You've not done anything with us since school started and you met this fag."

"Seth is turning me against you?" I repeated. I could feel my blood pressure rising. "You don't need Seth to turn me against you. You guys are doing a damn good job for your-selves!"

"What's that supposed to mean?" Asher spoke up for the first time.

"It's supposed to mean that I'm always the tag-along. Nobody ever calls me unless nobody else is available. It means that I'm not really a part of your little group, and I'm being con-stantly reminded of that fact. It means that nobody ever cared what I was doing or how I was doing until it started looking like I might have my own mind. It means that if I don't do exactly as you say and perform exactly as you expect me to perform, I get check-ups and lectures. I'm not your friend. I'm your mascot. At least Seth treats me like a person."

"You're a fag too, aren't you?" Zack said in the sudden silence left after my heated outburst.

"Go to hell, Zack!" I said between clenched teeth. "And get away from my car while you're at it or I'll run over you!"

"You're gonna be sorry, Killian," Zack warned as he, Asher, and Jesse started walking away. "You and your boyfriend."

That threat echoed through my head all the way home. What did that mean, and how much did they know? I sure hoped Seth would be a good friend, because I had just alienated the only three friends I'd ever had.

I went home and did all my homework for the weekend, and it was still only 4:30. I still had two and a half hours to wait before I went to meet Seth at the park. Calling Asher was out, I never called Zack or Jesse anyway, and I didn't have any other friends, so I signed onto the net.

None of my net friends were on. I usually talked to them later at night, so I decided to look up some articles on being gay. I went to my favorite search engine and typed in "gay." I was shocked when it came back with thousands and thousands of hits. Then I realized that 99% of them were porno sites. I was very curious, but I decided not to check them out. Well, maybe just one. I clicked on a link and waited. I almost fell off my chair when the site finally finished loading. I had never seen anything even close to this. I was hard in seconds; I didn't even know you could get hard that fast. My eyes almost popped out of my head, and this was just the title page. After I caught my breath again I tried clicking on the enter button. A form came up asking me to join, so I exited the whole site. No way were they getting my name, and besides, I didn't have a credit card. I sat in front of my computer with an aching hard-on trying to decide if I should try another site. I finally decided against it. I could see how that could get addicting and I didn't want to tempt fate.

I signed off, stood up, and was immediately reminded of my state of arousal. Well, I thought. I guess this settles the whole gay thing. I snickered at the tent in my pants and decided to do something about it. After checking to make sure my door was locked, I stripped, lay down on my bed, and jerked off. This wasn't the first time I'd ever done it by a long shot, but it was the first time I'd ever allowed myself to think of guys while I did. Not that my mind hadn't tried to go there before, but I'd always felt guilty and made myself think of girls from school. Talk about frustrating! I now found my mind wandering from the guys on the porno site, to Seth, and to my surprise, Asher. I quickly pushed Asher out of my thoughts since he hated me now and definitely wasn't gay anyway.

I finished and got cleaned up just as Mom called me down to dinner. I was surprised to find that it was just Mom when I got downstairs.

"Where's Dad?" I asked.

"He called and said he had a meeting, so it's just us," she said and smiled. My mom was very pretty in a held-back kind of way. She had me when she was young, only 18, so that made her

34 now. I looked at her closely as if seeing her for the first time. She wore her straight blonde hair shoulder length and tucked behind her ears. She didn't have any wrinkles yet. Her soft blue eyes were very seldom enhanced by make-up, but they were pretty even without any. In fact, she hardly ever wore make-up at all. Suddenly, I wondered why. Dad was always asking her to. The way she did everything else he wanted. The fact that she didn't do this small thing suddenly took me by surprise. Then I thought about the whole church thing. That was another place she stood up to my father. Maybe I had been underestimating her all this time.

"Why don't you wear make-up?" I asked her.

She looked at me in surprise, "What an odd question!"

"Not really. Dad is always asking you to."

She smiled a funny little smile, "Then maybe that's why."

"What?" I was suddenly very confused. Could the chief priest at the shrine of my father really not be as devoted as she seemed?

Her smile broadened. "You've never expressed much interest in my personal appearance before. What brought this on?"

I shook my head silently and she laughed. She blessed the food and we began to eat and make small talk, but my mind was busy trying to find other instances of my mother's rebellion. They were there. I'd just never noticed them before. I think they call it passive-aggressive behavior. I suddenly had a new respect for my mother.

"You don't like him very much, do you," I interrupted her in mid-sentence. I hadn't been paying attention, but I think she was talking about church.

"Pastor Mason?" she asked in a shocked voice.

"No, Dad."

"Oh," she said simply and sat there for a few seconds, fork still suspended half way between her plate and her mouth. When she spoke again, her voice was softer, so that I had to almost strain to hear her. "Your father is a very difficult man, Killian. So was his father. I've never told you this, but I think you are old enough to handle it. We weren't married when I became pregnant with you. I wouldn't even consider an abortion, so his father, your grandfather, practically forced us to get married."

She let the fork slowly drop to her plate and folded her hands in her lap before continuing. "You're right. I don't like him very much. My mother told me I'd grow to love him," she paused and I could see the pain in her eyes, "but it hasn't happened yet. Don't get me wrong; I don't regret having you. You're the best thing that in my life. I see the way he treats you, and it makes my heart ache. I've always tried to make sure you've had everything you needed, everything you wanted; the car, the computer." She shook her head as if to say it wasn't enough.

"Then why don't you leave him?" I asked equally quietly.

"It doesn't work that way, Killian baby," she said. "Your father's a very powerful man in this area. He'd take you away, and I'd never be able to get a job. I never finished college because I was pregnant, and your father never let me go back, so I have no marketable skills. I'm stuck. And I'm afraid that means you are, too, at least for a few more years. Maybe once you're in college, I'll have the nerve to make a break for it, but I don't want you to get caught in the crossfire. It would be ugly, trust me."

"I do," I told her sincerely.

She nodded and we went back to eating. The rest of the meal was somewhat solemn. I had a new image of my mother now and my respect for her had gone up considerably. All these years she had stayed in an unhappy relationship because she didn't want to lose me. I was almost in tears. When she stood up to clear the table, I gave her a hug and insisted she let me do it.

By the time I got the dishes finished it was almost time to meet Seth at the park. I figured that by the time I walked there, it would be just about right. I could have driven, but I didn't want to get there too early and have to sit around waiting. It was almost dusk, and it was a little creepy by the pond at night.

I told Mom that I was going for a walk and left. I had plenty of time on the 15-minute walk to think about things. And I had a lot to think about. So much had happened in the last two weeks. I'd realized I was gay and admitted it to myself. I'd come out to one of the pastors at my church and a new friend who was also gay. Then I'd alienated all my old friends, maybe for good. I had been kissed for the first time, and it was by a guy. (I wondered briefly if it counted if you hit them afterwards, but decided it did.) Then to top it all off, I'd found out that my mother was a real person after all. And I liked her.

I wondered what Seth would add to my list tonight. Would he kiss me again? I wondered if I wanted him to. I wasn't sure. Part of me did, but part of me was scared, too. I finally decided that if he did, I wouldn't stop him this time.

I was so lost in thought that I almost walked past the trail to the pond. The pond was a man-made pond that sat back in a copse of trees. The forest was small but thick with lots of undergrowth and high weeds on either side of the narrow trail that circled around the pond. The pond itself was a green, nasty looking thing that was fed by drainage ditches. They had built cutesy little arched bridges over the ditches, but it still all looked kind of seedy and creepy, even in the middle of the day. At night, it was downright scary.

It was just at the edge of dusk, the time when it's hardest to see because everything is like an old black-and-white movie with bad contrast. I couldn't see anybody around the pond, but I couldn't be sure, so I started to walk around it. Maybe I'd gotten here before Seth.

Then I thought I saw some movement on the far side of the pond. I started towards it at a faster pace as I called out in a hushed voice, "Seth?" If it was Seth, I thought, he would never recognize my voice. I wasn't sure why I wasn't louder, but I was feeling very terrified all of a sudden. I had goose bumps all over my arms and the hairs were standing up on the back of my neck. I almost turned and ran, but I told myself I was being stupid and kept walking toward the area where I'd last seen the movement. "Seth?" I called again in my new raspy voice.

Still no one had answered me, so I wasn't sure if I'd even seen anything. When I got closer to the spot where I thought I had seen the motion, I saw something lying on the ground, so I headed in that direction. Before I could get close enough to see what it was, something suddenly flew out of the undergrowth at me with a fierce howl.

Before I could even scream, it slammed into me, and the impact sent us both rolling across the ground. It was a person, I was sure of that much as I grappled tried to get away. I thought maybe it was Seth playing a sick joke, but I couldn't get turned around to see, since my attacker now had me from behind in a tight grip.

One hand abruptly let go, but before I could take advantage of that, the person raised an arm and quickly brought it down. In that spilt second of motion, I saw a flash in the moonlight. It was a knife! Everything seemed to go in slow motion. I felt the impact of the knife in my stomach, and the air rushed out of me with an audible "oof." Almost instantly, searing pain spread through my entire body as I felt my own warm blood gush out.

I'd been stabbed.

The person let go of me with the other arm and yanked the knife out. I fell back onto the ground as my attacker sat up over me. I tried to get a look at my assailant, but the pain had blinded me. I couldn't make out any facial features. The arm raised again, but then stopped. I lay there looking helplessly up at the faceless monster above me, but I couldn't do anything but whimper.

"Shit," the person hissed, then lurched up and took off running.

I didn't move for a few seconds. The pain was all I could think about, and I seemed to be having difficulty breathing. Each breath felt like a whole new stab. I struggled to sit up, but the pain flashed through my body again, and I felt myself blacking out. "I don't want to die," I thought, as the darkness surrounded me. I fought back and managed to get myself onto my hands and knees. I put pressure on the stab wound with one hand and tried to stand up, but my head was spinning too much.

I wanted to scream, but still couldn't seem to get enough air. I was also afraid that the person with the knife would come back and finish me if he realized I was still alive. I looked around for help, but I couldn't see over the weeds. I could see the lights of nearby houses faintly through the trees, but I knew my chances of getting through the underbrush in my condition were next to none. I had better chances of getting found here on the trail. Sometimes, people walked their dogs out here. Then I saw the figure lying on the ground again. I realized it was a person. Maybe I had interrupted a mugging and the victim was just unconscious. Maybe I could wake the person up to get help.

I painfully crawled over to the still figure, every movement bringing a wave of intense agony. I felt like I was going to get sick. As long as I didn't pass out, I didn't care. My shirt was soaked with my blood by this time. I knew I was losing a lot and that was why I was getting so light headed.

Finally, I reached the figure's side; it was lying on its side facing away from me, so I grabbed its shoulder and rolled it towards me. As soon as the body fell flat on its back, I knew I wouldn't be waking it up. Its throat had been slashed open, the gash angry and raw. It's amazing the little things you notice in a moment like that. I saw the leaves and small pebbles stuck in the drying blood around the wound, and I wanted to brush them off. It looked unspeakably obscene, as if the gaping slit wasn't obscene enough.

I felt the blackness swirling around me again and I didn't think I'd fight it this time. In the last second before I allowed the darkness to overwhelm me I looked at the face. My last thought before succumbing to the void was, "Oh God, not Seth."

Chapter 4

It felt as if I were floating. That's the first thing I remember. Then I became aware of a bright white light that I could see through my closed eyelids. The events leading up to my blackout flooded back into my consciousness and I found myself wishing for the bliss of the darkness again. Then I realized I wasn't in pain. Was I in heaven? I forced my eyes open, but shut them again quickly. The light was blinding. I tried again, a little more cautiously this time.

Well, I wasn't in heaven, not unless they hooked you up to machines and painted their rooms a nasty puke green. When would hospitals ever learn?

Just then, a nurse walked into my field of vision. She was wearing the typical nurses uniform of a brightly colored top over white pants and white shoes. She looked like she was maybe in her 60s, with close-cropped gray hair and a don't-mess-with-me look in her eyes.

"Ah, I see you're back with us again," she said. "How do you feel?"

"I'm not sure yet. How long was I out? Was I in a coma?" I asked. My voice sounded scratchy and harsh. The pain was starting to come back now, a little more with each breath.

"No, no comas," she told me as she started checking machines and making little notes on her clipboard. "You were unconscious when they found you, and then they doped you up for the surgery. You're just now coming around. Starting to feel some pain?"

I nodded. I liked her. She was very straightforward.

"Alrighty then, we'll take care of that," she made some adjustments to the keypad on the IV stand and changed the bag at the top. "There, that should help soon."

"What happened?" I asked her. "Am I ok?"

"You're going to be fine, but the doctor will be in shortly to tell you more. If you need anything from me, like more of the good stuff to knock you out or something to drink, whatever, just push this little red button here." She showed me a small tube-shaped thingy with a wire that ran out of the bottom of it to the wall behind me. A red button was on one end of it. "This will page us at the nurses' station. Someone will come and check on you, although it might not always be me. Ok?" I nodded again.

She bustled about busily for a few more minutes, then breezed out, waggling her fingers at me as she went.

The medicine started kicking in soon after, and I was about to go back to sleep when a tall black man with a thin mustache, wearing a white doctor's coat and a stethoscope around his neck, walked into the room. I assumed he was the doctor.

"Hello there, Killian," he said. He pulled up one of the chairs in the room (they were a lovely shade of orange, to go with the puke green walls, I can only assume) and sat down so he was more or less on an eye level with me. "My name is Dr. Murray. I'm your doctor. It's good to see you awake. You're looking a lot better than the first time I saw you. You've been through a lot in the last 24 hours."

"Like what?" I asked.

"Well, do you remember what happened?" he asked.

I nodded, "Aren't the police going to ask me questions now that I'm awake?"

The doctor laughed, "You've watched too many cops shows on TV. No, they aren't going to need to ask you any questions. They're saying you interrupted a mugging, classic case of wrong place at the wrong time. They haven't caught the guy yet, but they are looking. Now, as for you, this guy did a number on you. You're going to be just fine, but it's going to take a while, several weeks at least. The knife entered at a perfect angle considering he missed all the important stuff, but he did puncture your lung. We've stitched up what needed stitching. Now you just need rest to finish up the job. It's not going to be real fast, and it's going to hurt like hell, but that's why God invented drugs. I'll be keeping an eye on you, and I'm sure someone showed you how to contact the nurses if you need anything."

He stood up as if to leave, but I noticed he'd left out some important information. I struggled to stay awake as the medicine was really kicking in about now. "Wait, what about Seth?" I said. Maybe I had been wrong. Maybe it wasn't really Seth, or maybe they had been able to save him, too.

"That was the other young man?" Dr. Murray asked me. His slightly joking manner was gone now, and I knew the news wasn't good.

I nodded.

"Did you know him?" he asked.

Past tense. Definitely not good. I nodded again.

"I'm sorry," he said simply. "He was dead when the police got there."

I felt a tear roll down my cheek. The doctor looked at me sympathetically and patted me awkwardly on the hand. "Try to get some rest," he said. "That's what's going to help you heal."

I wondered if he meant physically or emotionally. I suspected I would heal much faster from my stab wound.

The next time I awoke, my parents were in the room with me. As soon as my eyes were open, Mom was at the side of the bed.

"Are you ok?" she asked me.

"I'm not sure," I told her truthfully. The meds had me pretty groggy.

"Of course he's ok," Dad barked from his chair across the room. "Don't baby him. He's 16 for God's sake."

Mom looked into my eyes, and our new bond let me know that she was still concerned for me. In the interest of domestic peace, however, she moved away from the bed and sat back down.

"What I want to know is what you were doing with that fag anyway," Dad went on as if we were in the middle of a conversation. "Your mother said you went out for a walk. You weren't meeting him were you?"

I closed my eyes and hoped he'd get the hint. I didn't feel

like dealing with him right now. I hadn't even taken in the fact that Seth was dead, and I had come too close to dying myself. I was still in the freaking, hospital for God's sake, and all he could do was start interrogating me.

"Killian," he went on when I didn't answer, "if somebody hadn't seen that guy run out of the woods, then you would be dead. I want some answers."

Join the club, I thought. I fumbled around for the call button with my eyes still closed, found it and pushed the button.

"Were you meeting him there in the woods?" He was relentless. I mean I was in a hospital bed, with a stab wound, and he was grilling me like a defense witness at one of his trials.

"Gary," Mom interrupted. "He's tired, he's hurt, why don't we just let him be for now? You can ask him all these questions later."

"Did I ask you?" he said to her in his I'm-so-calm-it-hurts voice.

I was about to page the nurse again when I heard someone come into the room.

"Did someone need me?" she asked in a chipper voice. "Oh, I bet I know who it is!" Oh great, a perky nurse. Just what I always wanted.

I opened one eye and couldn't help but open the other one, too. She looked amazingly like Britney Spears in a nurse's uniform. I wondered if the meds they were giving me were causing me to have hallucinations. If so, I think I'd rather deal with the pain.

"Are you hurting again?" she asked me. If she only knew how much, I thought. Then she went on before I could even answer, "Well, we just gave you some pain medication not that long ago, so I can't give you anymore right now. I think you just need some rest." She turned towards my parents and smiled brightly at them. "He really needs his sleep, maybe you could come back later and visit with him." I liked her better already.

Dad glared at her for a second, then stood up and motioned for Mom to come with him. She started after him but paused by my bed for a second, rested her hand on my arm, then followed him out of the room.

Nurse Britney turned her thousand-watt smile on me once they were gone. "Is that what you wanted maybe?" she asked.

I managed a chuckle but immediately winced. "You're good," I told her.

"Thanks, but you'd be surprised how many kids use that thing to get rid of their parents." She laughed and started back out the door. "If you need anything else, don't hesitate to page me."

And I was alone with my thoughts finally. I was still a bit groggy from the pain medication, but I needed to think. Seth was dead. Someone had killed him and come very close to killing me as well. From what Dr. Murray had said, the police had pretty much closed the case; saying that I had interrupted a mugging. Somehow that didn't make sense to me. I thought about how the killer had frozen when he saw me clearly for the first time. It was right after that when he ran away, almost like he knew me. He'd even cursed. I racked my brain trying to see if I could recognize the voice, but I had been too scared and the voice had just been a whisper.

Then my mind turned to the unthinkable. *Why would someone want to kill Seth?* Maybe it was just a random killing. It was easier to think about that than think he had been killed for personal reasons. Again I asked myself, *Why would anyone want to kill Seth?* In my heart, I knew the answer. I could hear it in Seth's own words, "I mean, I'm used to everybody hating me. My own family hates me, so why shouldn't you..."

"Why would I hate you?" I had asked him.

"Because I'm gay," he had answered, simply and honestly. And now he was dead. *What if he had been killed because he was gay?* That thought was especially scary since I was still dealing with my own homosexuality. I knew it happened all the time, though. I remembered Matthew Shepard from all the news coverage, and I knew there were many others who didn't get national news exposure, that were simply swept under the rug.

Suddenly I found myself crying, softly at first and then harder, until my entire body was trembling from the sobs. They seemed to start from somewhere deep within me, somewhere I had never tapped before. I was weeping for Seth. I was weeping for Matthew Shepard. I was weeping for all those who were killed, or killed themselves, because of something they had no control over. In my mind, they were both the same. Society had killed the suicide victims just as surely as they had killed Matthew Shepard, and now, I knew in my heart, Seth.

But most of all, I think I was weeping for myself. I felt deep sense of loss for what had happened in the park. Not even so much for Seth—I really barely knew him, even though I had

liked him and thought we would have been good friends, if not
more. I wept for what it represented. Eventually, I cried myself
to sleep.

When I awoke again, Nurse Britney was gently sliding my
arm into a blood pressure cuff.

"Sorry to wake you up, Sport," she said, "but I have to take
your blood pressure. Someone was here earlier to visit you, but
only family can see you just yet, so they had to leave."

"Who was it?" I asked her, still not quite awake.

"Cute kid about your age, I think his name was Ashley, or
no wait..."

"Asher?" I asked.

"Yes, that's it Asher."

Asher had come to see me? Why? After the way things had
ended after school the day before, he was the last person I would
have expected to come see me.

They kept me in the hospital for a few days, and then I was
sent home to complete my recovery. Thank goodness Dad hadn't
come after me again, but I knew it was just a matter of time. He
hadn't been home much, but that was too good to last. Asher
hadn't come around anymore either. I was pretty much bed rid-
den most of the time, so I had lots of time to think about what
had happened.

I had come to a few conclusions. They were fairly simple, at
least in my mind. Number one, whoever had killed Seth couldn't
be allowed to get away with it. If the police weren't going to find
him, and it didn't seem to me like they were trying all that hard,
then I would.

Number two, it was fairly obvious, to me at least, that Seth
had been killed because he was gay. I didn't buy into the myste-
rious mugger theory. It was just too coincidental.

My last conclusion was that the killer had to have known me
judging by his reaction when he saw me. It was this last conclusion that scared me the most. It meant that someone I knew,
maybe knew very well, was a cold-blooded murderer.

I had been having nightmares almost every night since I had

come home. They were almost always the same: I was at the park again, by the pond. The shadows were dark and almost seemed to be alive. I was so scared. And then, there was Seth. He was standing on the bridge and he kept asking me, "Why Killian? Why me?" I would try to answer him, but no words would come out of my mouth no matter how hard I tried. And then I would feel someone come up behind me. I would awake, wet with cold sweat, my heart pounding in my chest, unable to get back to sleep.

Between my dark thoughts, the nightmares, and the accompanying lack of sleep, I found myself slipping deeper and deeper into depression. After what had happened to Seth, I knew I could never come out myself. I felt trapped by things I knew I had no control over. I wanted out, but I was too much of a coward to do anything about it but hate myself.

About a week after the murder and my stabbing, there was a knock at our door. Mom left to answer it. I could hear the conversation from my post in the living room. I could tell it was a man, but I didn't recognize the voice. Then he introduced himself.

"I'm Adam Connelly," I heard him say, "Seth's father. I'd like to see Killian if he's up to it."

My mother was silent for a moment, then she spoke softy, "I'll check."

As soon as she appeared in the door, I nodded. She turned and motioned to Mr. Connelly. When he came into the room, I almost gasped. He looked like an older version of Seth, except tired and worn out. I wondered if he had looked that way before Seth's murder or if it was a by-product of that horrible event.

"Hello, Killian," he said, extending his hand for me to shake.

"Hi, Mr. Connelly," I said.

"Please, call me Adam," he told me. "Seth spoke so much of you, I feel like I know you. You were his only friend..." He choked up and had to stop speaking. My eyes shifted to Mom. She was staring at me with a funny look on her face that I couldn't quite interpret.

"I'll be in the kitchen," she said and walked away. I forced my mind back to Adam. I turned to him just as he was sitting down in the chair closest to my makeshift bed on the sofa.

"I'm sorry," I said, feeling horribly inadequate. "I'm sorry for what happened..."

He waved his hand to stop me and I faded out. "You don't have anything to be sorry for. You're maybe the only person I know in this pathetic town who doesn't have anything to be sorry for." He shook his head as if to clear it. "I'm sorry. I'm still dealing with a lot of anger, but finger pointing doesn't accomplish anything. You're probably wondering why I'm here."

I couldn't argue with that, so I simply nodded.

"I have something for you, Killian," he said, pulling an envelope out of his pocket. "I found it as I was cleaning out Seth's room. It's a letter that he wrote to you. I hope you don't mind that I read it. I thought he'd like for you to have it."

He handed me the letter, and I looked at it for a moment.

"Please, open it and read it while I'm here," he asked me. I could hear the pain in his voice. How could I say no? So I opened it with trembling hands and pulled out a single sheet of lined notebook paper. I unfolded the letter and looked at the date on the top. It had been written the day he kissed me. I forced my eyes down the page and began to read.

"Hey Killer," it began. "I'm really sorry about what happened today. I don't know what I was thinking. Maybe that's the whole problem. I wasn't thinking. I wanted so badly for you to be gay, that I guess I imposed it on you. I get so lonely here in this town. I wanted to find someone I could love and who could love me. I guess I was expecting too much. I know I've probably ruined everything by now, but if not, if you can forgive me, I'd still like to be your friend. If you don't hate me that is."

The letter stopped here and then picked up again in different color ink.

"Wow. I just got off the internet after talking to you. I can't believe I was right! You are gay! But I'm not getting my hopes up or anything. I'm just glad you don't hate me and you still want to be my friend.

"After you signed off I looked up your middle name. I think it's very interesting what it meant. Maybe you will, too. Travers means 'the crossing.' Do you see it? I think it means that you are at a crossroads right now. You know you're gay, but you don't know what to do about it. There are several paths you can take, but only you can decide what path is right for you. And there really is only one path that's right for you.

"I hope you find it and I hope that maybe I can help you along that path."

It was signed, "Your friend, Seth."

By the time I reached the signature, tears were streaming freely down my face. I looked up to see that Adam was crying as well. I cleared my throat, "Why didn't he give it to me?" I asked.

"I don't know," he said simply, "but I think he'd like for you to have it now." Then he stood up. "That's all really. I wanted to give you the letter. Thank you for being a friend to my son. I can let myself out."

He started out of the room, then stopped in the doorway. He stood there for a few moments and then turned. "He's right, you know. You are at a crossroads. What path you choose now will have an impact on the rest of your life in a way that you can't even begin to fathom now. Choose carefully." And he was gone.

Mom came back into the room a few minutes later. She took in my tear-stained face and the letter in my hands and then sat down in the chair Adam had just vacated. She sat for a few moments in silence.

"Killian," she said finally, "are you gay?"

I opened my mouth but no sound came out. I sat like this for what seemed like an eternity before I finally pulled myself together enough to shut my mouth. I nodded instead.

She sat there for a few more minutes without saying a word. Just when I thought the silence would deafen me, she simply stood up and walked out of the room. I felt as if my heart had been ripped out. I know that sounds like a cliché, but that's exactly what it felt like, as if suddenly there was a gaping hole where my heart had been.

I began to cry, and then once again I was racked by sobs. I don't know how long I cried, but suddenly I became aware that a storm had come up. I could hear the rain beating against the house and slight rumbles of thunder in the distance coming closer with each crash.

I struggled up from the sofa, ignoring the physical pain. The emotional pain had taken precedence for the moment. I opened the shades at the window and stared out at the storm and thought about how it reflected the storm I was feeling inside, slowly building up to the point where it was a force that couldn't be stopped.

I was at a crossroads. What path should I take?

Chapter 5

I was sitting at the window overlooking the garden, watching the wind blow furiously through the brightly colored flowers. Many of the plants had already lost their petals, but so far the bleeding hearts were holding their own, which is more than I could say for myself. I was feeling more and more lost every second.

I stood up and went outside into the storm. No one said anything to me, and I wasn't surprised. Once outside, the wind buffeted my body and the driving rain almost instantly soaked me, my tears mixing with the raindrops. I didn't care. I was half hoping the raging storm would blow me away—or at least blow away the storm raging inside me.

I fell to my knees in the middle of the yard. I had never felt so alone. In the course of the last two weeks I had lost everyone I cared about. I had alienated my best friends. Seth had been murdered. And now my mother knew that I was gay, something I'd only figured out a few days ago. There was no one I could turn to, no one to talk to. I found myself wishing that the guy who had killed Seth had finished me off, too. I wanted to die.

I had never had thoughts like this before. I'd never understood how anyone could even consider hurting themselves, let alone killing themselves. And here I was trying to think of the best way. I knew where Dad kept a gun in his bedroom. He'd made me learn how to shoot and I was good, but I didn't like guns. There was no way I could follow through with that. I could swallow some pills, but I didn't know what kind or how many or even if we had anything that would work. I didn't want to get halfway done and have it not work. I didn't think I was strong enough to slit my wrists. Maybe I could just lie out here and hope I would die of exposure. The temperature had dropped quickly, and even though it was only the middle of September, it was only in the upper 40s. I was shivering violently as I knelt in the middle of my back yard in the pouring rain with lightning flashing and thunder crashing all around me.

I don't know how long I had been sitting there when a voice penetrated my dark reverie. "Killian!" I got the impression it wasn't the first time it had called my name. Before I could even raise my head, someone was at my side. I looked up through the rain pouring down my face and couldn't believe my eyes. It was Asher!

"What are you doing here?" I asked. My voice was thick from crying.

"I came to see how you were doing, but I can see for myself. Obviously, not well. Come on. You have to come inside. It's freezing out here, and you're soaked." When I didn't move he picked me up and carried me inside. I let him. I was past putting up a fight.

We came back in through the sliding glass doors just as Mom came into the room.

"Oh my God," she gasped when she saw us. "What happened?"

I guess we did look pretty bad. I was soaked to the bone from the torrential downpour, and Asher had gotten pretty wet, too, even in just the few minutes that he was out there. At least Asher was wearing a jacket, although I was pretty sure the black suede would be ruined. He came the rest of the way in and lowered me to the couch before turning back to my mother.

"He's ok physically, but he's really upset. I found him in the backyard," he said. "He needs to get into some dry clothes, though."

My mom stood, staring at me with one hand over her mouth. After what seemed like forever she still hadn't responded, so Asher said, "Mrs. Kendall?"

She looked at him as if she'd just noticed him for the first time. "Oh, Asher, could you leave us alone for just a minute.

Don't leave; I think I'll need your help. I just need a few minutes alone..."

"Ok, I'll go get some towels," he said after she had faded out, and he left the room.

Mom walked slowly to my side and knelt on the floor. She reached out a trembling hand and smoothed back the wet hair that was plastered to my forehead.

"Baby, what were you doing out there?" she said, almost in a whisper.

I turned my head so I didn't have to look into her eyes. "I wanted to die," I whispered back.

Her hand on my arm began to tremble and she began to cry softly.

"Oh, God! Killian, I'm so sorry," she cried. She reached up and turned my face towards her. "Baby, I don't care if you are gay or...or...whatever. I love you with all my heart and that will never change. I think I've always known you were different. And that's not a bad thing, it's just...it's going to take some adjustment on my part. I don't know anything about being gay, but I'll learn. I love you."

We were both crying by now, and I rolled onto my side and hugged her tightly, ignoring the pain that I still felt in my stomach. My adventure outside didn't seem to have helped much.

"I love you, too," I told her through my tears. I think this was the first time we'd ever said those words to each other.

"You need to get out of those wet clothes," she said, pulling away. I was reluctant to let go. "Asher?" she called out.

He was there in a moment so he must have been waiting around the corner so as not to disturb us. He had taken off his jacket, and his long-sleeved shirt underneath was still dry, so that meant that only his pants were still damp. He looked as if he'd dried off a bit already himself. His curly hair, even darker when wet, was standing out in tufts.

Mom took the towels and handed them to me. "Can you help Killian upstairs to his room so he can change?" she asked Asher.

"Of course, Mrs. Kendall," he said. They both helped me up and Asher put his arm around me for me to lean on and we started out towards the stairs.

"And Asher?" Mom called. We stopped at the bottom step, "Thank you."

"For what?" Asher called back.

"For finding Killian and being such a good friend."

We stood there for a second before Asher nudged me into moving again. The climb up the stairs, which was slow and rather difficult, was taken one step at a time and mostly in silence. Finally we made it to my room and Asher helped me to my bed, then turned around. I thought he was leaving, but instead he shut the door and came back over to me.

"What are you doing?" I asked him.

"Your mom's wrong, you know," he said quietly. "I've not been a very good friend."

"You're friends with Zack and Jesse," I said. "They obviously come first. Like I said, I'm the back-up plan. Or I used to be. I'm nothing anymore. Why are you here?"

He ignored my question and started rummaging through my drawers, pulling out dry clothes. I winced when he opened my underwear drawer, but he just pulled out a pair of boxers and tossed them onto the bed.

"His getting killed really upset you, huh?" he asked me, still digging through my dresser.

"Geez, Asher, what do you think? I found him. And whoever killed him tried to kill me, too. No, I'm not upset, I'm just flippin' fine and dandy here." Then to my great embarrassment I burst into tears.

"Dammit," he said rushing over to me. "Killian, I'm sorry, I didn't mean to upset you. I'm so dumb sometimes. It's just...I didn't realize you were so close to him and all."

"We weren't that close," I sniffled. I was really getting tired of crying.

Asher picked up one of the towels and gently wiped off my face and then started drying my hair. I felt like a little kid again. "What are you doing?" I asked him again.

"I guess this is my way of saying I'm sorry for being such a jerk," he said, then he continued. "I had a big fight with Zack and Jesse. Earlier this week. I haven't talked to them since."

"You did? Why? What in the world happened?"

"I wanted to come see you after...well, you know, but they didn't think I should."

"Shouldn't hang around with fags, huh?" I said bitterly.

Asher froze. We sat there for a few seconds, neither of us speaking or moving. Then Asher got up and picked up the shirt and sweat pants that he'd dropped when I had started crying. He brought them over and set them on the bed. He stood there for a second, as if trying to decide what to do. Suddenly he reached down, took off my glasses, and began pulling up my shirt.

"Hey!" I yelped.

"I'm just helping you with your shirt, dude," he laughed.

"I don't need help, I can do it," I insisted.

"Oh, you can, huh? You can pull this wet shirt over your head without an extreme amount of pain?" he said in a teasing voice. "Just let me help. It's ok. I'm not gonna rape you or anything."

He had a point. I gave him a dirty look then allowed him to help me untangle my arms from the wet material and pull it over my head. The maneuver still caused quite a bit of discomfort, and I knew he could tell. Once my shirt was off and all I was wearing were some wet bandages and soaked shorts, I suddenly became very self-conscious. I wasn't unattractive or anything, but I also knew I wasn't anywhere near as built as Asher was.

"Help me get my shirt on," I mumbled reaching for the dry one.

"You need to change those bandages first, Kill," Asher said.

I sighed. He was right again, of course. "The stuff is in a basket by the couch downstairs," I told him and he was gone in a flash. I decided to change my pants while he was gone, since it was much easier pulling on pants then pulling on a shirt, but I only got as far as my dry boxers before he was back. It didn't seem like he could have had time to even get downstairs, and here he was back with the basket with me sitting in my boxers.

"Your mom was bringing it up. I told her I would help you this time," he explained.

"You don't have to," I said quickly.

"I know I don't have to, I want to. Will you just stop fighting me and let me help you?" He was starting to sound exasperated, so once again I gave in.

He gently unwound the wet wrappings and applied fresh salve to the wound, which was not healing quite as quickly as the doctors had hoped. They said my lungs were doing great, however.

"Arms up," he said, and began to wrap the new bandages around me. He sat to one side of me, which meant he had to wrap his arms around me each time around. He seemed to be going much slower than was absolutely necessary. I tried not to enjoy the closeness of his body too much. After all, he was still strictly off limits.

"You shouldn't be so nervous about your body, Kill," he

said softly into my ear making me jump.

"Wh-wh-what?" I stuttered.

"I could tell you felt weird about me seeing you without a shirt," he said. "It's no big deal. I've seen you before like when we go swimming and stuff."

"I'm not nervous," I argued, then after a few seconds. "It's just that you're so much more built than I am."

"So? Who cares? You're fine. There, all finished." He stepped back to admire his handiwork, then grabbed my shirt and helped me into it. After handing me back my glasses, he picked up the sweats. He stood there with them for a few seconds, unsure of what to do. He looked so awkward; it was all I could do not to start laughing.

"I think I can manage those on my own," I told him, trying not to smile. "But thanks for all the help, Ash."

"You're welcome, Killian." He paused for a second, "I have to go now, but I want you to know that I'm really sorry I haven't been a better friend. I promise I'm gonna do better from now on." Then he totally shocked me by leaning in and kissing me on the cheek.

I was speechless, which Asher used to his advantage to quickly slip out of my room. He paused in the doorway on his way out and called over his shoulder, "I'll be back tomorrow."

I didn't know what to think about Asher's sudden about-face. It seemed like he was honestly making an effort to be a real friend, but I was a little skeptical. He said he'd had a big fight with Zack and Jesse, over me no less, but what if he was really just spying on me? I wouldn't put it past them. Kind of a "let's see what Killian-the-fag is up to." But it felt like Asher was sincere to me. And what was up with that kiss? He wouldn't have thrown that in just to be convincing, would he? I wouldn't even allow myself to think that he might be gay.

Thinking about being gay reminded me about Mom. Now she knew that I was gay, too, and she still loved me anyway. I felt so good knowing that. The earlier thoughts of killing myself seemed so far away. But what about Dad? He couldn't find out.

Suddenly I was tired. All this conjecture, combined with my very emotional roller-coaster ride of a day, had worn me out. I didn't have enough energy to tackle the stairs again, so I crawled up on my bed. *I'll just take a short nap*, I thought.

Chapter
6

I had a vague impression that someone looked in on me at some point, but the next time I awoke, the sun was streaming brightly through the windows in my room. I had slept all night and it seemed the storm had passed. I looked at the clock and gasped. It was almost 11 AM. I must have been more worn out than I had thought.

I sat up and winced at the pain. I fought my way to my feet and almost fell back onto my bed. Asher was sitting on my floor, reading a book. He was wearing jeans and a white Billabong sweatshirt that made him look paler than usual. His curly dark brown hair shone in the sunlight that fell across him like a spotlight. He looked like an angel sitting there. He looked up at me and smiled.

"Good morning, Sleeping Beauty," he said.

"How'd you get in here?" I asked him.

"Your mom let me in. I've been sitting here for about an hour. By the way, she had to leave to do some chores. She asked me to keep an eye on you, so I did." He grinned up at me. Gosh, he was cute when he grinned. "You need some help getting into the bathroom?"

"I dunno," I said. "I think I can handle it. I can walk, you know."

He still hadn't stopped grinning. "Barely. How about that?"

he asked me, pointing to my crotch. "Think you can handle that?"

I almost died. There, in all its glory, not hidden at all by my boxers, was my morning wood. I tried to pull my T-shirt down over it, but to my further embarrassment it was still fairly obvious. I glared at Asher and walked off to the bathroom, trying to spare some dignity while he rolled on the floor laughing.

Thanks to my extreme mortification, it didn't take long for Mr. Woody to go away. I decided while I was in the bathroom to go ahead and take my bath. Besides, it would make Asher wait that much longer. Maybe he'd go home before I got out. I stripped down and carefully took off the bandages while the water ran. I usually was a shower person, but showers were a little more than I could handle right then. I had to wash carefully around the wound and especially had to keep soap away from it or it stung like crazy, but it was looking much better this morning. I might be able to get the stitches out soon.

When I came out of the bathroom in just a towel, I was surprised to see Asher reclining on my bed, still reading.

"Make yourself at home," I said dryly.

"Thanks, I will," he grinned. Man, that grin got to me. "By the way, nice towel."

I stuck my tongue out at him and went to get clothes out of my dresser.

"You really shouldn't be worried about your body, Kill," Asher said coming up behind me. "You have a natural definition like your dad. You don't even need to work out."

I blushed. "Um...thanks, Ash," I mumbled.

He examined my wound. "It looks a lot better this morning," he said, running his fingers lightly around it. "Must be my magic touch. Sit down and I'll put the bandages back on it for you."

"Oh crap, I left the bandage in the bathroom," I told him. His closeness was starting to get to me. I still didn't know what to make of his sudden interest.

While Asher was getting the bandage from the bathroom, I quickly pulled on my boxers and a pair of jeans.

"Ok," he said in a bad Dr. Ruth imitation as he came back in. "Have a seat, the doctor will see you now."

I chuckled as I perched on the edge of the bed. I had to admit, I liked having him around. I hadn't felt this good since before...I felt my face fall with the thought of Seth. How could I be laughing and having fun when Seth had been murdered?

"You're thinking about Seth, aren't you?" Asher asked me, suddenly serious.

I nodded. Asher pulled the tube of salve out of the basket and squeezed some on to the stitches. "You know," he said as he worked, "you have to move on eventually. You can't help it that he was killed, but you don't have to go around sad all the time either."

"I know. And I'm not sad all the time," I argued, "but it just doesn't seem right that he could be murdered like that in cold blood and no one is trying harder to catch the killer. I could have been killed, too."

Asher looked up at me from where he had knelt on the floor. "I know," he said almost under his breath. Then he went on, louder now, "It was just a mugger, Killian. They'll catch him eventually."

"Maybe not just a mugger."

Asher looked at me intently, "What do you mean?"

"What if it wasn't just a mugger? What if he was murdered on purpose?"

"Why would anyone kill Seth?"

"Because he was gay."

"Then why would they stab you?"

I paused for a second, then rushed on, hoping he wouldn't catch the pause, "Maybe because I was just in the wrong place at the wrong time. They stopped when they saw who I was, you know. They were gonna kill me too, but when they sat up and saw me more clearly, they said 'Shit,' jumped up and ran. They recognized me."

Asher sat back onto the floor. "You're kidding," he whispered.

I shook my head. "I wish I was," I said.

"That's scary, Kill, but that doesn't mean he was killed because he was gay. Maybe the mugger knew you."

"I've been thinking a lot about this, Asher, and I don't think it was just a mugger. I was there, remember? Call it intuition, call it a hunch...I don't know what it is exactly. I just know in my heart that it wasn't a random mugging."

Asher sat in silence for a minute, then got back up on his knees and reached for the bandage. "If you've thought so much about it, who do you think it was?"

"I don't know," I told him. "I hadn't really thought about

that part of it yet."

"Well, arms up then," he said, and as soon as I'd complied he started wrapping me up again.

While he wrapped I thought about his question. Who could it have been? I was surprised I hadn't thought about this before. I felt kind of dumb actually. Isn't that the obvious first question? But as I began to think about it I realized that maybe I just hadn't wanted to think about it. The first person that popped into my mind was Zack. I thought about his threat earlier that same day. He had said that I'd be sorry; me and my boyfriend, and we all knew he meant Seth. Then I thought of Asher and his words that day last week in this same room, "If he hurt you, I'll kill him." Immediately, my body stiffened involuntarily.

Asher noticed right away, "What? Did I hurt you?" he asked me.

"No, it's nothing," I said, then, "Can I ask you a question?"

"Sure, Kill, you know you can ask me anything."

"Asher, why are you being so nice to me all of a sudden?"

He didn't answer at first. He just finished up the bandaging job and then sat back on his heels, leaving his hands still resting lightly on my sides, his eyes turned down, not looking at me.

"I told you before," he said.

"Tell me again," I insisted.

He took a deep breath. "When I thought I was losing you as a friend to Seth, I realized how much you meant to me. When you started acting so different, I wasn't sure what was going on. You were always snapping at people and getting mad and yelling. It wasn't like you, so I got worried." He looked up to see if I was listening, then, quickly looking away again, he continued. "I didn't really like what Zack and Jesse were saying and all, but it was just easier to go along with them. But then when you got hurt, almost killed, it really scared me. I realized that I had almost lost you...er...lost the chance to tell you...I mean..."

"Tell me what?" I asked softly.

He sat there for a second then looked back up at me. Our eyes locked.

"Did you love Seth?" he asked me.

"What?" I gasped.

Then he leaned forward onto his knees again and kissed me softly on the lips.

Time seemed to slow down when Asher kissed me. In the few seconds that our lips were pressed together I had a whole conversation in my head.

"*Does this mean that Asher is gay? Well, duh! Straight guys do not generally kiss their friends on the lips like this. Not unless they are in the Mafia and I'm pretty sure Asher isn't—his dad maybe, but not Asher. But then why didn't he ever tell me? Maybe for the same reason I didn't. But then again, I didn't know until last week really. Oh, who am I kidding? I've always known in my heart. Nothing has ever felt more right than Asher kissing me.* Wait a minute! Asher is kissing me!"

With that last thought, I jerked back and stared at Asher wide-eyed. He slowly sat back on his heels and looked up at me. I could read in his eyes the fear of rejection and the depth of his feelings. For a long time neither of us spoke. Finally I pulled myself together.

"Why did you kiss me?" I asked. My voice came out shaky and a little hoarse, as if I'd just woke up, which is kind of how I felt, too.

"I...I...I'm sorry," he said shakily. "I shouldn't have. It's just...I found that letter that you left on the couch last night when I was looking for you, the one from Seth. I know I shouldn't have read it, but I did."

I had completely forgotten about the letter. What if Dad had found it? I was very glad that Asher had found it instead. Especially considering what had just happened.

He continued, "When I read that you were gay..." He stopped again and seemed to search for words, "Killian, I've had a crush on you for years. I've always known I was gay, but who was I going to tell? Zack? Jesse? No way! I finally got up enough nerve to come see you and I found that letter. When I read that you were gay, I had to find you. And then when I saw you outside in the rain like that, my heart broke for you. And for me too, maybe, cuz I thought that you must have been in love with Seth to be so upset. I was so jealous of him, Kill. I was afraid that he would steal you away from me. I want to be with you, Killian Travers Kendall. Seth said that you were at a crossroads. Last night you almost went down the wrong path. Let me help you, please. I want to walk with you down whatever path you choose."

He seemed to run out of words and so he just sat there staring at me expectantly. I wasn't sure what he expected, however. I wasn't sure what I felt. I needed time to think.

"Ash," I began, speaking slowly and deliberately, "I need

some time to figure stuff out. All I can tell you right now is that yes, I am gay. No, I didn't love Seth. Not in that way at least. I didn't even really know him, although I wanted to know him better."

"So you don't want me?" Asher whispered.

"Ash, I didn't say that. I just meant..." I stopped as a large tear slipped out of the corner of his eye and rolled down his cheek. I followed its shiny path all the way to his chin, mesmerized by that small drop of saline.

"It's ok, Killian. I understand. Why would you want me? I'm just a dumb jock who treated you like dirt." With that, he began to cry in earnest, not great body-shuddering sobs, just quiet acceptance. In a way, it was worse. I slowly slipped off the bed until I was sitting next to him on the floor. I reached out to him and drew him to me and let him cry quietly on my shoulder for a minute. Then I cupped my hand under his chin and lifted his face until he was looking me in the eye. I kissed him softly on the lips, just for a few seconds before breaking away.

"Asher, right now I don't know what I want. I like you. I do. It's not that at all, it's just...I don't know how to explain it to you. I need more time. I mean, there's a lot going on right now. Seth hasn't even been buried yet."

Asher nodded and sat up, pulling gently away from me.

"His memorial service is this afternoon you know," he told me, wiping his tears on the back of his hand. "He was buried already back up around Baltimore somewhere, but his dad wanted to have a service down here, too." He looked at his watch. "Actually, it's in like one hour."

"I didn't know," I said softly. "I want to go. Can you take me?"

"I dunno, Killian. Maybe that's not such a good idea. I mean, everyone's talking already cuz you were with him in the park and all."

"Please?" I begged him. "It would mean a lot to me. Kind of like a chance to say good-bye."

He stared at me, then nodded. "Yeah, I'll take you. And I'll stay with you too so I can bring you home afterwards. We'll leave a note for your mom. Let's get you changed. You can't go dressed like that."

The next 45 minutes were spent with the two of us changing my clothes (it was a two-person job) and then swinging by Asher's house while he changed his clothes. I sat in the car while he ran in, giving me a few precious minutes to think, the first I'd had since Asher's big revelation.

I still wasn't sure how I felt about Asher. I knew I liked him, but did I trust him enough to give him a chance? My heart screamed yes, but my head was still having doubts. Especially troubling was the idea that maybe Asher was the attacker. He'd admitted that he was jealous of Seth and he felt as if Seth was taking me away from him. And his words that day in my room kept echoing through my head over and over, "If he hurt you, I'll kill him." Somehow I just couldn't believe that about him, but it still kept me from jumping in the way I wanted to.

And what about what he'd said earlier, that everyone was talking about me? That meant that they suspected I was gay. I was still coming to terms with it myself; I wasn't ready to deal with everyone else. Why did life have to be so confusing?

Finally Asher came back out dressed almost identically to me, all in black. He looked a whole lot sexier, however, at least in my opinion. The black silk shirt clung to his chest in a way that almost made me dizzy.

"What?" he asked me.

I tore my gaze away from him and tried to remember why we dressed like this. I felt guilty for finding myself so attracted to one friend on my way to the funeral of another. "Nothing," I mumbled.

"No, tell me. Should I go change? Do I look stupid?"

"Definitely not," I told him. "Let's go, we're gonna be late."

The memorial service was being held at the park, of all places. I was scared about going back, but I tried to tell myself that it was broad daylight and Asher would be with me. I'd never even been to a memorial service before, or a funeral either. I wasn't sure what to expect.

We drove in silence, neither of us knowing quite what to say. When we arrived at the park, there were hardly any other cars. As we approached the pavilion where the service was taking place, I could just about count on one hand the number of people who had showed up to remember Seth. I recognized Adam Connelly, Seth's dad, standing next to a handsome man of about the same age. He was talking to a man wearing a black suit and a clerical collar who I assumed must be the minister or priest or whatever. I didn't know the other several people there.

Adam noticed us as we approached, and he broke away from

the man in black and walked towards us. The other man with him followed a few steps behind.

"Killian, thank you for coming," he said simply and embraced me gently, watching out for my injury. "You should be at home recuperating, but I appreciate your being here. I'm glad there will be at least one person here that cared about Seth beside Steve and I." He turned to the man who had followed him over and motioned him forward.

"Killian, this is Steve Redden, my very good friend. Steve, this is Killian Kendall, he was Seth's friend."

I shook Steve's hand and exchanged nice-to-meet-you's.

"This is my friend, Asher Davis," I said.

After another round of hand shaking, Adam turned to Steve. "Killian was attacked that night as well, but thank goodness he survived."

I shuddered at the implication; that Seth hadn't been so fortunate. It was a grim reminder of why we were standing here now.

"Come on," Adam said, taking my shudder for a sign of my physical weakness, "you need to have a seat."

With Adam on one side, Asher on the other, and Steve trailing behind, I felt a little like royalty as we approached the pavilion. I scanned the group that had gathered. It had grown to maybe 15 people while we were talking; I suspected that some of them were police and others reporters. All in all, it was a sad testament to a sad, broken life. It seemed so unfair that such a good person had been struck down so young. And I was convinced that it was over something so incredibly stupid. In fact, his killer could be here today, pretending to mourn for the very life he took.

Then I noticed a particular face and stopped cold. Steve almost ran into me from behind. What was my father doing here? Political posturing most likely, it was after all an election year. I didn't think he had noticed me yet, but then he slowly turned and stared right at me. His eyes were intense and I knew the fight I had been avoiding since the hospital wouldn't be put off much longer.

I looked away and decided that I wouldn't let him distract me from the reason I was there. Adam insisted we sit on the front row with him and Steve. I felt very conspicuous and I could tell Asher felt uncomfortable as well, but I couldn't say no.

As soon as we were seated, the priest stepped forward to the podium. I noticed the table set off to one side for the first time. It had pictures set up all over it; all of them had Seth in them somewhere. Many of them were the ones I had seen at his house, but there were some new ones, too.

"We are here today for a very solemn purpose," the priest began, "to remember the life of a young man cut off before his time. Seth David Connelly's life was ended much too soon in a senseless and tragic act of violence. Perhaps we will never understand what provoked such a horrible event, but we can rest assured that Seth is no longer in a world filled with hate and prejudice. I am going to keep my comments very brief today to allow you time to remember Seth in your own very special ways. But first Seth's father, Adam, has some words he'd like to share with you." I got the impression that the priest really didn't know Seth at all.

Adam stood up and walked to the podium. He stood for a minute without saying a word; just stood there, gripping the podium as if it was all that was holding him up. I thought he was going to break down, but he fought for control and won.

"My son was taken from me last week. He was taken from me by an act of violence so horrible that it physically sickens me every time I think about it. Most of you here didn't even know him; you're only here because your editor or superior sent you. You're just doing your job. Well, let me introduce him to you. Seth David Connelly was a beautiful, brilliant, clever, and kind-hearted 16-year-old. He enjoyed running on the beach. He liked reading mysteries. He did well in all his classes, but theater was his favorite. He loved acting. He wanted to be an actor, but now he'll never get that opportunity."

He choked up and dropped his head. When he looked up again his eyes were bright with unshed tears, but he was once again in control. I admired him for his strength.

"There is so much more I could tell you about my son. He was the greatest joy of my life. Nothing will ever be able to fill the void that his death has left in my life. But I haven't told you something very important about my son. He was gay. And he wasn't afraid or ashamed of it either, even though he had suffered so much in his young life because of it. He was a hero to me. He should have been a hero to all of us. He had the courage to accept himself in a society where he was told that what he was is wrong, that it's dirty and perverted. But he knew differently. He saw things with his poet's heart. To him the world was always beautiful and exciting. He trusted inherently. We moved to this town in the hopes of finding a safe place to live—it's ironic isn't it? It's even more ironic that this town that prides itself on being welcoming so totally rejected my son. In fact, there was only one person at his whole school who would even speak to him without calling him names and insulting him. To me, he is also a hero." He looked at me and smiled a sad, teary-eyed smile. "Thank you, Killian.

"I want to leave you with this thought. The police and our state's attorney have been quick to tell us that Seth's death was a random mugging. Why do they believe that when there is so little evidence? All his money was still in his wallet. I believe that this was a hate crime, pure and simple. I told the police investigating about the threatening notes that we found and they wrote them off as childish pranks. I don't think having your throat slit is childish." Several people gasped and Adam seemed to be struggling for control again. "His killer may never be brought to justice, but I take comfort in the fact that one day he will have to stand before the Great Judge. Goodbye, Seth. I love you!"

Adam stepped down from the podium, took his seat and began to weep softly. Steve pulled him into himself and allowed him to cry on his shoulder. No one moved for what seemed like an eternity, then the priest slowly walked back up to the podium. "Does anyone have anything they would like to say in memory of Seth?" He almost sounded as if he hoped not. Again, another eternity seemed to pass. No one dared even move. It was almost like they were holding their collective breath. Just as the priest cleared his throat to give some final words, I stood up.

Every eye was fastened on me, including the furious glare of my father. I looked him straight in the eye before turning to Adam.

"I am truly sorry for your loss, Mr. Connelly...Adam," I began. "It's not just your loss, though. It was a loss to every person who never got the chance to know him. I didn't know Seth that long, only two weeks really, but he was my friend. He was a truly good person and that's something we don't have enough of in this world. He helped me through what could have been one of the hardest things I've ever been through. I'll miss him."

I collapsed back into my seat and tried not to cry. I felt Asher's hand fumble discreetly with mine for a second, then it slipped into my hand and he held it below the sight of the people sitting behind us. It was not, however, out of sight of the priest who looked at us in surprise before once again clearing his throat.

"Well, if that's all, then I'd like to thank you all on behalf of the family for coming out to show your respects. Donations can be made in Seth's memory to the Theater Club at the high school. Thank you." And he quickly hurried away.

At the priest's dismissal the crowd quickly dispersed, my father shooting me a lethal look, until finally it was just Asher, Adam, Steve, and myself.

"So you don't think it was a mugger either?" I asked Adam quietly.

"Either?" he asked me with a raised eyebrow.

"I didn't believe that from the beginning," I told him, "but what can we do?"

"*We* can't do anything," Adam said, stressing the 'we,' "and there's not much I can do, for that matter. I'm thinking about hiring a private detective, but the few I've contacted so far turned me down cold. They said this isn't some TV show where private detectives run around with guns. They mostly just do insurance stuff and spy on cheating spouses. They told me to drop it and let the cops handle it. Who cares if they sweep it under a rug?"

We both sighed at the same time.

"Maybe I can ask some questions around school," I suggested.

"Are you crazy?" Asher jumped in.

"Asher's right," Adam said. "That wouldn't be safe, Killian. We're talking about a murderer here. He killed Seth and he tried to kill you."

"No, he didn't try to kill me. If he wanted to kill me, I would be dead. He had the opportunity and he didn't take it."

"Two things there," Steve interjected. "One, you say 'he,' do you know for sure it's a man? And two, what do you mean he had the opportunity and didn't take it?"

I thought for a minute. "No, I don't know for sure it was a man. It could have been a very strong woman, I guess. Or a well built teenager, easily. I didn't get a good sense of his size because he jumped on me and we were wrestling on the ground before he stabbed me. I never really heard his voice cuz he just whispered. He was wearing a stocking on his head so I couldn't see his face in the dark." I took a deep breath. Talking about it was still a little hard. "And after he stabbed me in the stomach, he was going to stab me again, but when he raised up and saw me, he said 'shit' and ran away."

"And you told the police this?" Adam asked me.

"They never asked me," I told him.

"You were never questioned?" Steve asked incredulously.

"Nope."

"What kind of investigation is this?" Steve shook his head in disgust.

"It's not an investigation," Adam said sadly, "it's a cover-up."

"Oh come on, Adam," Steve said gently, "don't go all conspiracy theory on me. It's just small town police ineptness."

"This police force is anything but inept," Adam told him. "I looked into it when I was looking for a community to settle into. I'm nothing if not thorough. They have an excellent force here. No, they aren't keystone cops, they are well-trained professionals."

"You said something about threatening letters?" I asked him.

"Yeah, there were three of them all together. Each one printed out on a computer. Virtually untraceable, anyway, so they wouldn't have really led to anyone, but they could at least be taking the idea of murder more seriously. They didn't even take the letters. They were nasty, hateful. They said things like 'God hates fags' and 'Go away. We don't want queers here.'"

"The police said if they were death threats they would have taken them into consideration," Steve chipped in.

"How did he get them?" I asked.

"They were stuffed in his locker at school."

"So it had to be someone at school!" I exclaimed. "See, you do need me to help. Where else can you get inside information from the school? I was Seth's only friend; it'll be natural for me to be asking questions."

"It's not safe, Killian," Asher said again. He sounded a little worried. I had almost forgotten he was even there, he'd been quiet for so long.

"Well, actually," Steve began as we all turned to look at him, "if you just stick to general questions, it can't hurt anything. It's not likely to be anything more than a mugging, but on the off chance that it is, I doubt they will do anything to hurt Killian if they didn't when they had their chance the first time."

We all sat in silence for a few minutes thinking about what Steve had said. Finally Adam nodded.

"Ok," he said, "If you promise to be careful and not do anything stupid or obvious, you can ask some questions. But check in with us every day and don't go off half-cocked." He turned to Asher. "And you, please keep an eye on him. If anything happens to either one of you, I don't think I could live with myself."

"Killian is looking a bit tired," Steve said. "Maybe you should get him home, Asher."

"Yeah, I am feeling a little drained," I admitted. "Although I can't say I'm looking forward to dealing with my father when I get home. You should be able to hear the fireworks from here."

"Your father was here?" Adam asked me. "I must admit that surprises me."

"It's an election year," I joked half-heartedly.

We all stood up and exchanged hugs this time around instead of handshakes, and Asher and I started off for home. When we arrived, Dad's car was parked next to Mom's in the driveway. Asher parked behind Mom and turned off the car. We both sat there in silence for a few minutes, neither of us wanting to face what was waiting for us inside.

"Do you ever wonder why you drive on a parkway and park on a driveway?" I asked no one in particular.

Asher, being the wise person that he is, chose not to answer that, but instead got out of the car and came around to help me out. We approached the front door with more than a little trepidation. Before he opened it, Asher wrapped his arms around me for a brief hug. We barely had the door closed behind us when Dad stepped into the hallway, Mom a few steps behind him. I could tell by the look on Mom's face that this wasn't going to be pretty. I braced myself for the barrage.

Chapter
7

"Asher," Dad said in that horrible controlled voice of his, "I think it would be best if you went on home now. Your dad's waiting for you. We just got off the phone."

Asher shot me a look that was easier to read than a book. He was terrified.

"Yes, sir," he said softly, and turned and left. Now I was left standing alone facing my father. I still hadn't even gotten out of the entrance hall.

"You," Dad said. "What were you doing at that place today?"

"I felt like I should go," I said firmly.

"You felt like you should go?" he mocked. "Well isn't that nice, Meg?" He addressed this to my mother. "You waited till your mother was gone and then you and Asher couldn't get out of here quick enough."

I decided that this wasn't a good time to point out that I'd had no way of knowing that Mom was going anywhere this morning, so it wasn't like it had been planned.

"I left you alone after the whole stabbing incident at your mother's insistence," he growled this as if the 'whole stabbing incident' was my fault, "but this is too much. I want answers and I want them now. How could you publicly humiliate me like that? There must have been reporters from three different newspapers in attendance and you sit on the front row. Then if that isn't enough, you stand up and make your little tear-jerking speech. That's going to be all over the place in the morning."

I was warmed by his concern for the family of the deceased. He was making me more and more angry by the second, but I struggled to remain silent.

"Start explaining, and let's start with the park. I find out today that you were friends with that...that faggot Connelly boy after I explicitly told you to stay away from him."

"You can't tell me who I can and can't be friends with," I said matching him in the control department. I had learned well.

"Yes...I...can," he was starting to lose his veneer of control and I was loving it. "That's why I'm the father and you are not. You were going to meet him that night, weren't you?"

"Yes, I was," I told him defiantly.

"Then you deserved what you got," he snarled, for the first time losing control. He took three large steps towards me, covering the entire length of the hallway in those few strides, and struck me across the face open-handed. I reeled backwards into the door and slid down to the floor. I vaguely heard Mom screaming in the background, but the ringing in my ears almost deafened me.

"I won't have my son associated with faggots," he bellowed over me.

I looked up at him with all the hate and contempt that I felt for him at the moment and he actually took an involuntary step back when he looked at me. "I will associate with who I want to associate with," I spat out. It was almost like someone else speaking.

With an animal-like roar he reached down and yanked me to my feet, only to strike me again, this time with a closed fist. I slammed into the door and slid to the floor once again. This time I tasted the metallic taste of blood. Mom shrieked again and tried to get to me, but Dad shoved her back roughly.

"You listen to me and you listen to me well, boy," he rasped, "I'm telling you to stay away from that Connelly man. You stay away from Asher Davis from now on, too. I don't know why he helped you, what you did to make him take you, but you are not to see him anymore. If I find out you've been sneaking around again, this beating will look like fun. This is my house and you will respect what I say."

"Fuck you," I screamed at him. "You think you can just beat

me and I'll respect you? You lost that a long time ago."

He jerked me up again and held me for a second, suspended in the air. Once again, time slowed down in that eerie way it has of doing at important moments, as if to underline their importance. I could hear Mom moaning softly behind him, a low keening sound. I was only inches from Dad's face. I could see each vein as it bulged and the fury in his eyes. A small rivulet of spittle made its way down his chin from the corner of his mouth. The pain in my face and stomach was intense, but somehow it only served to sharpen my senses.

In that instant that I hung in mid-air and he drew back to strike me yet again, I made a decision.

"Guess what?" I gasped. "I'm gay."

Everything froze. Before, time seemed to slow down. But now it stopped completely. Mom fell silent. Dad's fist ceased its swing. We all held our positions, a strange tableau of the dysfunctional family in the twenty-first century.

Then suddenly, it all shifted. Dad released his grip on me and I collapsed. His fist dropped to his side, although it remained clenched. For a moment, all remained silent. Then he looked down at me. For a brief second, I could read utter hatred in his eyes, but then they went dead, as if someone had flipped a switch.

"Get out of my house," he whispered. "Get your stuff and get the hell out. I never want to see you again. You are not my son." Then he drew back and kicked me so hard I rolled across the floor. I heard his footsteps retreating, then I heard the back door slam shut.

Mom was at my side before he was halfway to the door.

"Oh God," she wept. "I'm so sorry, Killian. I'm so sorry."

I tried to sit up, but the pain was excruciating. My vision blurred and suddenly I wasn't in my hallway with my mother weeping over me. I was lying on the ground by the pond once again with a murderer bending over me, knife raised ready to plunge. I screamed and struck out.

"Killian!" Mom's frightened voice brought me back to the house. "Do we need to go to the hospital?"

"Yes," I managed to gasp, but she was too small to lift me and I was in too much pain to help.

"Should I call an ambulance?" she asked me. I don't know when I got to make all the decisions, but I was glad she asked me this time.

"Call Adam Connelly," I said through gritted teeth.

She looked at me blankly for a moment. "Seth's dad," I added.

"Oh, but I don't know his number," she said, running to the phone. She dialed information and had them connect her.

I faded in and out after that. I remember Adam arriving and cursing a great deal. He lifted me like a doll and we were off to the hospital, my second trip in as many weeks. I vaguely remember the hospital and a doctor telling Mom that I was fine overall. Amazingly enough, the wound hadn't reopened. I did, however, have some bruised ribs and a few contusions. He also told her that I had had a psychosomatic episode; that I had reverted back to the night of the stabbing and experienced it all over again, even to the point of believing I was there. He said it was similar to what war veterans experienced.

In the end they released me, and Mom and Adam decided that I would go home with Adam. We decided not to file any charges and just said that I'd been beat up by a gang of bullies. Mom kissed me good-bye at Adam's car and promised she would bring my clothes and stuff I needed tomorrow and we would sort things out. I was too tired at the moment, since the painkillers that they had given me were starting to kick in. My last conscious thought was that I sincerely hoped Asher had made out better than I had.

Chapter 8

I awoke to a strange room and for a few moments I was very disoriented before I remembered what had happened the night before and where I was. I sat up and gingerly felt around my ribs. Definitely sore, but I could live with that. I took time to look around the room since I hadn't before. I caught my breath as I realized where I was. Adam had settled me into Seth's room. It unmistakably had his mark. There were track trophies on a shelf and posters on the wall proclaimed "Gay and Proud!" and "Stop the Violence!" My eyes were especially drawn to a poster from the MTV campaign "Fight for Your Rights: Take a Stand Against Violence!" Nearby was a smaller poster of Matthew Shepard with the dates 1976-1998 printed at the bottom. The irony was so thick it was sickening.

Just then someone knocked lightly on the door.

"Yes?" I called.

"I take it you're awake?" Adam called back through the door.

"Yes, you can come in." I said, and so he did.

"How are you feeling?" he asked.

"Well, I've been better, but I could've been worse. Over all, I'm ok."

"Good! Your mom is on her way over with some stuff for you. I told her and I'm telling you, you are welcome to stay here as long as you need to."

"Thank you, Adam. This means so much, I don't know how to even tell you..." I choked up and had to stop.

"There's no need to thank me, Killian. I would have wanted someone to do the same thing for Seth if he found himself in the same situation." He pointed to the Fight for Your Rights poster, "I'm going to do everything in my power to stop the kind of violence that took my son's life and sent you to the hospital twice now. I can't do much, but I can offer you shelter and care when you need it the most. My house is now your house. Seth would have wanted it that way."

I nodded, too overcome with emotion to even speak.

The doorbell chimes broke the moment and Adam hurried off to answer it. He was back in a few minutes with Mom...and Asher.

Mom noticed my eyes light up when I saw him and she broke into a grin.

"He insisted on coming along, I guess I made the right decision in letting him," she joked. After greetings and hugs were over she asked me, "Are you ok? How are you feeling?"

"A little sore, but I'm ok," I told her. "How are you?"

"Your father never came home last night, which is just as well. I'm not sure what I'm going to do. I'm going to see a lawyer this afternoon."

I turned to Asher, "What about you?"

He broke into a grin, "You won't believe it!"

"Well, while you get filled in, Adam and I are going to get your stuff out of the car," Mom jumped in quickly before Asher could go on.

After they had left, Asher settled down on the bed next to me. "'K, now tell me all about what I'm not gonna believe," I said, snuggling up next to him.

"Wow, you really seem to be feeling better," he said.

"That pain medicine is good stuff. I'm sure I'll be hurting when it wears off. Now talk."

"It's my dad. I told him I was gay...and he was fine with it. Well, maybe fine with it is a little strong, but he didn't freak out. It turns out my Uncle Rick is gay. I never even knew it. But anyway, Dad and Uncle Rick have always been close so it didn't weird him out too bad." He said all of this without taking a breath.

Meanwhile, I was stunned. Not only had Asher come out to

his parents, but they were ok with it, too. Asher took advantage of my speechless state to sneak a quick kiss. I looked at him in surprise for a moment; I still wasn't used to him kissing me. Suddenly I decided to throw all caution to the wind. I reached up with one hand and pulled his face to mine while my other arm snaked around his waist. I kissed him much more forcefully than we had kissed before. It was a slow, sensual kiss. I felt his tongue against my lips and I parted them.

The kiss lasted for what seemed like only seconds, or maybe years...who could tell? When he finally pulled away I lay back onto the bed and Asher laid his head on my chest.

"Wow," he whispered after a moment.

"Yeah, wow," I agreed.

We heard footsteps coming down the hall and Asher sat up quickly. Adam entered with a box and gave us a funny look—I suppose we looked guilty—but he didn't say anything. Mom followed a few seconds later with another box.

"This is all your clothes," she said. "When you are feeling better Adam will bring you to get your car. You'll be staying here until I figure some stuff out. I've got to run now, that appointment with the lawyer. Asher, do you want to go now or stay awhile? Adam said he could take you home later if you want to stay."

"I'll stay, if you're sure it's ok?" Asher said immediately.

"It's fine," Adam assured him.

Mom came over and gave me a hug and a few words about being a good guest for Adam and then she was gone. Adam walked her out to her car, so Asher and I were alone again.

"Um, Asher?" I said as soon as they were gone.

"Yeah?" he said cautiously.

"What do you think that kiss meant?"

"I dunno," he whispered. "Maybe that you like me?"

"I told you I did, Ash," I told him gently. I reached out and took his hand in mine. "I'm just confused about some stuff right now. I probably shouldn't have kissed you like that."

"Are you kidding?" he exclaimed. "I am so glad you did. I want to do it again right now. And again. And again. But what are you confused about?"

I didn't know whether to tell him or not. How do you tell someone that you can't give them your heart because you are afraid they might have killed your friend? I almost started laughing at that thought. It sounded like the plot off of some soap opera. I decided to be honest and let the chips fall where they would.

"Asher, I have to ask you a question. Please don't get offended. It's really important to me, ok?" I said.

"Sure, anything for you, Killian."

"Where were you when Seth was killed and I was stabbed?"

For a long time, neither of us said a word. Asher never looked away from my eyes. I watched the light slowly go out in them, like someone was turning a dimmer switch. The affection and warm love were replaced by hurt and cold anger. He slowly stood to his feet and stared down at me. I sat up, worried that I had gone too far.

"So that's it," he said softly, almost to himself. Then louder and full of anger, "That's why you can't love me? You think I killed Seth and stabbed you? You think I'm a murderer."

The anger faded as quickly as it had come up and Asher suddenly burst into tears.

"I love you, Killian," he sobbed. "I've loved you for years. How can you think I would ever, ever hurt you? Do you really think I'm the kind of person that could kill someone and then lie here with you like nothing happened? Is that what you think of me?"

My mouth was opened to speak, but nothing would come out. He spun around and ran out of the room. Finally I found my voice and called out after him, but it was too late.

Adam appeared in my doorway. "What happened?" he asked sharply.

"I was stupid and hurt Asher," I said quickly. "Please, go after him."

Thankfully, Adam ran off after Asher without asking a bunch of questions first. I collapsed back on my pillow and let out a long, shaky sigh. I seemed to have quite a talent for hurting those I cared about. I wonder whom I could alienate next?

The next week was spent in recovery. Adam would allow me to walk to the living room and that was about it. He waited on me hand and foot. I was starting to get a bit spoiled. I missed Asher, but he didn't come around. Adam had caught up to him and they had had a good talk, but Adam said he wasn't ready to come back yet. Give it time, Adam kept telling me. Asher did bring my make-up work from school as far as the front door, where he handed them over to Adam, so I figured that was a good sign.

Meanwhile, I grew closer to Adam and learned more and more about Seth. It turned out that Adam had another son who still lived with his mother. She still wouldn't allow Adam to see him at all. His name was Kane, and Seth had missed him terribly after he had come to live with Adam. Adam got quite choked up whenever he talked about him. Kane's 15th birthday party was coming up in a week and this especially saddened Adam since he wouldn't get to see him.

He showed me pictures of Seth and Kane together. Where Seth had the long gangly frame of a runner, Kane was stockier, more solid looking. That wasn't the only difference. Kane was also quite a bit shorter than Seth and his curly hair was darker, more auburn. But if Seth had looked a bit like an elf, Kane looked like an elfin prince. From the one close up Adam had I could see that Kane's eyes were the same intensely piercing green that Seth's were. Adam said they got that from their mother and it was completely natural. His face was delicate, beautiful but hard to describe.

I felt for Adam. I could tell just by the way he looked at the pictures how much he loved Kane. I knew it would be a great comfort to see him right now as he dealt with his grief. What a hard woman his ex-wife must be not to allow him to see his only living son at a time like this.

When I asked Adam about it, he simply said that it was more hopeless now than ever since his ex-wife was blaming him for Seth's death.

By the end of the week I was feeling much better. I thought I might try to go back to school on Monday. On Saturday, we went and picked up my car. I wanted to go see Asher, but Adam said to wait some more.

I talked to Mom almost every day. She said the lawyers were advising her to get out of the house as soon as possible, but she was still afraid of what Dad might do if she tried to leave him. She said he was hardly speaking to her since the beating and when he did it was like I had never existed. I was worried about her, though, worried he'd become violent again and there would be no one there to help her.

As Kane's birthday drew nearer and nearer, Adam became more and more withdrawn and depressed. I wanted to do something so desperately, but what? His birthday was on Wednesday;

it was Sunday afternoon when I had my brainstorm. As soon as
Adam left to go visit Steve on Sunday evening (he lived one
town over), I went to work. My idea was simple. But first I had
to find some information.

I felt a little guilty as I began to dig through Adam's desk,
but I decided that the ends would justify the means. I didn't find
what I was looking for, so I decided to check Seth's desk. After
about ten minutes of searching I was rewarded with the object of
my quest.

I ran to the phone and excitedly dialed the number I had
found on a scrap of paper. It rang. Once. Twice. Three times. I
was getting tense.

"Hello?" a voice answered. I couldn't quite tell if it was a
woman or a boy whose voice hadn't yet changed.

"Hello?" I said hesitantly. Now I wasn't sure what to do.

"Hello?" they said again.

"Um...is this Kane?" I asked.

"Yeah. Who's this?" I sighed with relief.

"You don't know me," I started, talking fast, "but my name
is Killian Kendall. I know your dad. Actually, I'm living with
him right now cuz my dad kicked me out of my house and your
dad took me in. I was Seth's friend." I paused to take a breath
and Kane jumped in.

"You live with my dad?" he sounded excited. "Is he there
now? Can I talk to him?"

"No, he isn't here now and actually that's why I called."

"What do you mean?" he sounded confused.

"Your birthday is this Wednesday, right?"

"Yeah?" he sounded even more confused.

"It's all your dad has talked about for the last week. He's so
sad cuz he can't see you. He wants to see you so bad, so I
thought maybe if you called that day, it would be better than
nothing. I thought it might cheer him up."

"What do you mean? Why can't he see me? Mom said he
never calls and that he didn't want to see me."

My heart went out to Kane. I knew how it felt to not be
wanted by your father. But it wasn't true in Kane's case.

"No, that's not true. He wants to see you so badly. He cries
when he talks about you. Can you call?"

"Definitely. I would love to talk to him. I miss him so
much," Kane sounded somewhat distant, as if he was thinking
about something else.

"Are you ok?" I asked him.

"Yeah, maybe. I don't know. Why would my mom lie to me?"

"Um," I didn't know how much to tell him. "Do you know why Seth moved in with your dad?"

"Mom said because he wanted to," Kane said thoughtfully, "but I know Seth was happy here. He was gay, but I guess you knew that if you were his friend. He didn't hide it. I always thought that it might have something to do with that, since he moved right after he came out to Mom."

"Yeah, I knew. Were you ok with that?"

"Yeah, why not? He was still the same guy as always. He was a great brother," he choked up a little. "I still miss him."

"Me too," I said simply. I made my decision. "And so does your dad. He's gay too, you know."

"He is?" he asked with just the tiniest hint of surprise in his voice. "I guess I kind of suspected in the back of my mind, with the whole Seth thing. Are you, too?"

"Yes, I am," I said. It still felt strange to say that, but very right.

"Were you Seth's boyfriend or something?"

"No, we were just friends."

"Oh. Well it doesn't matter about my dad. I still love him and want to talk to him."

"So you'll call him on Wednesday?"

"You bet I will and I can't wait."

I gave the phone number and he asked for the address so he could send letters.

"Thank you for calling, Killian," he said just before we hung up. "You are a good person. I'm glad you were Seth's friend. He didn't have many."

"I'm glad I was Seth's friend, too," I said sincerely.

We said our good-byes and we hung up. I felt very satisfied with what I had accomplished. I couldn't wait for Wednesday.

Chapter 9

I woke up the next morning excited about my day for the first time in quite some time. I was excited for three reasons. One, I was still excited about my conversation the night before with Kane. I couldn't wait to see Adam's face when he called on Wednesday.

The second reason I was excited was that I was going back to school today. After missing two weeks, I was anxious to get back. I was a little nervous, too, since I knew I had been a main topic of conversation.

The third reason was that before I went to school, Mom was picking me up and taking me to the optometrist to get new glasses, since mine had broken when Dad punched me. I hadn't had any since then.

I was ready and dressed in my best pair of baggy jeans and a new long-sleeved T-shirt when Mom arrived to pick me up for my appointment. We made small talk all the way to the office. After Dr. Sanchez did a check up to see if my prescription was still accurate, he asked me the question he always did every time I got new glasses.

"So, Killian, have you thought any more about getting contacts?" he asked me.

I started to answer with my usual no thanks, but for some reason I stopped and thought about it. Why not? It wouldn't be to please Dad anymore and if other people could get used to putting them in then maybe I could, too. It was time for some changes. I was going to take control of my life and I would start by getting contacts.

"Yeah, I think I'd like to try them," I told him.

He looked up in surprise, "You would?"

"Yeah, I'm ready for something new."

"Ok, let's take another look at a few things then," he said. He moved the machines back over to my eyes and looked at them from different angles. After a while he sat back and said, "You have great eyes for contacts. You shouldn't have any problems. I think we even have your prescription in stock. You can take them home today."

I had to choose between disposable and permanent; I went with disposable. Then I had to decide what kind, I settled on a new kind that I was supposed to be able to put in and leave in for a month at a time. Apparently they breathed or something, whatever that meant.

Then I had to practice putting them in, over and over till I could do it relatively well. It wasn't as hard as I had feared, although it did take me about 20 minutes on each eye the first time.

I decided to wear them to school. I also asked Mom if I could get a haircut after school since I was ready for a change. Besides, my hair had grown a lot since my last haircut and it was looking a little shaggy. Mom decided that we would just go now since I was already late for school.

"You might as well look your best for your first day back," she said philosophically. Who was I to argue?

We arrived at the salon Mom goes to and I was turned over to a stylish woman improbably named Bambi. Bambi asked me what I wanted, but since I didn't really know I told her to do whatever she wanted. She let out a little squeal and said I was her dream client come true.

About a half hour later she spun me around to get my first look at the finished product. It was a short stylish cut, very different from the longish style that I had come in with. The cut was short around the ears and in the back and a little longer in the front. Bambi had parted it down the center and my naturally wavy hair had actually curled slightly.

"So whatcha think?" she asked me.

"I love it!" I told her.

After we paid for my haircut and I tipped Bambi generously, we were off for school. I was more than a little nervous by this time. I had been out for two weeks, I knew I was the main topic in the rumor mills, and I had a new look that for all I knew everyone would hate. I tried to summon up the courage that I had found earlier, the courage from the new Killian, but apparently he had stepped out for the moment.

Mom noticed, of course.

"You're gonna be fine, Killian," she encouraged me. "I know I'm just your mom and my opinion doesn't really count, but I think your new look is super. You look very cute. The girls will be all over you." She paused for a moment and then added, "Too bad you won't be interested."

I stared at her in surprise for a second, my mouth hanging open in shock, and then she burst into laughter. I realized she was making a joke, and I joined her in the laughter.

"You should have seen your face," she gasped as we pulled into the school drop-off point.

I grabbed my backpack and then impulsively leaned over and kissed her on the cheek.

"Thanks, Mom," I said. "Thanks for everything."

As I jumped out of the car I saw tears forming in her eyes. "I love you," she called, "Have a great day!" She pulled away as I turned and faced the school.

I let out a little sigh and started for the main doors. I had to check in at the office since I was late. They were all overly nice to me, telling me not to worry about being late and writing me passes and essentially telling me I could have come in 5 minutes before the final bell and it would have been hunky dory with them. I guess that's one of the benefits of being stabbed and having it splashed all over the newspapers.

At my school, we have 4-period days, meaning that each period is much longer than with the traditional 7-period days. I came in right at the end of my second period. The rest of the day went fairly smoothly, with everyone going out of their way to be nice to me. Frankly, it was getting annoying. I'd rather have just been ignored as always.

After final bell I looked for Asher. My newfound confidence was back, and I was ready to make an attempt at least to patch things up. I wanted to ask him to forgive me and see if we couldn't work things out. Unfortunately, I couldn't find him anywhere.

Adam was supposed to pick me up, since Mom had dropped me off, so I was waiting outside when Zack and Jesse approached me.

"Killian," Zack said as they took up positions on either side of me.

"Hi, Zack. Hi, Jesse," I said nervously.

"I think we need to talk," Zack continued.

"Yeah? What about?"

"I think you know," he countered.

"Maybe, but I'd rather you said," I told him cautiously.

"Stop playing games, Killian," the ever-helpful Jesse chipped in.

"I'm not playing games. You guys are the ones that haven't so much as spoken to me in weeks. I've been in the hospital and then stuck at home."

"Well, you're not at home anymore, are you?" Zack said.

"No, I'm not, but what's that got to do with anything?"

"It has everything to do with everything," Zack explained patiently. "Look, we're not dumb. You start hanging out with Seth, you ditch us, you're in the park at night with Seth, you get kicked out of your house, and now you're back with a whole new look. You're gay aren't you?"

I figured it was coming but somehow it still caught me off guard. I wasn't ready to come out to the whole school yet, and telling Zack and Jesse would be the equivalent of just that. But what could I say that they would believe? I thought frantically for a few seconds, then decided that the truth was always the best way to go...or in this case, part of the truth.

"Look, Seth and I were just friends. We were meeting in the park to talk, I swear. And my dad kicked me out because I went to his funeral. You know how my dad is."

They stared at me for a minute in silence, then Zack pushed off away from the building.

"Ok, Killian," he said finally. "I'll buy that for now, but we'll be watching you. I just hope that now that the fag's gone you can get back to normal."

I was suddenly so furious that my sight actually blurred. I've always heard the saying 'seeing red' but now I knew what it meant. It took all I was to remain outwardly calm and quiet as they walked away.

I was still trying to calm my pounding heart when Adam pulled up. I jumped in the car and slumped down in my seat.

"What's wrong?" Adam asked.

"Nothing," I said. "Just stupid people."

"No shortage of those," he agreed. "Anything in particular or just your everyday, average, run-of-the-mill stupidity?"

"Zack and Jesse just make me so mad. I don't really wanna talk about it."

"No problem. If you change your mind, I'm here for you."

"Thanks, Adam," I said sincerely. "When I get back to your house I'm gonna take my car and go talk to Asher. We need to talk about what happened."

"Ok, he might be ready by now, but don't push it. If he doesn't want to talk, let it go again for now."

I drove over to Asher's house and knocked on the door. His mom answered. She was a slightly plump lady with short curly brown hair almost just like Asher's. She always seemed to be in a good mood. I loved hanging out at Asher's house just so I could be around her. Her first name is Deb and she's always telling me to call her that, but for some reason I've always called her Mrs. Davis. She was wearing jeans and a fuzzy purple sweater.

"Killian," she said, sounding surprised, "I haven't seen you in ages. How are you doing?"

"I'm fine," I said. "Is Asher home?"

"No, he went out with Zack and Jesse."

"Oh, ok, well...can you tell him I came by to talk to him," I paused for a moment, then added. "Tell him I said I'm sorry."

"I'll do that, Killian," she said. "And you take care of yourself, ok?"

"Yes, Mrs. Davis. I'll try."

Tuesday and Wednesday were pretty much repeats of Monday except I drove so there were no more awkward conversations with Zack and Jesse. Asher was either still avoiding me or he'd dropped off the face of the earth, but since I hadn't heard any rumors of his sudden disappearance I could only assume the former. I was a little hurt that he wouldn't even talk to me, but Adam kept saying that he would come around eventually, to just give him time. I wondered how much time it would take. I really missed him.

I was distracted the whole last period of school on Wednesday because I knew Kane was calling that night. I couldn't wait to see the look on Adam's face. I drove straight to Adam's house and walked in to find Steve cooking at the stove in the kitchen. I smelled spaghetti sauce.

"Hey there, kiddo," he called out when I came in, then he caught sight of me. "Whoa, new look! I like!"

"Hi, Steve. Thanks," I said. "Smells good. I didn't know you were coming over tonight."

"It was one of those last-minute kind of things," he told me. "I know today is Kane's birthday and it's always really hard on Adam, so I thought I'd come over and cook dinner for you guys and offer a little moral support."

"Well, I have a surprise that ought to cheer him up," I said with a huge grin.

"Oh yeah? And what's that?"

"If I told you then it wouldn't be a surprise, now, would it?" I teased.

"What wouldn't be a surprise?" Adam asked walking into the kitchen.

"Ah ah ah," Steve called over his shoulder as he dumped the spaghetti noodles into the boiling water. "If I can't know then neither can you."

Adam walked over and slipped his arms around Steve's waist and kissed him on the back of the neck.

"Hey, don't distract the cook," Steve laughed. "And if you're trying to get the secret out of me, it won't work because I don't know it."

Adam let his arms slip out from around Steve and he picked up a spaghetti strainer and advanced on me.

"Tell me the secret or I'll strain you," he said menacingly.

I burst out laughing and Steve and Adam quickly joined in. It was quite a festive atmosphere in the Connelly kitchen, and I felt totally relaxed and happy for the first time in just about as long as I could remember. I sat at the kitchen table under the warm yellow light from the overhead lamp while I did my homework. Steve and Adam puttered happily around me as they finished preparing the dinner. At some point someone put on a Santana CD and the sounds of guitar mixed with the pungent smell of garlic and oregano, filling the house. I was home.

We had just settled around the table to eat when the doorbell rang.

"Who could that be?" Adam wondered.

"I'll get it," I offered, jumping up before anyone else could.

I opened to the door and almost passed out. It was Kane!

"Kane?" I hissed. "Oh my gosh...I thought you were gonna

call. How'd you get here?"

"You must be Killian," he whispered and with a shy smile offered his hand.

I nodded as I shook it. I couldn't believe he was here. He stood there in black baggy shorts (even though it was very chilly outside) and an oversized gray sweatshirt with a red T-shirt peeking out around the collar. He looked like a lost little boy. He was even shorter than I was, maybe about 5'6" or so. His hair was a beautiful reddish-brown color that shone in the porch light. He was absolutely beautiful.

"Um...is my dad here?" he asked me after a few seconds.

I realized I was staring and quickly looked down.

"Um, uh, yeah," I stuttered. "He's, uh, in the kitchen."

I stepped back to allow him in, and as he stepped by I noticed he had a backpack slung over his shoulder and he was carrying a skateboard by the front axle.

"Who is it, Killian?" Adam called from the kitchen.

Kane's eyes lit up at the sound of his father's voice.

"Just a sec," I called back, then spun back to Kane. "How did you get here? Are you staying?" I was trying to keep my voice down but it kept climbing up.

"I caught a bus and then a taxi," he explained, trying to match my low tones. His eyes kept sliding down the hallway towards the kitchen doorway. "I don't know what I'm doing. Mom'll flip when she finds out I'm not really at Chad's house. But I don't care. I just had to see Dad."

"Well, hold on a second," I told him. "I'll go in and set it up. Oh man, this is so much better than just a phone call."

Kane giggled nervously and I shushed him. I motioned him to follow me as far as the kitchen door. He stayed just out of sight as I walked on in.

"Who was it?" Adam asked. He and Steve had started eating already.

"Well, remember that surprise I mentioned earlier?"

Steve and Adam both looked up curiously now.

"Yeah?" Adam said.

"Well, it didn't turn out quite how I expected, but I'm pretty sure you'll like this even better."

"Like what, Killian?" Adam asked me. "Whatever it is I'm sure I'll love it."

I took a deep breath and motioned to Kane. He stepped slowly into the light of the kitchen.

For a few moments you could have heard the proverbial pin drop. Then suddenly Adam leaped up from the table with a clatter of discarded silverware and ran towards Kane, lifting him up off his feet in a huge bear hug.

They spun around silently for a few moments before Adam set him down gently on his feet. When he pulled back there were tears running down his cheeks.

He cupped Kane's face in his hands, "Kane! How did you get here? Does your mother know you're here?"

"I caught a bus and, no, she doesn't know yet," Kane answered. He sounded just as emotional as Adam.

Adam pulled him in for another hug and turned to me.

"This was your doing?" he asked me.

"Sort of," I admitted, "but I just thought he was gonna call."

"Well, thank you," he said as he reached out and drew me in the hug as well. "Thank you from the bottom of my heart."

Steve cleared his throat and our little huddle broke up.

"I think some phone calls might be in order," he suggested gently. Steve seemed to be the voice of reason around here.

"Yes," Adam agreed. "We need to call your mother. But first let's eat, before the food gets cold. And oh...how could I forget? Let's sing 'Happy Birthday' to Kane!"

After singing a rousing chorus of "Happy Birthday," we set another place at the table and once again settled down to eat. There was a lot of excited conversation and explanations, how I'd found Kane, how he'd gotten there. It felt like a real family. Maybe not a family in the traditional sense, but a family nonetheless. When everyone was finished and the dishes had been rinsed and stacked in the dishwasher, Adam sighed.

"Well, I think we've put this off long enough," he said. "Let's call your mother, Kane."

Kane took the phone and called home. After a few rings, he began to talk, explaining quickly where he was. It seemed to go downhill from there. We could only hear his side of the conversation, but things obviously weren't going well.

"But Mom," he kept saying, but she apparently kept cutting him off. Finally he just sighed and held the phone out to Adam, who visibly winced. He reluctantly took the phone.

"Hello, Eve," he said evenly. He listened for a moment with his eyes closed. "No, I had no idea he was coming here." Pause. "No, I didn't secretly sneak him down here." Pause. "No, Eve, this is not a kidnapping, don't call the police. There's no sense in blowing this out of proportion." Long pause. "That's fine, then, I'll look forward to seeing you." He hung up the phone. "About as much as I look forward to a having all my teeth ripped from my head while having all my body hair plucked and being set on fire and...and..."

I couldn't help it; I started giggling. Adam looked over at me with a half-smile and after a few seconds began to chuckle. Soon we were all laughing and the easy feeling from earlier was back.

"So what was said?" Steve asked.

"A lot that I won't repeat, thank you," Adam said with a wry smile, "but the gist of it once we'd established that I was a no-good kidnapping bastard was that she'll be down late tomorrow afternoon to pick you up, Kane."

"So I get to stay the night?" he asked excitedly.

"Yep," Adam said. "And we'd better make the most of it, cuz it might be the last time for awhile."

We sat around talking and laughing for the next hour. Kane turned out to very funny and clever once he got used to everyone. Things got a little bogged down once when we started talked and reminiscing about Seth. We all cried a little, but eventually Kane and Adam got to telling anecdotes about Seth when he was younger and soon we were all laughing again, but now with a bittersweet undercurrent. Suddenly the doorbell rang again. Everyone turned and looked at me.

"What?" I said.

"Another surprise?" Steve asked.

"If so, it isn't mine," I told them. "But I'll go get it anyway."

I got up off the couch and walked to the front door. I flipped on the light as I opened the door, then froze.

"Hi, Killian," Asher said.

I stood staring at Asher with my mouth hanging open. He was just about the last person I expected to see.

"Mom said you stopped by," he said in the silence.

"Two days ago," I answered.

"Look, can we talk?" he asked. "Either inside or out, it doesn't matter, but I feel dumb standing at the door."

I thought for a second then called into the house, "It's for me. I'll be a few minutes."

I stepped out onto the porch without waiting for an answer, shutting the door behind me. I stared at him expectantly. He was wearing a green World Jungle jacket over a sweatshirt and cargo pants. I waited and he waited. Finally, I couldn't stand the silence any more.

"So you said you wanted to talk?" I asked.

"Yeah, look, I'm sorry, Killian. I'm sorry I got mad the other day and I'm sorry I've been avoiding you. Adam explained to me how upset this whole thing has got you. How when something like that happens it scares you. Takes away your sense of safety and makes it harder for you to trust people."

"He said all that?" I was amazed.

"Yeah. I guess I should've accepted it then, but I wasn't ready. I've been thinking about it a lot, and I think I'm ready to forgive you and move on if you want to try."

"I do want to try," I told him, "but I don't know."

"What do you mean you don't know?" Asher said with confusion in his voice.

"What if every time we have a problem you run off like that? Plus after you told me all that stuff that Adam said, maybe I shouldn't even be in a relationship right now. And I'm not ready to come out to the school. I don't want to end up like Seth."

I ended on a choked note and suddenly started crying. Why did I always seem to start bawling whenever Asher was around?

Asher stood awkwardly for a moment, then moved closer and wrapped his arms around me. I cried on his shoulder for about a minute before he started talking.

"As far as my running goes, I don't know. I'll try my best not to, but I don't guess I can make any guarantees. It's my personality. I hate conflict and I'll do whatever I can to avoid it."

"Like I enjoy it," I sniffled into his arm.

"No, I know you don't enjoy it, but you don't run from it, either, like I do. Look how you stood up to Zack and Jesse and then your dad. But only you can know whether you are ready for a relationship or not, but I'm willing to take the risk if you are. And as far as coming out at school, I have no intentions of doing that whether we are together or not. Whatever you decide, I'm here for you."

I nodded against his shoulder and pulled back a little so I could look into his face. I'd never really noticed his eyes before. They were an odd color, kind of a silvery-gray color. They were beautiful.

"What?" he asked.

"It's...nothing," I said. "Can I have some time to think about it? I'll call you tomorrow after school. I promise."

Asher nodded and stepped back, quickly stepped in close again and kissed me softly on the lips. And then he was gone.

I stood alone on the porch for a few minutes before going back inside. If anyone noticed that I'd been crying, they were all too polite to ask why. After a few more hours of talking, Adam announced that it was time for bed. This caused a bit more discussion about where Kane was going to sleep. Finally, it was decided that he would share my room. Steve, of course, was sleeping with Adam. We all took turns in the bathroom and then we went into our respective rooms.

Seth's bed was pretty large, so Kane and I decided to share it instead of one of us having to sleep on the floor. I was a little worried that he wouldn't want to share a bed with a gay guy, but it didn't seem to faze him in the least. We stripped down to our T-shirts and boxers and climbed into bed. I snapped out the light and we settled in, squirming and wiggling to get comfortable. We said our good nights and then silence fell.

Just as I was about to drift off, Kane cleared his throat. "Thanks a lot for calling me, Killian." he said quietly. "I don't even know how to thank you."

He sounded a bit choked up and for just the briefest second all I could think was, *Oh no, not more tears.* Then I got a hold of myself and found my voice.

"You don't have to thank me, Kane," I told him. "I'm just glad to see how happy you guys are. This is the closest I've ever felt to what a real family must be like. That's all the thanks I need."

"You are so awesome," he said, still sounding a bit weepy. "Why are you living here?"

I decided to give him the condensed version. "My dad kicked me out when he found out I was gay."

"How did he find out?" Apparently he wasn't satisfied with just an abridged tale.

"I went to Seth's memorial service and he was there and he got really angry and started yelling at me and I just told him."

"How did you know you were gay?" he asked me.

I thought for a minute. I guess all the questions were normal. This whole thing must be so confusing for him. My heart went out to him as I thought about all he'd been through—losing his father and not seeing him for years, then losing his brother, first when he moved away and then in death, then finding out that both his father and his brother are gay.

Finally, I answered slowly, "You just know, really. Seth told me that he thought I was. He kissed me and I freaked out, but afterwards it made me think and I realized that I knew I was in my heart. I had just been blind. Seth said the same thing; that he just knew."

"I have to tell you something. Please don't be mad at me," he said.

Could he be gay, too? Or maybe he actually hates gays and he's going to tell me to go sleep on the couch. Or maybe...

"I went to check on you when you were gone for awhile tonight and saw that guy kiss you on the front porch. I didn't mean to, like, spy on you or anything. I hope you're not mad."

"No, it's ok," I said quietly and with a little relief.

"Is he your boyfriend?" Boy, Kane was just full of questions.

"I don't know. Maybe. His name is Asher. We've been friends since we were kids. He just told recently that he's had a crush on me for years. We're still working stuff out. I don't know if we'll end up together or not."

He was quiet for a while and I thought he must have gone to sleep so I started relaxing.

"I hope you find someone that makes you happy, Killian," he said suddenly, making me jump. "You deserve that. You're the nicest guy I've ever met. Will you be my big brother now that Seth is gone?"

And then he was crying, of course. And by now we all know how easy I cry; it takes a lot less than that to get me started. I rolled over and wrapped my arms around him and just held him till he was cried out.

"Thanks," he sniffled. "I don't usually act like this, really."

"Kane, you don't have to apologize to me. You've been through a lot and I would be more than honored to be your big brother."

"I wish I lived with Dad," he said wistfully. "Then I could be with you guys all the time."

I gave him a final squeeze and then let go and rolled back over. "We'd better get some sleep now, Kane. I have school in the morning still."

"Yeah, you're right. Good night, Killian."

"Good night, Kane."

Chapter 10

How I ever got any sleep with that incredibly beautiful boy sleeping just inches from me I'll never know, but I did. I slept like a rock. (A strange saying that. Just how do rocks sleep?)

All I could think about all day at school was what I was going to tell Asher when I got home. And when I wasn't thinking about that, I was thinking about Kane. He'd captured my attention in much the same way that Seth had, and yet they were so different. But why was I even worrying about Kane? He lived in Baltimore and, more importantly, he was straight.

As soon as school was over I rushed right back to Adam's house, or what I was starting to think of as home. There was a strange car in the driveway when I got there.

When I got inside I found the queen of the fairies sitting on the couch in the living room. She could only be Seth and Kane's mother. She was tiny, not just in height but also in weight. She couldn't have been over 5 foot tall, and if she weighed 100 lbs I'd be shocked. She had short, spiky fiery red hair and the same piercing green eyes that both Seth and Kane had shared. Her skin was as white and translucent as alabaster, in sharp contrast with her blood red lipstick. All in all, she looked as if she'd be quite at home with wings sprouting from her back.

She turned and looked at me with cold eyes and I realized that while they might be the same color as Seth and Kane's, they held none of the warmth and compassion that was so evident in her sons'.

"And who might you be?" she asked me. Her voice was just as brittle and cold as her gaze.

"I'm Killian. Are you Mrs. Connelly?"

"Ms. Douglas. I stopped being Mrs. Connelly years ago."

"Oh, well, I'll go put this in my room," I said as I backed out of the room.

"If you mean the room at the end of the hall, you might as well have a seat. My dear son, Kane, has locked himself in and refuses to come out. Adam has been talking to him for twenty minutes now. I'm getting ready to go find an axe and hack the damn door down."

"Oh, um, maybe I can talk to him," I said weakly. I spun around and ran upstairs. Sure enough, there was Adam sitting on the floor with his forehead against the door. He looked up when I appeared.

"Killian," he said. "Maybe you could..." He pointed help-lessly at the door. "He won't open it."

I tapped lightly on the door.

"God, why can't you all just leave me alone?" came Kane's anguished voice through the door.

"Kane?" I called back. "It's Killian. Can I come in?"

There was no response for a while so I called again, "Kane?"

"Ok," he said finally, his voice muffled by the door, "but if I let you in, only you can come in. Nobody else."

I looked at Adam and he nodded.

"Deal," I said.

I heard the lock turn and the door opened about an inch. I opened it the rest of the way and stepped into the room, shutting the door again behind me. Kane had thrown himself across the bed face-first. I went over and sat down next to him. I didn't say anything at first, but eventually, after he made no move to speak or even acknowledge my presence, I began to gently rub his back.

"Kane?" I said softly. "What's wrong? How come you're locked in here like this?"

He mumbled something into the bed, but I couldn't under-stand him. It sounded vaguely like "I ate one."

"What?" I asked.

He rolled over and looked up at me with red swollen eyes

and a tear-stained face. "I said I hate her," he clarified.

"Oh," I said stupidly.

I didn't know what else to say. Thank goodness, Kane didn't need any prompting. He went on, "She waltzes in here and starts yelling at Dad, like it was his fault. She was calling him names and saying dumb stuff. Then she told me to go get in the car. I said no, that I wanted to talk to her first. She said she didn't care what I wanted, that I'd just better do what she said because I was in enough trouble already. I got mad and I yelled at her. I don't even know what all I said. I told her I knew that she'd been lying to me all these years about how Dad didn't want to see me. I told her that Seth was dead because of her and I didn't want to live with her anymore. I said I hated her and I do." He broke down crying again.

I felt so helpless. I reached out and smoothed his hair back from his forehead. He stretched his arms out to me and it felt as if my heart was being ripped apart. How could a mother hurt her own child like this? I lay down next to him and he curled into me. I wrapped my arms around him and let him sob, just like the night before. He had so much pain bottled up inside him; he just needed to let it out. After a short time he sat up.

"I have to go with her, don't I?" he stated more than asked.

"Yeah," I said as I sat up.

"I'll be back, somehow," he vowed. "Can I call you?"

"Of course. Any time."

"Do you have e-mail?"

"I do at home, but I've never even used this one," I said pointing to the computer on the desk in the corner.

"Well, if you have AOL like Seth did then you can use this computer, too, and we can talk. You just sign on as a guest. What's your screen name?"

I told him and he wrote it on a notepad he found on the desk and stuck it in his pocket. He started for the door, but then he paused, turned, walked back to me, and threw his arms around my neck for a big hug.

"Thank you," he whispered into my ear.

"Like I said last night, there's nothing to thank me for," I told him.

He pulled away and wiped his face, although there was no hiding the fact that he'd been crying. He threw his shoulders back, lifted his chin high, and yanking open the door, marched resolutely down the stairs. I followed much less impressively behind.

As soon as she saw Kane, Ms. Douglas started for the door without saying a word. She stopped in the open doorway and glared at Adam as he gave Kane a hug. She threw a calculating look at me, as if measuring up a potential enemy, then turned on her heel and stalked off to the car. I had to give it to her; she knew how to make a dramatic exit.

"I love you, Dad," Kane said.

"I love you too, son," Adam said thickly. He sounded on the verge of tears. There was entirely too much crying going on around here.

Kane waved at me sadly and followed his mother to the car. Adam and I stood in the doorway until they were out of sight.

"Quite a piece of work, isn't she?" Adam said as he closed the door.

"I guess you could say that," I said.

"What else would you say?"

"That she's a class-A bitch," I answered.

"I'll have to give you that one," he chuckled, and we went into the living room, where I started my homework and Adam went back to work on the computer.

About a half-hour later the phone rang and Adam answered it, since it was right next to the computer.

"Killian, it's for you," he said after speaking to the person on the phone. "It's Asher."

Oh, crap! In all the excitement I had forgotten that I'd promised to call Asher and give him my decision as soon as I got home from school. I jumped up and grabbed the phone, wishing it was a cordless so I could have a little more privacy.

"Asher, hi. I'm sorry I forgot to call. There was a lot going on..." I started as soon as I had the phone.

"It's ok, Killian," he interrupted me. "Can we talk now?"

"Yeah, well no...I mean." I took a deep breath. "Can I come pick you up?"

"Yeah, that's fine," he said.

"Ok, I'll be there in a few minutes."

"Is everything ok?" Adam asked me as I hung up.

"I'm not sure," I told him honestly.

"Take a second and tell me what's going on," he invited me, getting up from the computer desk and sitting on the couch.

I sat down next to him and let out a sigh.

"You know Asher likes me, right?" I began.

"I'd have to be blind to not see that." Funny choice of words.

"Well, I know you know how I hurt his feelings and he got mad at me, cuz he told me you talked to him."

He nodded.

"He came last night and said he forgave me and asked me to forgive him for ignoring me. Then he said that he wants us to be together."

"And what's the problem?" he asked me.

"I don't know exactly," I exclaimed. "I mean, I know I like Asher. I've liked him for years. And now I find out that he likes me, too. I should be thrilled. I should be running into his arms. But I can't. Something is holding me back."

"Are you still afraid he had something to do with the attacks?"

"I dunno, maybe. But I don't think it's that, cuz in my heart I know Asher couldn't do something like that."

"Do you think you are afraid of losing him altogether if the couple thing doesn't work out?"

I thought for a minute. "I'm just not sure. I don't know what I'm afraid of. I just..." I seemed to run out of words. I just didn't know how to explain it.

"What are you going to tell Asher?"

"I don't know that either," I sighed. "I guess I'll figure it out when the time comes."

Adam ruffled my hair and stood up. "Well, you better get going. You told Asher you'd be there in a few minutes. I hope you figure out your heart on the way there."

As I drove to my old neighborhood, I thought about what Adam had said. Figure out my heart. That was the problem. I couldn't figure it out; I didn't trust my own heart. I was so scared of giving it to someone and having it crushed. I thought about the storm and how I'd watched the flowers being buffeted by the winds. That's still how I felt. I felt as if my heart was bleeding. It was still raw and maybe it would never heal.

My thoughts were interrupted when I pulled into Asher's driveway. He was out the door and in the car almost before I'd stopped rolling.

I backed out on to the street and asked, "Where do you want to go?"

"It doesn't matter, anywhere."

"How about the inlet?" I asked.

"That's fine."

We made small talk all the way there, both of us carefully avoiding the whole purpose of this little trip. I parked, dropped a few quarters in the meter, and we walked out on the beach. The wind off the ocean was more than a little chilly, and I wished I'd thought to put on more than just a T-shirt. Asher noticed.

"Here," he said taking his jacket off and handing it to me.

"No, it's ok. You need it," I argued.

"Just take it, Killian, please. Why do you always have to fight me about everything? Just let me do something for you," he said, frustration in his voice. "Besides I have a sweatshirt on and you just have that T-shirt."

I silently took the jacket and pulled it on.

"Thanks," I said softly. He nodded.

The beach was deserted except for the two of us and a man and his dog way off down the beach. The sun was quickly making its way towards the horizon. We walked towards the pier for a while, neither of us talking. Finally, Asher spoke up.

"Did you think about what we talked about last night?"

"A little," I said quietly. Asher took a step closer to me so that he could hear over the sound of the waves. We were now walking almost shoulder to shoulder. I felt his hand brush against mine.

"And?" he prompted.

"I'm scared," I told him. His hand brushed mine again and this time he took it and held it in his.

"Of what?"

"I don't know how to explain it."

"Do you still think I killed Seth?"

"No, I honestly don't. I just don't know how to explain it to you." I thought for a moment and he didn't push. Suddenly, I stopped walking. It was like a dam burst inside me, and words began to tumble out of my mouth almost faster than I could speak them. "I've been hurt so many times. When I was a kid, I used to worship the ground my father walked on. I thought the sun rose and set on him. I learned differently the hard way over many broken promises and hurt feelings. I didn't understand my mom. I never thought she cared about me until recently. I was never accepted at school. I guess I've learned how to keep people away. I thought I was safe behind my defenses, and then along came Seth and he saw right through me. That really shook me up. I was ready to trust him and then he was taken away from me. I'm scared to give someone my heart, Asher. I'm scared of getting hurt again." We were under the pier now. I dropped his hand and walked a few feet away. Asher followed me closely.

"I've already given you my heart, Killian," he said.

"But that's just it. What if I don't want it? What if I don't know what to do with it? What if I hurt you the same way I've been hurt?"

I felt Asher's hand gently grip my shoulder and turn me around so that I was facing him. He put his other hand on my other shoulder.

"I told you last night that I was willing to risk it if you were. I still am." Then he pulled me closer and, wrapping his arms around me, kissed me hard on the lips. I didn't respond at first, but I slowly melted into his embrace and began to kiss him back. The kiss just kept getting more and more passionate. Asher gently lowered me to the sand and then I felt his body follow, pressing his length against mine. We kissed for a little while longer and then suddenly I remembered where we were.

"Asher!" I gasped, my breath coming in short bursts.

"Mmmm?" Asher asked, his face buried in my neck.

A tingling sensation flooded through my body and I gasped again.

"Asher! We're on the beach!" I managed to get out.

He raised his head and looked at me. "So?"

I grinned and kissed him on the lips again then pulled back. "So, let's go home and finish this in private."

"You mean it?" he asked excitedly.

"Yup. Think you can spend the night?"

Chapter 11

Asher and I burst through the front door of Adam's house, or as I was quickly coming to think of it, my house. We were giggling and tripping over each other in our haste.

"Well," Adam said coming into the hall to see what was going on. "You two sound like a herd of elephants. I thought I was being invaded. Make that a herd of giddy elephants."

"Can Asher spend the night?" I asked breathlessly.

Adam's left eyebrow flew up so high it almost shot off his forehead.

"Well, I don't know," he said slowly.

"What?" I was shocked. I hadn't expected any problems.

"I think I'd rather talk to your mother first," he said.

"What do you mean?"

"Can I talk to you for a second in the other room?" he asked.

"Yeah, sure."

We left Asher standing in the hall and walked into the living room.

"Obviously your talk went well and you made up your mind, but are you sure this is the best thing right now?" Adam said once we were alone.

"I don't understand what you mean," I told him.

"Well, number one, I'm not naïve. I know you two intend to

do more than talk up there." I blushed. "You're so young, Killian. I know I'm not your father and therefore I have no right to tell you what you can and cannot do with your life, but I've grown to care for you very deeply and I don't want to see you get hurt. Don't rush into a sexual relationship. If what you have is real, then it will wait. Let your relationship grow first. You are both just beginning to explore this new side of yourselves. Don't do something you may regret later. I've seen too many friendships ruined by sex.

"Number two," he continued, "is that you just went through a very traumatic experience; two in fact, Seth's murder and then your father's abuse. I don't think you've really dealt with either one. You don't need to add the emotional stress of a serious relationship until you've worked through those things first."

"I'm fine," I told him. "I don't know what you mean about dealing with them. It seems like all I do is cry anymore. Isn't that dealing with it?"

"No, that's releasing the pressure, and that's better than holding it in, but it's not dealing with the underlying issues. Until you address them, you will always be dealing with that pressure."

"I don't know what to do."

"I know, Killian. We'll work through it together, huh?" He pulled me in for a quick hug. "I'll talk to your mom tomorrow and see what we can do about maybe finding a good counselor for both of us."

I nodded although I still wasn't convinced I needed to see a counselor. I mean, I thought I was doing great considering.

"What about Asher?" I asked.

"I still don't think it's a good idea for him to stay over. How 'bout if we watch a movie together and then you can drive him home? I have a great one that I know you guys will love and I guarantee you that you've never seen it before."

"What is it?" I asked suspiciously.

"Just wait, it'll be a surprise. But I will say that it's one of the most wonderful movies I've ever seen. I watch it over and over."

I went and filled Asher in. He was disappointed, but agreed to the movie idea. It was better than nothing.

Asher and I settled in on the couch with a blanket while Adam popped some popcorn. When the lights were dimmed and everyone was situated, Adam pushed play on the remote control and the movie started. It lived up to his glowing review. The movie was called "Beautiful Thing." It's the story of two teenage boys who fall in love and their families and their struggles. That doesn't even come close to describing it. I related so much to the characters. One of the guys was a 17-year-old named Ste. His father abused him and I started crying I related to him so much. Asher held me tightly during those parts.

It was a little hard to understand because it was a British movie. Their accents were quite heavy and they used a lot of English slang terms that I wasn't familiar with, but Adam kept us up to speed.

I also enjoyed snuggling with Asher. It felt so good to have his warm body curved around mine, to feel his breath on my cheek and his arms around me. When the last notes of Mama Cass died away, Adam lowered the volume and stopped the tape and started it rewinding.

"Did you like it?" Adam asked us.

"Yes!" we answered in unison and Adam just chuckled a bit, then turned his attention to the TV, where the news was on. We all got a bit engrossed in the top story and it wasn't long before I realized that Asher's breathing had become very regular and his body had relaxed. He had fallen asleep.

"Asher's asleep," I whispered to Adam.

He looked over and smiled at us. "You two look so peaceful," he said softly. "Just like Ste and Jamie. I hate to disturb him."

"Then don't," I countered. "Let us sleep here. We won't do anything. I promise."

He thought for a moment, then seemed to make up his mind. "I'm going to trust you on this, Killian," he said. "Please, don't let me down."

I broke into a wide grin. "I won't," I promised.

"I need to call his mother, then, and let her know where he is," he said, getting up.

I gave him Asher's phone number and he made the call. After speaking for a brief time, he hung up and snapped off the last lamp.

"I guess that means it was ok," I whispered.

"You guessed correctly."

"Good night, Killian."

"Good night, Adam."

He started from the room, "Adam?" I called out softly.

"Yes?"

"Thank you...for everything. I'm glad you were there for me. You're like the dad mine never was."

He stood silhouetted in the hall light for a few moments, his back to me, and I wondered if he was going to respond. Then he turned and slowly walked back over to me, bent over and gently kissed my forehead. I felt a drop of wetness land on my cheek and I realized he was crying. Before I could say anything else, though, he quickly moved from the room and turned off the hall light. I heard him go up the stairs and his door close, then silence descended on the house. It wasn't long before I joined Asher in sleep.

Chapter 12

I was standing in the park by the pond. I could feel more than see the other presence in the shadows that seemed to writhe and dance around me, slowly closing in. I was turning, trying to watch all sides at once, but it was hopeless. Then the shadows seemed to take form, become more solid, and from them stepped a figure.

He was dressed all in black but I couldn't see his face at first, and then I realized it was because there wasn't one. Then I knew who it was without being told. It was my attacker, Seth's murderer. He'd come back to finish off what he'd started.

I wanted to run, but it was as if my feet wouldn't respond to my brain's commands. I was frozen where I stood as he slowly came towards me. And then somehow, before I knew it, he was behind me. His arm snaked around my neck and I felt the cold steel of a knife blade cutting into my throat. I felt a trickle of blood run down my collarbone. Then suddenly it was as if whatever spell had me frozen had been broken and I was fighting for all I was worth - kicking, screaming, thrashing. I didn't want to die.

"Killian! Killian!" A voice was calling me.

My eyes flew open and I sat bolt upright. I was sticky with sweat and my heart was pounding in my chest so hard that I thought they must be able to hear it in the next county. Everything was dark and I looked around frantically for the attacker. I couldn't see. Where was he?

I felt an arm slide across my shoulders. I cried out and flailed blindly at it. I hit flesh and I heard a startled "oof" from the darkness.

"Killian, it's ok! It's just me, Asher."

"Asher?" I whispered.

"Yes, I'm right here."

"It was a dream?" I said shakily, remembering where I was and what had happened.

I felt his arms slide around me again and this time I didn't fight. "Yeah, I guess so. It must have been a bad one. You woke me up throwing your arms around and kicking and crying like."

"I'm sorry," I said, burying my face in his chest.

"Don't be sorry. It's ok. It's not like you can help what you dream. Do you remember what you were dreaming about?"

"Yeah," I said. "It was Seth's killer. He was after me and I was fighting. Oh God, it was so horrible." I squeezed Asher harder.

"I'm here, it's ok, Killian," he murmured into my hair, "It was just a dream. Go back to sleep, baby. I've got you. You're safe."

It took quite a while, but finally my body won out over my fear and sleep overcame me.

I awoke the next morning with Asher's arms still wrapped around me. It made me feel safe and warm, even though the dream from the night before still lingered around like the last shreds of mist in the morning sun. I just wanted to stay like this forever, but nature's call was coming in loud and clear, and if I didn't get up soon I'd have an embarrassing problem on my hands.

I tried to slip out of his embrace without waking him, but he just tightened his grip. I tried again with the same results, so I gave up on not waking him.

"Asher," I said. When he didn't respond I got a little louder, "Asher!"

"Huh? Wha?" he said sleepily.

"I hafta piss, man," I told him. "You gotta let me up."

"Oh yuh, sorry," he mumbled, letting go and falling immediately back to sleep. Well, that was a bit of information to file away for future use: don't worry about disturbing Asher's sleep.

After I went to the bathroom I was wide-awake, so I went ahead and went upstairs for a shower. When I came downstairs after dressing I smelled bacon cooking and knew Adam was up. I padded into the kitchen in my stocking feet and sat down at the table.

"Good morning," Adam said. He was quite chipper. I hate morning people.

"Morning," I said.

"How'd you two make out on the couch?"

"With our lips," I shot back.

Adam gave me a warning glance and I sighed.

"We made out fine," I told him. "I had a nightmare, though, and Asher had to wake me up."

Adam looked at me again, more seriously this time. "What was it about?"

I sighed, "Scary. It was the killer. He tried to kill me."

Adam left the stove and came over to sit across from me.

"What did he look like? Did you remember anything else?"

"No, I couldn't see his face again. It was like he didn't have one. He didn't speak, either. But I'm pretty sure it was a guy in my dream at least, but that doesn't really mean anything, does it?"

"I don't know. I'm going to call today to find out about counseling," he said.

I nodded and noticed smoke starting to come from the frying pan on the stove.

"I think the bacon is burning," I told Adam. He jumped up and dashed over to the stove.

"No, not burnt, but it'll be crispy. Go get Asher up so by the time he gets out of the shower breakfast should be ready."

I went into the living room where Asher was still asleep on the couch. I gently shook his shoulder while I called his name. When that didn't work, a rather mean idea popped into my head. Of course, I loved it. I started tickling him.

He sat up so suddenly that his head smacked into mine, and while he fell off the couch I fell backwards.

"Dammit, Killian!" he whined with his hand on his forehead. "Why'd you have to go and do that?"

"I thought it would be funny," I responded; hand on my nose. "Is it bleeding?"

"No, and I think it lost something in the translation, cuz it sure wasn't funny."

That started me giggling and soon we were both lying on the floor laughing. Finally I got control of myself and told him that he needed to hurry up and get his shower.

The rest of the day flew by. School was pretty uneventful. Things finally seemed to be falling back into their same old patterns and I was relieved. I was tired of the whole special treatment scene.

I was walking down the hall after the last bell when suddenly a person appeared on either side of me and grabbed my arms. It was Zack and Jesse. I struggled but they lifted me off my feet and swept me down a side hall and into an empty classroom. They set me down and spun me around to face them.

"What was that about?" I demanded.

"We need to have a little talk," Zack said threateningly.

"I'm sick of our 'little talks.' I'm leaving," I tried to push past them, but they shoved me back roughly. I was starting to get a little scared.

"We know what you and Asher were doing on the beach last night," Jesse growled.

"What?" I gasped.

"Someone saw you, dumbass," Zack taunted, jabbing me in the ribs for effect. "So now we know for sure that you're a faggot and we know Asher is too."

"Yeah, and you're both going down," Jesse piped up. "We don't want no fags at our school."

"How very enlightened of you, Jesse," I said, my anger building by the second. "But guess what? I'm not going anywhere. Yeah, you're right. I am gay. And I'm not gonna be ashamed of that. But guess what else? That's none of your business. You can't intimidate me or scare me."

"Well we can beat the crap outta you," Jesse said as he took a menacing step towards me.

I took a step back and glanced over my shoulder. There was only the one door to this room, and Zack and Jesse were between it and me. My mind was racing almost as fast as my heart. Zack and Jesse began closing in on me. My foot shot out, catching Jesse by surprise and nailing him in the balls. He screamed like a girl and collapsed to the floor as Zack launched himself at me. I tried to jump out of the way, but he caught my shoulder and I spun as I fell. We ended up in a pile on the floor when the light came on.

"What's going on in here?" a voice demanded.

I sat up, disentangling myself from Zack. It was Mr. Dou kas, my physical science teacher from last year.

"Nothing, we were just messing around," I told him.

"Well, mess around somewhere else. Get going before I escort you to the office." I could tell he didn't believe me. He cast a suspicious look at Jesse, who was struggling to get up, obviously still in pain. He was looking a little ill.

"Are you feeling alright, Mr. O'Donnell?" Mr. Doukas asked him.

"Not really," he answered truthfully.

I grabbed my backpack that I had dropped when Zack tackled me and started out of the room.

"We'll talk later," Zack called after me meaningfully.

"We'll see," I called back.

I searched all over for Asher, but I couldn't find him anywhere and no one I talked to had seen him, so I drove straight to his house. Mrs. Davis answered the door and said Asher was in his room and for me to go right in.

I tapped on the door and I heard his muffled voice tell me to come in. I opened the door and couldn't help but gasp. He was lying on the bed with the worst black eye I've ever seen, and his lip was busted and swollen.

"Oh my God," I said, rushing to his side. "What happened?"

"Zack and Jesse happened," he spoke carefully because of his lip.

"Oh geez," I whimpered hugging him tightly. "They tried to get me after school, but I fought back and luckily Mr. Doukas came in before things got ugly. I didn't squeal."

"Maybe you should've. They aren't gonna give up that easy, you know."

"What do you mean?" I asked, sitting up.

"They'll be back. And probably with back-up."

"We were careless last night, weren't we?" I said softly.

"Yeah, we were. I'm sorry," he said.

"Hey, what's done is done. Now we have to live with the consequences, but there's no sense in beating ourselves up over it. Zack and Jesse will take care of that for us." I added with a grin. I continued seriously, "At least we have each other to talk to and lean on as we go through this. Seth didn't have anyone."

"Killian, I don't know if I want to go through this. I don't know if I can. Maybe it's too late, but maybe not. I mean if I can convince Zack and Jesse not to tell anyone, maybe I can save my reputation. I don't want to end up dead like Seth."

I stood up. "Ok, wait a minute. First of all, are you saying that your reputation is more important than us? And what do you mean end up dead like Seth? Do you think it was Jesse and Zack?"

He looked away. "I don't know," he mumbled.

"Asher, if you know something you have to tell someone," I told him, urgency creeping into my voice.

"I don't know anything," he said again, rolling over with his back towards me. "Maybe you should go, Killian. I'm not feeling so great."

"Asher," I pleaded. "If you know something, please tell me. It could help catch Seth's killer."

"I told you, I don't know anything," he shouted. "Please, just go."

I stood there for a second while he started sniffling, then I turned and left. I was so confused. What was wrong with Asher? Did he know something he wasn't saying? Or was he just having the same kinds of doubts and fears I was? It definitely seemed he wasn't ready to be outed.

I drove right home and went in to find a note from Adam saying that he'd be home soon and that Steve was coming with him. They would bring dinner home with them. I went up to what had become my room and decided to log on to AOL and see if Kane had e-mailed me.

To my surprise there were several from him just since the day before. The first one simply said that they were back and the ride had been horrible. The second one was a bit longer. He thanked me again for being there for him and he said that he felt very close to me. He also said that he and his mother had had a huge fight. *I just want to get out of here*, he wrote.

The last letter, though, was the real shocker. It had come just before I signed on.

Dear Killian, I'm still fighting with Mom. We've hardly spo-
ken since I called her a liar at dinner tonight. I'm so confused
about everything. Why would she lie to me? Why does she hate

Dad so much? Just because he's gay? But that doesn't make any sense. He's still the same as he used to be. I just wish I could live with you guys. Maybe I can. My friend Chad said he got to choose what parent he wanted to live with when his parents got divorced. He said I can go to court and fight if Mom won't let me.

Killian, I want to talk to you about something. If I can sneak out tonight after Mom's asleep, is it ok if I call you? I need to know how you know if you are gay or not. I wonder if maybe I am too. It's genetic, right? And Dad and Seth were. And I liked being held by you. I don't know. I'm just so confused.

I'll call you tonight.

Love, Kane.

Chapter
13

I sat stunned in front of my computer. I couldn't believe what I had just read, so I read it again, but the words hadn't changed since the last time. Kane thought he might be gay. My heart was racing at the very thought, but what about Asher? He was so unsure about what he wanted; I didn't even know where I stood with him.

Of course, Kane hadn't said he was interested in me, actually, just that he might be gay and he liked being held by me. That didn't mean much, really. I had to be careful to not influence his decision. It had to be completely his own; he had to be sure that he was gay.

It occurred to me that I didn't really know that much about why people are gay. I'd accepted the fact that I was and never wondered what made me that way. I didn't have any clue what to tell Kane if he asked me that. I minimized Kane's letter and typed in my favorite search engine, Google.com. After reading several articles I found that each one I read seemed to contradict the one before. None of them seemed to agree. One suggested that it was genetic, another that it was environmental, nature vs. nurture, on and on. They all seemed biased and stated their case as if they were absolutely right and everyone else was wrong. It was all very confusing and after half an hour I didn't know anymore than I did when I started. Then I found an article that seemed to be an unbiased balance of both views that made more sense to me than anything I had read so far. It was long and I was deeply immersed in it when I heard Adam calling me to come eat dinner with him and Steve. I hadn't even heard them come in. I quickly book-marked the site and sent Kane a short e-mail telling him to feel free to call me.

After dinner, Adam, Steve, and I were sitting around the table just chatting, talking about the day. I told them about what had happened with Zack and Jesse, and Asher's reaction.

"Asher's reaction is normal," Steve said when I'd finished, "especially if he's still uncertain about what he wants. I admit it sounds like he may know more than he is saying, but we can't know what, and it's useless to speculate. What concerns me more is Zack and Jesse. Something is going to have to be done about those boys. This is serious. It can't be allowed to continue. Someone is going to get hurt worse than a black eye."

"Maybe they already have," Adam said softly.

"You think they might have been involved in Seth's murder?" Steve asked him sharply.

"Maybe, and if not they probably know more than they are saying," Adam said.

Steve looked over to me, "Have you talked to anyone at school yet?"

"No, I'm not sure where to start and I was kinda waiting until things returned to normal," I told him.

He nodded. "Smart thinking. As for what to say, you'll have to play that by ear. Just be very careful. It sounds like Zack and Jesse are dangerous and now they know that you're gay, they may be more so."

"Speaking of being gay," I started, "I've been wondering why people are gay. I mean, why am I gay? Was I born this way? I've read some articles, but what do you think?"

"Well," Adam said, "I don't know if anyone knows for sure. It's actually something Steve and I have argued about." Steve nodded. "I believe you are born gay; that it's genetic. I mean, just look at me and Seth." And possibly Kane, I thought, but didn't say. "Steve thinks it's more a matter of environment. If you've been reading articles then I'm sure you've heard both sides and I don't need to go into a lot of detail. I think we can discard the choice theory. I don't know anyone who chose to be gay."

"I sure didn't," I agreed. "I read an article this afternoon, or started it at least, that suggested that it's a mixture of both genes and environment. It made a lot of sense to me."

"I'd like to read that if you still know where it is," Steve said.

"Me too," Adam agreed.

"Sure, I book-marked it," I told them. "C'mon, I can show it to you now."

We all went up to my room and I signed on and went to the site. We all read it together and discussed it as we went. In the end we agreed that, while no one could be sure, this theory was as good as any other.

I stayed up late waiting for Kane's call, but it never came. I slept fitfully that night, worrying about Kane. Was he ok? He had sounded like it was urgent that he talk to me. I hoped nothing was wrong. In my head I knew that he probably just didn't manage to get to the phone, but that didn't stop me from worrying.

I finally dozed off after tossing and turning for what seemed like hours. I don't know how long I was asleep before the attacker was there. I don't even know how long he was there before I noticed him. Suddenly there he was, on the edge of my consciousness, as if he were taunting me. As I became more aware of him he grew in clarity, although he still didn't have a face. He didn't attack me this time. He just stood there and stared at me. I don't know how to explain how I knew he was staring at me since I couldn't see his eyes; I just knew he was. Somehow his staring was worse than an actual attack, like I knew he was saying he could have me whenever he wanted me. He began to fade back into the shadows and I woke suddenly, my heart pounding, feeling quite unsettled. There was no Asher to help me get back to sleep this time.

I didn't sleep much after that; I was afraid he'd come back. As a result I was tired and cranky at breakfast, and my bad mood continued throughout the rest of the weekend. I stayed in my room a lot since Asher was still avoiding me and I wasn't very good company anyway. I didn't hear any more from Kane and I continued to fret about that as well. At least it helped distract me from the whole Asher thing.

Finally Monday rolled around and it was back to school. I was still thinking about Kane and Asher and found it hard to concentrate in class.

I was getting some stuff out my locker in between first and

second periods when Gillian Sheridan appeared at my side and leaned her back against the locker next to mine.

"Hi, Killian," she said. Gillian, or Gilly as everyone called her, was the girl who had been after me forever. She was in my first-period class this semester, and except for that one incident when she cornered me in the hall, I hadn't talked to her all that much this year. If I had to say one way or the other, I guess I would say that Gilly was cool, I just wasn't interested in her like that. She was about the same height as me with long straight white-blonde hair, light blue eyes, and just a hint of freckles across her nose. I suppose she was very pretty, although I'd never really noticed before. I had always just thought of her as a pest.

"Hi, Gilly," I said with my head as far in the locker as I could get it without stepping inside.

"Uh, can I talk to you?"

"Sure."

"I mean without your head stuck in the locker."

I reluctantly withdrew my head, shut the locker, and looked at her. She looked worried, or maybe just concerned.

"Are you ok, Killian?" she asked.

"Yeah, why wouldn't I be?"

"You seem distracted in class this morning and, well...I've heard some stuff."

Now she had my full attention. "Like what?"

"Just...stuff," she said lamely.

The bell rang and she pushed away from the locker. "Maybe we can talk later," she said.

"What lunch shift are you on?" I asked her. She was on a different shift, but she said she thought she could meet me at mine. We agreed and went our separate ways.

I waited for Gilly in the cafeteria, and once she got there we settled into a table away from the main crowds.

"So what is this stuff you've been hearing about me?" I said as soon as we'd sat down.

"Well, you know I don't believe any of it, but...um...Zack and Jesse are saying that you are...um...gay," she said awkwardly.

I thought for a minute, then decided it was best to be honest. I was sick and tired of lying, to myself and to others. I took a deep breath.

"They are telling the truth for once," I said quickly and

looked down at my sandwich, which I had yet to touch.

She didn't say anything for so long that finally I had to look up. She was looking at me with a curious expression on her face. I was relieved to see curiosity instead of hatred or revulsion, but this had me almost as worried.

"Is that why you'd never go out with me?" she asked finally.

I nodded, "I guess so."

"Well, at least I don't feel like a total loser now," she said and started to giggle.

I smiled at her a little, although I was still nervous.

"Killian, don't look so worried. You look like you're gonna puke. I won't tell anybody. If you wanna keep it quiet I'll even pretend to date you. It would be the closest I'll ever get to the real thing."

I laughed with her this time.

"I don't know about that, Gilly," I said. Then it occurred to me that it might be beneficial when I started asking questions to have an in with some of the popular crowds. I liked Gilly well enough. Maybe I should take her up on her offer. "Can I think about it?" I asked.

"Of course," she said. "Here, I'll give you my number. Maybe we can go get dinner or something one night this week and talk about it." She scribbled her number on a sheet of paper and handed it over to me. "Call me later tonight if you want."

I thanked her and she ran off to get back to class. I sat and nibbled on my sandwich while I thought about her offer. It didn't seem to bother her at all that I was gay. I knew she had a reputation for being nice to everyone and just a good girl in general. As far as I knew, she'd only dated a few guys for very short periods of time. I would talk to Adam tonight and see what he thought about the idea of me "dating" her.

The rest of the day passed quickly and I didn't see any opportunities to talk to anyone about Seth. I wanted it to be natural when I did, so natural that they wouldn't think enough of it to mention it to the wrong person. I saw Zack and Jesse once and ducked into a classroom to avoid them. I got some funny stares, but I didn't care as long as I didn't have to deal with the dynamic duo.

I waited till after dinner to bring up the subject of Gilly with Adam. When I'd finished telling him he thought for a minute.

"If you are sure she knows what she's asking, then maybe it

would be a good idea, at least until you are ready to come out to everyone. Just be careful to be very up-front with her. Sometimes girls think they can change you if they are just given a chance. Gillian sounds like a very nice girl, though. She'd be a good friend if nothing else."

After we'd cleaned up the dishes I checked my mail. There was an e-mail from Kane. It just briefly said that he was sorry he couldn't call me last week, but he was still trying and that things were still bad between him and his mother. I felt so bad for him. He seemed so much younger than 15; I felt like I should protect him, but I wasn't sure from what, or how, or what I could do. I had enough problems of my own.

After I got off the computer, I decided to call Gilly and see if we were on the same wavelength. A man answered and called Gilly to the phone.

"Hi, Gilly. It's Killian."

"Hey! I'm glad you called," she said, and she sounded like she meant it.

"I was thinking about what you said today, about us pretending to date? Are you sure you want to do that? I mean, that's not really fair to you."

"Hey, don't worry about me. I offered didn't I? Look, I've been thinking a lot about it. When I offered it was kind of a spur-of-the-moment thing, but now that I've thought about it, I still want to do it. I'm not really into any of the guys at school right now, so it's not like I'll be missing out on anyone. If something changes, we officially break up. No biggie. I want to be your friend and this is something I can do to help you out."

"That means a lot to me, Gilly," I said. "I don't know why you are being so nice to me. I've never done anything for you. Doesn't it bother you that I'm gay?"

"Ok, look, you don't have to do anything for me, Killian. I'm not asking for anything, just your friendship. I'm not one of those Kleenex people who use you and then throw you away. And no, it doesn't bother me that you are gay. I have an Uncle Rick who is gay so I know you're not some sort of pervert or anything."

"What's up with everybody having an Uncle Rick?" I asked.

"Huh?" was Gilly's confused response.

"Asher has a gay Uncle Rick too," I told her before I thought better of it. I immediately regretted revealing Asher's personal information, but it was too late now. Gilly started laughing. "What's so funny?" I asked.

"Asher's Uncle Rick and my Uncle Rick is the same person. Asher's my cousin. I thought you knew that. His dad and my mom are brother and sister."

"I had no clue."

"Oh, well, we have a huge family. Besides my mom, Uncle Alex and Uncle Rick, there's also Aunt Judy. And that's just my aunts and uncles, not even counting all the cousins. Aunt Judy, by the way, is a little nutty. She thinks she's some sort of psychic or something. She says we have gypsy blood in our veins. Don't I look like a gypsy?" She started giggling again.

I heard a kid's voice in the background saying, "No, you look like Jar Jar Binks," followed by childish giggles.

"Who was that?" I asked.

"My little brother, Jamie," she said. "He's a huge Star Wars fan. Anakin Skywalker is his hero."

"I didn't know you had any brothers."

"I have three. My older brother, Todd, is a senior, Jacob, or Jake, as everybody calls him, is 14, and Jamie is 5."

"Wow. I didn't know that. I'm an only child."

"Yeah, I know. There're a lot of things you don't know about me. I have the advantage since I've been obsessed with you for years. Why don't you come over for dinner tomorrow after school so you can meet my family? If you're gonna be my pretend boyfriend then you need to know them."

"Ok, I'll check with Adam but I'm sure it'll be fine."

"Who's Adam?"

"Adam is Seth's dad. I live with him now. My dad kicked me out when he found out I was gay."

"Oh, Killian. That's horrible. I'm so sorry."

"It's not as big a deal as it sounds. I hated him anyway. I like living with Adam. He's cool. He's more like my dad than my dad. I miss my mom, though."

"She stayed?"

"Yeah, she's afraid of him."

"Well, he is pretty influential around here."

"Yeah."

"Hey, Gill, I need to use the phone, time's up," I heard another voice say, this time a deeper male voice, though not the one who had answered the phone.

"Ok, Todd, hang on," Gilly's voice was a bit muffled, so she must have put her hand over the mouthpiece, then she came back again, "Hey I have to go; Todd wants to use the phone. So you'll come over tomorrow?"

"Yeah, I'll try anyway."

"Ok, I'll see you in school tomorrow. Buhbye."

"Bye."

I lay back on the bed and thought for a while about what had just happened. It seemed I had gone from dating Asher (however short-lived it had been) to dating his cousin...who was a girl. Curiouser and curiouser. Of course, Gilly was just a cover. I felt like a spy. Just call me Bond. Killian Bond. I giggled to myself.

I was still flopped on my bed when the phone rang in my hand. I yelped and then started giggling at myself all over again. I was still laughing when I answered the phone. By now I was in a very silly mood.

"Hello. This is Bond. Killian Bond," I said in my best English accent.

"Killian?" a shaky voice said uncertainly. It was Kane.

"Kane, hey, are you ok?" I asked in my normal voice, all silliness gone.

"No."

"What's wrong?"

"I've got to get out of here. It's horrible."

"What's horrible, Kane?"

"Mom, she watches every move I make now. I can't do anything with any of my friends. I go to school and have to come right home. At home, she never speaks to me except to scream. She's going through my stuff. I have to sneak onto the computer or the phone. Yesterday she slapped me because she caught me on the computer trying to e-mail you. She's never hit me before. I hate her. She lied to me about Dad, she sent Seth away. I can't stand it anymore. I'm running away. I'm coming down there."

"Kane, whoa, slow down," I said quickly. "Look, if you come down here your mom will just come get you again. You're going to have to do this the right way."

"What right way?"

"I don't know, but I know running away isn't it. What about that legal stuff you were talking about?"

"That would take too long. I want out now."

"I don't know what to tell you, Kane. Wait, hang on, lemme go get your dad," I said and took off to the living room, where Adam was reading a book.

"Adam, it's Kane and he's really upset. I think you'd better talk to him. He wants to run away."

Adam snatched the phone.

"Kane?" he said into the phone, his voice filled with tension.

He listened for a while, making comforting noises occasionally. Finally he said, "Kane, listen to me, son. Hang in there for a few more days. I'll call my lawyer in the morning and see what's involved here. But if she hits you again, call me and I'll come get you. I don't give a damn about her lawyers. You'll be with me soon."

They talked for a few more minutes, then they said goodbye and Adam hung up.

"Thank you, Killian," he said when he'd hung up.

"For what?" I asked.

"For being there for Kane. He told me he talked to you and what you told him. You are a good friend and a good person. You've proven that I can trust you. I couldn't talk the other night when you said I was like a father to you. I was too overcome with emotion. But I want you to know that I have come to think of you as a son as well."

I took the few steps between us in one leap and gave him a huge hug. I didn't cry though. I was getting better.

The dreams came back with a vengeance that night and I woke up in a cold sweat. It was so bad I had to go wake Adam up. He let me sleep in his bed and I finally got some rest.

I overslept a little and was late getting to class, so I didn't get to talk to Gilly until after first period. We met by the door and everyone grinned at us as they walked by.

"Does everyone know already?" I asked. It never ceases to amaze me how fast news travels in a high school.

"Yeah," she said with a grin. "I told a few people and it spread like wildfire. After the rumors that Zack and Jesse were spreading this is hot stuff." She giggled.

I laughed and she gave me a hug before running off to her next class. I was eating lunch later that day when someone sat down beside me. I looked up to find Asher sitting there with a confused look on his face. I hadn't spoken to Asher since the day Zack and Jesse tried to beat me up.

"You're dating Gilly?" he asked in an accusatory voice.

"Well, yeah, kinda," I said meekly.

"You're dating my cousin...*who's a girl*," he hissed the last part, leaning in towards me intensely.

"Look, Asher, it's not how it seems..." I started, but he broke in.

"Then how is it? Huh? Tell me, Killian. Are you just gonna sweep through the whole family? Who's next, my brother, Marcus? Or maybe you'd rather go after my sister, Bethany? Hell, maybe you want both of them since you can't seem to make up your mind."

"I can't make up my mind?" I was getting angry now. My voice was climbing and a few people near us glanced over at us curiously, so I made an effort to speak more quietly. "Who was it that said they didn't want to ruin their precious reputation? Who was the one that backed off with us? Who was it that said they couldn't handle all this? Here's a clue; it wasn't me!"

"Yeah, well, I didn't run off and start dating your cousin, *who's a girl*, less than a week later."

"It's none of your business who I date, Asher," I lowered my voice even more and leaned in until our noses were almost touching. He refused to back off or look away. "You had your chance and you blew it. Sorry, babe."

I stood up, grabbed my backpack, and walked away without looking back. I should have felt great. I'd just told Asher off, something I never did. I don't even know what came over me, it was almost like it was someone else speaking and I was just as shocked as he was at what I was saying. But I didn't feel great; I felt awful for hurting Asher. Why didn't I just tell him the truth?

Chapter 14

By the end of the day, the whole school knew about Gilly and me. I had guys I hardly knew clapping me on the back and telling me way to go; girls who had never had the time of day for me before waving and smiling at me and calling me by name from across the hall. It was truly bizarre. Like popularity in a box, just add beautiful girlfriend.

I didn't run into Asher anymore that day, although I was half hoping I would so I could apologize. I was supposed to be at Gilly's house for dinner at 5:00 so that gave me a couple hours to kill. I drove home, but Adam wasn't there. I found a note on the refrigerator saying he was seeing his lawyer and wouldn't be home before I went to Gilly's, but he would see me later that night.

I made myself a light snack and was just sitting down to eat it and work on my homework when the doorbell rang. I got up to answer it. I hated that frosted door. I could never see who was there, just shadows and movements. For a split second panic swept over me as I was reminded of my dream and I almost didn't open the door, but the moment passed and I did. I immediately wished I hadn't. There stood Zack and Jesse.

I froze for just the briefest second but it was long enough; when I tried to slam the door Zack was already in motion and managed to shove the door back open.

"That's not very hospitable, Killian," he said. "We're just here to pay you a quick visit. I promise it won't be long."

I wasn't about to let them into the house so I stood where I was, feet apart and arms crossed to try and hide their shaking.

"What do you want?" I demanded. I refused to let them see how scared I was.

"What kind of game are you playing, Killian?" Zack asked casually as he leaned against the doorjamb.

"What do you mean?" I asked.

"Don't play games, faggot," Jesse entered the conversation for the first time with his usual wit and charm.

"I don't know what you are talking about? What games?"

"What's going on with Gilly? We know you're a fag, you told us so yourself. Plus we saw you with Asher," Zack explained patiently.

"I'm going out with Gilly," I said simply.

"We got that much, what we want to know is why. Why date Gilly if you're gay?" Zack said.

"Maybe I changed my mind," I almost giggled at the thought but I restrained myself out of fear. I could feel the sweat trickling down my back I was so nervous.

"You can do that?" Jesse asked in surprise.

Zack shot him a disgusted look and said, "Look Killian, I don't know what you are up to, but don't forget we're watching you. If you hurt Gilly, we'll hurt you. Got that?"

"Yeah, I got it, Zack. You know, you guys are pretty pathetic if you don't have anything better to do than follow me around all the time and keep tabs on my love life."

Zack pulled himself up straight and squared his shoulders. Jesse moved into position behind him and it became very evident that my big mouth was about to get me in trouble again. Just as I was about to try and talk myself out of whatever was coming, Adam pulled into the driveway.

Zack glanced over his shoulder and started backing up.

"We'll talk more later," he said loudly enough for Adam to hear as he got out of his car.

"Are we leaving?" Jesse asked. I swear Jesse would be out of his depth in a parking lot puddle.

"Yeah, we're done here for now," Zack told him.

"Who was that?" Adam asked as they got in their car and pulled off.

"Zack and Jesse, also known as Tweedle-dum and Tweedledumber."

"What did they want?" he asked sharply.

"They were trying to figure out what I'm doing with Gilly. I think it really confused them; more than their insignificant intellect can handle."

Adam laughed. He put his arm around me and steered me into the house. "That mouth of yours is going to get you in trouble one of these days. I think your lips move before your brain gets done thinking."

"It almost just did. I'm glad you got here when you did," I went on to recount the whole scene with Zack and Jesse.

"I don't want you coming home alone anymore," he said when I was finished. "If I can't be here I'll have to figure something out. It's just not safe. That could have gone so many ways."

"But it didn't," I said. "I'm ok. I just won't be so stupid as to open the door before I know who's there anymore. So what happened with the lawyer? I didn't think you were supposed to be back this early."

"Nice change of subject. It went well. Ilana thinks we have a good chance. She's very confident"

"Ilana?"

"My lawyer, Ilana Constantino. She's going to go ahead and start the wheels turning on this custody thing. She's going to contact Eve's lawyer. I told her to expect all hell to break loose when Eve finds out."

"What happens if Eve gets ugly?"

"Oh, it's not a matter of if, and I guess I'll just have to get ugly back. This is my kid we're talking about. I'm not playing around any more. I'm tired of being the nice guy while my kids get hurt."

We'd settled in the living room by now. We talked for a while about all the legal ins and outs of the situation and what it would be like to have Kane move in with us. We would be sharing Seth's old room; Adam said he would get twin beds. Some time later, Adam looked at his watch.

"Aren't you supposed to be getting ready for your dinner with Gilly's family?" he asked me.

"Getting ready?"

"Meeting the girlfriend's family is a big deal, you know," he was grinning now.

"Gilly's not my girlfriend, not really," I said defensively, thinking about Asher and my angry words earlier that day.

"I know, Killian, I'm just kidding. But you should still make an effort to look nice."

"What's wrong with what I'm wearing now?"

"Nothing...if you're going to school. Why don't you just go change? Doesn't have to be anything too dressy, just a little less...beachy."

I looked down at my T-shirt and faded jeans and realized that maybe he had a point. I ran upstairs and changed into a pair of cargo khakis and a dark green button-up shirt over a white T-shirt. I checked myself out in the mirror and thought I didn't look half bad. My hair was even curlier than usual. I decided not to brush it out since I kind of liked the way it looked curly.

I went back down and presented myself to Adam. After getting his approval I decided it was about the right time to head over to Gilly's house; a little early, but not too much. I hated being last minute.

I followed the directions Gilly had given me, but I was sure I must have messed up somewhere when I pulled into the drive of the address she'd written down. The house was a huge, old plantation manor; it could almost be described as a mansion. After I double-checked the directions and address, I parked the car and walked up to the front door. It opened before I could even knock. Gilly stood there grinning ear to ear.

"Are you sure you're ready for this?" she said before I could even say hi.

"What do you mean?" I asked.

"Think you're prepared to meet my crazy family? They all turned out to meet you."

"W-w-what?" I stuttered nervously.

"Aunt Judy's in town for a few days, she lives in California, so everybody will be there to see her. I kinda forgot that when I invited you, but Mom said what's one more mouth?"

"Oh great," I thought. "I'm walking into a freaking family reunion. Now I have to impress the whole family." Then it struck me that Asher might be there and I almost headed back to the car, but Gilly had me by the arm and was dragging me in.

I shouldn't have worried though; from the moment I stepped through the door it was like being swept up into a whirlwind. People were everywhere, or so it seemed. As I was given a mini-tour of the downstairs of the house, I was introduced to everyone.

In the living room I met the famous Uncle Rick and Todd, who were both seated on the couch and seemed to be in a deep conversation. Alex, Asher's dad, was talking to Asher's sister, Bethany, who was home from college for the weekend and had extended her stay to see Judy. Rick was in his mid to late 30s with straight light brown hair that he wore in a stylish short cut brushed to one side. Todd was a year or two older than me with shoulder length blonde hair and the same sky blue eyes that Gilly had. He was the stereotypical surfer boy, tan and built from all the paddling and swimming. Alex had graying sandy blonde hair and gray eyes. Bethany had the same hair as her mother and Asher, but longer. It came to just past her shoulders and hung in shiny brown ringlets. She was very pretty, with a heart-shaped face and perfect pouty little lips. Asher said she had been doing some modeling where she was going to school and was trying to get into acting. I could picture her on a movie screen. She had that look about her; she carried herself like a star.

In the rec room, there was Marcus, Asher's brother, and Jacob ("Call me Jake") playing Nintendo 64, while Jamie divided his time between watching them and playing with a pile of Star Wars figures on the floor. Marcus looked like he was from a different family from Asher and Bethany. He had wavy sandy blonde hair and blue eyes, where both Asher's and Bethany's were a steely gray color. He looked more like Jake's brother than Asher's. Jake had blonde hair, too, although it was darker than Todd's and Gilly's. His eyes were the same shade of blue, though, as everyone in their family's seemed to be. His hair was longish, but not as long as Todd's. His look was more skater than surfer, even to his outfit—baggy jeans, wallet chain, and layered shirts. Jamie was adorable, same white-blonde hair and blue eyes as Gilly. He still maintained a little of his baby fat, not enough to be chubby, but enough to give him that soft baby look.

Everyone else was in the kitchen putting the finishing touches on dinner. Tom and Janice, Gilly's parents, were standing over an open oven arguing over who was going to take the ham out. Tom pulled an oven mitt off long enough to shake my hand and Janice took the opportunity to duck under our arms and grab the ham. He chased off after her, insisting that she let him carry it while she insisted that she was fine. Tom was slightly overweight with prematurely white hair and glasses. Janice looked much younger than he did with her blonde hair cut in a pageboy style. She was built like Gilly, thin and small with delicate, pretty features. Mrs. Davis—Deb—was scooping huge mounds of fluffy mashed potatoes into a bowl while Judy, Gilly's crazy aunt, was cutting a cake. Judy had piles of hair of an unnatural shade of red that towered over her head in a gravity-defying feat of hairdressing magic. She wore an abundance of make-up and looked rather like a carnival gypsy in her brightly colored muumuu. Her nails added to the effect; about two inches long and painted bright red, they looked like talons. I suspected they could be considered deadly weapons. When we were introduced, she dropped the knife she was using to slice the cake and swooped in on me for a big hug. It was like being attacked by a giant fluffy bat. It was almost impossible to pinpoint her age; she could have been the oldest or the youngest sibling in the Davis clan.

There was only one person I hadn't seen: Asher. I turned to Gilly as we went back to the rec room and asked, "Is Asher here?"

"No, he said he wasn't feeling well and wanted to stay home, so they left him," she explained.

"Oh," I breathed a small sigh of relief.

"Are you guys fighting?"

"Sort of," I said and left it at that. Thankfully, Jamie barreled into us at that moment and distracted Gilly from pursuing it further.

"Will you play Star Wars with me?" he asked as he wrapped himself around my legs and looked up at me with those big blue eyes. How could I say no to that?

I sat down in the floor with him and he handed me a Darth Maul figure. "You be him and I'll be Obi Wan Kenobi," he told me.

"Who can I be?" Gilly asked.

Jamie looked at her with a puzzled expression for a moment before saying, "I don't have any girls."

"What about Princess What's-her-name?"

"Amidala, and she was a queen, not a princess. And I didn't want her."

"Why not?" Gilly persisted.

"Cuz she's a girl," Jamie finished decisively, as if that explained everything. Gilly shrugged and moved over to watch Jake and Marcus battle it out on Goldeneye. I heard her mutter something about males and violence, but I couldn't catch all of it.

We fought with our figures, making light saber noises and other cool sound effects until we were called to dinner.

Dinner was another experience entirely, quite unlike any I'd ever had before. It was like one of those families you see on TV or in the movies, like those big Italian families in Mafia stories, except they weren't Italian and they weren't Mafia...at least as far as I knew. Everyone talked over each other and food just kept going round and round. I swear it seemed to keep multiplying like some sort of Biblical miracle. While on the surface everyone seemed quite genial and happy, I sensed an undercurrent of unspoken tension, especially with the Sheridans. I didn't really have time to think about it, though, since questions kept coming at me from every side. I tried to keep up with them, but I'm pretty sure I missed a few. I was very relieved when dessert was served.

After dinner, Asher's family had to leave, but everyone else headed for the living room where they settled down and continued chatting. After a few minutes, Judy excused herself to go smoke. A few minutes later, Gilly asked me if I wanted to take a walk, to which I quickly agreed. It wasn't that I didn't like her family; they were just a bit overwhelming.

We walked around the back yard for a while before finally settling on the back porch on a swing. We talked about nothing for a few minutes before Gilly excused herself to go to the bathroom. She hadn't even shut the door before Judy appeared from the bushes and sat down beside me on the porch swing. I wondered how long she'd been lurking in the shrubbery.

"You're not really Gilly's boyfriend, are you?"

"Huh?" I managed.

"You and Gilly, you aren't really boyfriend and girlfriend. I can see."

"What do you mean you can see?"

"I see many things. I see that you only love other boys, and since Gilly is not a boy..."

"How do you know that? How do you know I'm gay?" I hissed. I was getting panicky.

"Don't be scared. I don't judge, I simply see. I see many things most people don't. It's not that they can't see, they just often choose not to."

"What else do you see?" I asked hesitantly.

She reached out and took my hand. "I see you are scared. You have been hurt very much and you have not yet healed. You are in danger; someone wishes you harm. You must find them before they accomplish the task they have set before themselves. Your paths are intertwining; they converge repeatedly. From this point there are many paths you can chose, but there is only one that you will survive. Watch your step carefully."

She dropped my hand and stood up. She looked down at me for a second, then began to walk away.

"Wait!" I called after her. "Do you know who it is? Who's after me?"

She paused and turned back to me, her face was lost in the shadows so that her voice seemed to come from nowhere, "You must discover that for yourself. It is your path." I felt the hairs on my arms stand up, and then she turned and melted into the darkness.

Gilly came back out as soon as Judy was out of sight, but before she could even sit down her mom called her back inside.

"I'm sorry, Killian. I'll be right back, I promise," and she ducked back inside.

She hadn't even been gone for a minute before the door opened again. My mind was still swirling with Judy's words so it took a moment for me to realize that it wasn't Gilly, it was her brother Todd. He hadn't noticed me on the swing as he walked to the rail and leaned against it. I was debating whether or not to make my presence known when he turned around and noticed me. He started a little, then cursed under his breath.

"Sorry, I didn't see you there," he said.

"S'ok," I told him.

"You're awful quiet," he said as he came over and sat down beside me. I couldn't help but think that this was all like a carefully choreographed play or a TV sitcom, with everyone coming and going in such a seemingly synchronized way. "So you're Gilly's boyfriend now. You're the guy she's been after for so long."

"I guess," I laughed nervously, although it had been phrased as a statement and not a question. Good thing I was or some poor guy would be feeling really special right about now. I shifted a little because Todd had sat down closer to me than I was comfortable with. I was feeling a little flushed from his closeness; he was very attractive.

"You guys don't seem to be all that enthusiastic about it," he commented. He looked at me closely and again I felt vaguely uncomfortable, like he was seeing through me.

"What do you mean?" I asked warily.

"Just that you guys don't seem to have the body language you usually see with two people who are first going out."

"Get lost, Todd," Gilly said suddenly from behind us. We both jumped. I hadn't even heard the door open. "Since when are you an expert on body language?"

"Gilly, I'm just looking out for you. That's all," he said standing up and moving away from the swing.

"Thanks, Todd, I know. But you have to remember that I'm a big girl now. I'm only 18 months younger than you. I can take care of myself."

Todd looked at me one last time and I could tell that there was more that he wanted to say, but he just shrugged and walked back into the house.

"Sorry about that. I warned you that I had a weird family." Gilly said sitting in the once again vacant spot next to me.

"It's ok," I told her, "but I really think I need to be getting back home. I didn't finish my homework."

Gilly smiled, but it didn't look like she really meant it. "Ok," she said. "Will you come in and say good-bye to everyone first?"

"Yeah, of course," I said.

Then before I could react she leaned forward and kissed me. I jerked away without thinking.

"Gilly...I'm gay," I said softly.

"I know, but I thought maybe if we..." she never finished; instead she just burst into tears.

"Oh geez, Gilly," I said, feeling very helpless and unsure of what to do. I patted her awkwardly on the back. After a few minutes she managed to stop crying and wiped her eyes with the back of her hands.

"I'm sorry, Killian," she sniffled. "I promise I won't do it again."

"It's ok, Gilly," I said, still feeling very awkward. "It's not that you aren't a great girl, you are, it's just...if I wasn't gay, I'm sure I would like you a lot. I mean I like you now as a friend, but if I was straight I'm sure I'd like you as more than a friend..."

Gilly reached out and placed a finger on my lips to shut me up, "You don't have to apologize or explain anything, Killian. I was out of line and I'm sorry. We agreed that this was just for show. I just got carried away. Let's just pretend that never happened? Ok?"

I nodded and we both stood up and hugged briefly. We went back inside and after saying good-bye to everyone I went out to my car, but my strange night at Gilly's house wasn't over yet. Before I could get in my car someone tapped me on the shoulder. I spun around with a yelp, but it was only Rick.

"Sorry, didn't mean to startle you," he said. "I just wanted to say good-bye and tell you if you ever need to talk, I'm available."

"Um, thanks," I said uncertainly.

"I know this must be a confusing time for you right now. Asher talks to me and he told me what's been going on for both of you and as you know, he isn't handling things very well. But hang in there; hopefully he'll come around soon, and he'll need his friends when he does."

"He hasn't seemed to want me as his friend lately," I said. I was a little angry that Asher had told my personal business to Rick without even asking me.

"Asher doesn't know what he wants right now. In time, though, he'll sort things out, and so will you. Just give him time." He patted me on the back and started back towards the house. I got in my car and drove away from what had to have been one of the oddest nights of my entire life.

Chapter
15

I went to sleep thinking about what Judy had said and it was the first thing I thought of when I woke up. In fact, it totally distracted me all morning at school, as well. At one point I paid attention enough to realize that I had no idea what we were talking about and thought that this would be a bad thing come test time, and then I spaced out again.

I was still in my own little world at lunch when I realized someone had sat down next to me. Somehow, I wasn't surprised to see that it was the only member of Gilly's family, besides her parents, that hadn't cornered me the night before.

"Hey, Jake," I said.

"Hi, Killian. Can I talk to you for a few minutes?" he asked. He was wearing a baggy pair of carpenter's jeans and a long-sleeved Creed concert T-shirt, accessorized with the requisite wallet chain. Today he had thrown in a silver ball chain necklace. His blonde hair was tucked behind his ears in a way that I found very appealing. Was everyone in Gilly's family attractive or was it just me?

"Sure, why not?" I said.

"You were friends with Seth, right?"

Wow, that was about the last thing I had expected him to say. "Uh, yeah, I guess you could say that," I said finally.

"I heard that you're even living with his dad now."

"Yeah, I am." I wondered where this was leading.

He looked around at the tables near us then leaned in closer to me. "Wasn't Seth gay?" he asked quietly.

"Um, yes."

"Is it true that his dad is too?"

"Yes."

"Then, um...are you?"

Uh oh, dangerous waters; what should I say? "I'm dating your sister," I said, deciding to go with a non-answer.

"I know, but that's not what I asked." He was sharper than I had given him credit for.

"Look, Jake, do you think we could get together later maybe and talk about this?" I looked around meaningfully.

Jake thought for a moment then made up his mind. "Yeah, sure. Can I ask you one more question, though?"

I was hesitant but I agreed.

He again leaned in and lowered his voice even more. "Do you think Seth was really killed in a mugging? I mean, you were there, but that seems unlikely to me."

I was so shocked that for a minute I couldn't even say anything. At last I was able to ask, "What do you mean?"

"Just that it seems strange that the only openly gay student at our high school gets mugged and killed two weeks after school starts. Call me suspicious, but that sounds fishy to me."

I couldn't believe what I was hearing. I wondered for a second if I was being set up, red flags were going up everywhere. I remembered Judy's words, "Watch your step carefully," she had said. I decided that this was very good advice for this situation.

"Why does it matter to you?" I asked cautiously.

He looked around again. Why did he seem so paranoid? "We'll talk about it later, ok? When do you want to meet?"

"How about after school? You can meet me at my car. You know what I drive right?"

"A black Beetle, right?"

"Yeah."

"Todd parked next to it this morning. I'll meet you there, but wait for me; I have to talk to Mr. Johnson after school for a few minutes about an assignment that's late. I'll see you then."

"Ok," I said. "See you then."

Gilly and I were leaning against my car talking after school, Gilly waiting for Todd and me waiting for Jake. Neither of us had mentioned the kiss from the night before. We were studiously avoiding that topic. People were still straggling out but most of the cars were gone from the student parking lot by now.

"So how for real is your Aunt Judy?" I asked.

"Who knows? Why? Did she get to you last night while I was gone?" Gilly asked as she tucked a flyaway strand of blonde hair behind her ear. I nodded and she went on. "We don't really take her all that seriously, but there have been some eerie coincidences."

"Like what?"

"Well, by far the freakiest thing that ever happened was last Christmas. She told Uncle Rick that he was soon going to be alone and that's why she bought him a puppy. Uncle Rick was mad because Elliott, his partner, was allergic to dogs and they'd been together for a long time. A week after Christmas, Elliott died in a car accident. Uncle Rick still has the dog; he named it Enigma."

I felt the hairs on my arms stand up again. "So is she like a psychic or something?" I asked.

Gilly laughed. "Don't let her hear you say that. She gets so mad when somebody calls her psychic, even if they're just joking. She says for the most part she just sees stuff that other people miss, that she's just more sensitive. The rest, she says, comes from God. It's not like she's an operator for one of those cheesy 900 numbers. Why? What did she say to you?"

"It's nothing, really."

"When did she talk to you, anyway?"

"While you were inside."

"Her and Todd both?"

"Well, Judy when you went in the first time and Todd the second."

"Why is my family stalking you?"

We both laughed as Jake came running up to us.

"Speaking of stalkers." I laughed. "Here comes another one."

"What? Why am I a stalker?" Jake asked, confused.

Todd walked up just then. "Because you're a creepy little psycho," he said with a grin as he ruffled Jake's hair.

"Knock it off, Todd, or I'll tell everyone about the magazines under your bed," Jake said good-naturedly.

Todd shot him a strange look, as if he wasn't sure if he was serious or not, but apparently decided he wasn't. "Are you two goobers ready?" he asked.

"I'm going to go home with Killian and then he'll drive me home," Jake said as he shifted his backpack from one shoulder to the other.

Gilly gave me a surprised look, which I'm sure I returned in kind. Todd gave me a look I couldn't quite identify, then shrugged and said, "Suit yourself. Gilly, you ready?"

"Yeah, I'm ready," she said slowly and with a lingering look at me got in the car. After they had driven off and Jake and I were in my car, I asked him, "So, where to?"

"Wherever, somewhere we can talk in private and not be overheard," he said.

"What's all this cloak-and-dagger stuff about, Jake?" I asked him as I started the car and pulled out.

"I just need to talk to you about some stuff and I don't want to be heard."

"What stuff? About Seth?"

"Partly."

"Jake, we're in a moving car; as far as I know there is no one in the back seat, I think it's safe to talk."

"Ok. It's just that this isn't easy for me. I've never told anybody this before."

"Told anybody what?" I shouted in exasperation.

"I'm gay!" he shouted back.

I almost drove off the road. Once I had the car back under control, I looked over at him. He sat slumped in the seat, staring at his hands in his lap.

"It's ok, Jake," I said softly. "I'm not going to hate you or anything."

He looked up hopefully. "Really?"

"Yeah, really. You know why?"

"Why?"

"I'm gay, too."

His mouth dropped open and his eyes widened in surprise. "Wha...?" I couldn't help but laugh at his expression. "I mean I wondered...but what about Gilly?"

"Gilly and I are just friends."

"But...but...you told everybody that you are going out." His face was a study in confusion.

"It's kind of like a cover; so that no one knows I'm gay for right now. I think more people will talk to me about Seth if they don't know I'm gay. Not that I'm ashamed of it or anything. I was at first, I guess, like it was something I needed to hide, but

Adam has taught me that it's just a part of who I am, like being left- or right-handed."

"Adam?"

"Adam is Seth's dad."

"You live with him now, right? Were you and Seth...?"

"We were just friends."

"And you think that something happened besides a mugging, too? I mean, why else would you want to talk to people about Seth without them knowing you are gay?"

"Ya know what? You're a lot smarter than you let on," I told him.

"I'm not sure if should take that as a compliment or not," he said with an adorable grin. I noticed he had a dimple and almost ran off the road again.

"Take it as a compliment," I said as I blushed. I could tell he was still grinning even without looking at him.

"I'll do that, on one condition."

"What's that?"

"That you'll keep your eyes on the road while you're driving."

I burst out laughing and he quickly joined in. All of a sudden I realized that without having a clear destination in mind I had been driving on autopilot and now I found myself at home.

"Well, this is where I live now," I said as I pulled into the driveway. "I didn't really mean to come here; it's just where we ended up, but since we're here, you wanna come in for a few minutes?"

"Sure, why not?" he said. He flashed me another one of those killer smiles and I felt like I was melting.

We went in and I made introductions. After Adam went back to work on his computer, Jake and I wandered up to my room to talk. After we were settled at opposite ends of the bed, I started back into our earlier conversation.

"So you think Seth was murdered?" I asked him.

"Well, yeah, I mean, it's the only thing that makes sense to me. I just don't understand why the police aren't doing more."

"Well, we think it was more than just a mugging, too. Adam thinks that maybe the police are purposefully ignoring important information."

"Like what?"

"There were letters, in Seth's locker. The police dismissed them, but we think that means that the killer has to go to our school. Or at least has a contact there that must know something. Did you have any classes with Seth?"

"No, but I saw him a lot in the halls and stuff."

"Did you ever see him with anyone?"

"Mostly just you."

"Anybody else?"

He thought for a minute then spoke slowly as if he was carefully considering each word. "This is hard. Not just hard to remember who I saw him with, but I also feel like I'm casting suspicion on anyone I name. But anyway, I saw him with Zack, Jesse, and Asher once; another time I saw him with just Asher. I saw him with Becky Rosinski. And I think I saw him with my cousin, Marcus, once." He hesitated for a moment before continuing on quickly, "And I saw him with a few different people I don't really know but none of them looked like they were really 'with him' with him, maybe just talking to him after class, you know."

I started to ask him about the hesitation, but decided not to right now. It bothered me that Asher had talked to him twice. He never told me that. Could that be what he was hiding? Or was there more? I pulled my mind away from that line of thought and forced it back onto the present conversation.

"Did he look angry or scared or uncomfortable with any of them?"

Once again, he thought for a moment before answering. "It's hard to say; maybe so with Zack, Jesse, and Asher, and when it was just Asher. Not really with Becky. I couldn't tell with Marcus 'cuz I just saw them from behind."

"What about the others?"

"I'm not sure." His eyes flickered away and again I had the distinct impression that he wasn't telling me everything. This time I decided to not ignore it.

"You have to tell me everything, Jake," I told him gently.

"What do you mean?"

"I mean, whatever it is you're not telling me. I can tell you are trying to protect someone or something, but this is really important. I need to talk to everyone who had anything to do with Seth, because even if they didn't kill him they might know something, maybe even something they don't even know that they know."

He sat there for a few minutes before he finally seemed to make up his mind. "Look, Killian...there is another person that I saw him talking to, but let me talk to that person first please. Don't push it right now."

"Why are you protecting this person? What if they are the one that killed Seth?"

"I just can't believe that about them. Please, just give me a chance to talk to them first."

"Ok," I gave in with a sigh.

His whole face lit up with that smile as he impulsively jumped across the bed and tackled me. We wrestled on the bed for a few minutes before he finally got the advantage. He had my body pinned with his and my arms held down to the bed above my head. His face was just inches from mine when our eyes locked and we both froze. We stayed like that for what seemed like an eternity before he suddenly leaped back.

"I'm sorry," he said sounding slightly out of breath even though I knew we hadn't wrestled that hard.

"For what?"

He seemed at a lost for words, so I took pity on him and got up off the bed. "Never mind," I called over my shoulder as I turned on the computer.

"Hey, Killian," he said. "Can I ask you a question? You don't have to answer if you don't want to."

Well, that certainly piqued my curiosity. "Sure, ask me anything."

"Do you...like anybody?"

"Like how?" I asked him, even though I knew what he was asking; I just wanted to hear him say it.

"Like as in...are you attracted to anyone?" He blushed a furious red and I couldn't help but smile, so I quickly turned back to the computer so he wouldn't think I was laughing at him.

"Yes," I said simply.

"Can I ask who?" came his timid reply.

"Sure you can ask, doesn't mean I'll tell you, though," I was enjoying this way too much.

"Why not? Don't you trust me?" I could tell that this was serious question for him and I realized that I wasn't being very sensitive. I left the computer trying to log on to AOL and walked back over to the bed. I sat down next to him and looked directly into his eyes.

"Yes, I trust you, Jake. You seem to be a very honest person and I really like spending time with you. I hope we can be friends, but I'm not quite ready to talk about who I'm attracted to. Do you understand?"

"Yeah, I think so," he said. "I should be getting home. Do you think you can drive me home now?"

I felt awful. I could tell I'd disappointed him, but what could I do? Tell him I was attracted to both him and his cousin?

"Yeah, sure."

Just then I heard a familiar voice say "Welcome."

"You're online," Jake said with a small smile.

"Yup, sounds that way," I laughed.

"You've got mail," the voice continued.

"Let me shut this down and we can go," I told Jake.

"No, go ahead and check your mail since you're on. I can wait a few more minutes."

"Ok, thanks."

There wasn't anything of any importance except a short letter from Kane saying that nothing had changed, but at least Eve hadn't hit him again. I shut down the computer and I drove Jake home. We made small talk during the ride and he thanked me a dozen times for talking to him and giving him a ride before he got out of the car.

I was pulling out of the driveway, which had two enormous bushes on either side of it, when Aunt Judy stepped out in front of my car. I slammed on the brakes and managed to stop just short of hitting her. I was very glad I hadn't been going any faster. My heart was pounding in my chest as I went to open the car door, but she motioned me to stay where I was. She walked around and climbed into the passenger seat. Today she was wearing her hair loose and flowing, and it hung down almost to her waist. Her face was deathly pale and she was wearing a black loose-fitting dress that swept the ground as she walked. Her nails, which had been bright red the night before, were now painted black. All in all, she looked rather like a red-haired Morticia Adams.

"Do you always have to jump out of shrubbery? I could have hit you!" I accused her angrily once she was in.

"But you didn't," she said calmly. "I needed to speak to you in private."

"So you jump out in front of my car?" I was exasperated.

"It served its purpose. We're talking, aren't we?"

I shook my head in wonder. Obviously there was no winning with this strange woman. "So what was so important that you had to risk your life to tell me?"

"I'm leaving tomorrow."

"Well, thank you for the information. I'll miss you terribly."
I was still rather miffed about the whole situation.

"I needed to tell you before I left that you are in danger.
Things have been set in motion that you are powerless to stop. I
had a dream last night."

Now she had my attention. "What about?"

"There was a faceless man watching you, but you didn't see
him. He didn't come after you, but I fear he will soon. He had
evil intent."

At first I was speechless, when I finally found my voice it
came out a bit shaky. "I have that dream all the time."

She gave me a surprised look. "Perhaps you are more sensitive than I gave you credit for."

She sat staring at me for a few more seconds, then opened
the door and climbed out. She bent back over and spoke to me
again. "You are a remarkable young man with a promising
future. I tell you again to watch your step carefully. And guard
your heart, it is a fragile thing which bleeds ever so easily."

With that, she slammed the door and started back up the
drive towards the house. I sat there for another minute, thinking
about what she had said, before I drove off.

My sleep was troubled once again that night, but not with
the faceless man. My dreams were haunted by images of bleeding hearts—and I don't mean the flower—and Morticia Adams
leaping in front of my car. As a result, I was tired the next morning. I felt like I'd never even been to sleep. This was beginning
to be a pattern with me. I dragged myself down to breakfast and
then on to school. The day pretty much went by in a blur; my
grades were going to be mediocre at best this year if this kept up.
After school I saw Marcus, Asher's brother, walking towards his
bus. I ran to catch up with him. It was time to start my investigation.

"Marcus, can I talk to you for a second?" I asked when I'd
caught up.

"Hey, Killian. We can talk if you're fast, I've got to make
the bus or I'll be dead meat."

"This is going to sound weird, but humor me. Did you ever
talk to Seth?"

"Talk to him? Yeah, I guess so. He was in my Spanish class."

"I mean like ever have a real conversation, not just class stuff."

He gave me a funny look. "I don't know, maybe once."

"Do you remember what you talked about?"

He gave me that funny look again. "Not really. Nothing important, I'm sure."

"Well, if you think of anything, will you let me know?"

"Yeah, sure, Killian, whatever. I gotta go."

He turned to walk away, but I had one more question. "Did you ever see him talking to anyone else?"

"What's it to you, Killian? Why do you care who he talked to or what he talked about?"

"He was my friend. I'm just trying to find out what was going on with him before he died. Closure, you know?"

"You are weird, Killian. I don't know who he talked to. I didn't keep tabs on him." He started walking away then turned back around and kept walking backwards. "I do know that Asher talked to him a few times. Talk to him. He's the one still moping around 'cuz you guys broke up."

"What??" I called after him, but he was gone already, loping off toward the bus.

I thought about what he'd said all the way home. Asher was moping about us? Did he really feel as if we'd broken up? I didn't know we'd ever really been going out. Everything happened so fast. Did that mean there was a chance still for me and him? And what about Jake? I couldn't deny that I was attracted to him, and I was pretty sure he was attracted to me, too. And where did Aunt Judy's warning to guard my heart play into all this? Too many questions; I didn't know what to think.

I walked in the door and dropped my backpack by the door as I headed for the kitchen for a snack. Just then, the phone rang.

"Hello?" I answered.

"Hi, baby, it's me, Mom."

"Mom!" I said excitedly. It had been several days since we'd talked.

"Killian." Her voice sounded tired, or maybe weary is a better word. "I need to talk to you about something important. Is it a good time for me to come over?"

Chapter
16

I was waiting nervously in the living room, waiting for Mom to get here. She wouldn't say why she wanted to talk; all she would say was that she felt she needed to talk to me in person. So here I was, pacing back and forth like one of those bears I always see at the zoo. I was too tense to sit still.

Finally I heard a car pull up outside. I was at the door before she was even out of the car. Right away, I could tell something was wrong. Her clothes were rumpled and wrinkled, as if she'd slept in them. As she straightened up the wind caught her hair and blew it back from her face. Suddenly, I felt my knees buckle under me and I had to grab the doorjamb to keep from falling. One whole side of her face was an angry purple bruise. Her left eye was almost swollen shut and her lip was split and swollen as well. As she came towards me I noticed that she was walking with a slight limp.

I tried to swallow around the lump that had formed in my throat; I tried to say something, but I couldn't find my voice. All I could do was run to meet her and throw my arms around her in a giant bear hug.

"Oh!" she gasped as I came in contact with her. "Be careful, honey, I have a few cracked ribs."

I backed up quickly and looked at her again. It looked even worse up close.

"He did this to you, didn't he?" I finally managed to whisper hoarsely.

She looked at me for a minute, then linked her arm through mine and started walking toward the door. "Come on, let's go on inside."

Once we were settled in the living room, both of us on the couch—me with my head on her shoulder—she sighed a long heavy sigh and began to stroke my hair.

"I'm going to live with my sister, Aunt Kathy, in Pennsylvania," she said after awhile. "I want you to go with me."

I sat up and turned so I could look into her eyes. "What?"

"I can't stay here, Killian. That became very clear last night. I'm going to move in with Kathy and take care of the kids for a while. It's the only way I am going to be able to survive. I really want you to go with me. It's a nice town, good schools." Aunt Kathy had a slew of kids, I forget how many exactly. We didn't see them very often. Her husband had died the year before and I knew she had been having a hard time without him.

"What happened last night?"

"That doesn't matter now. What matters is that it's over and I'm not going back. I have everything that is mine packed in the car. I'm leaving tonight."

"But...but..."

"But what, Killian?"

"I don't want to go," I said awkwardly.

"You...don't want to go?" I could tell she was hurt.

"I don't want to leave. I like living with Adam. I don't want to move away right now. I..." I almost said that I couldn't leave until I found out who had killed Seth, but I stopped myself just in time. I don't think Mom would have understood.

"I don't understand," Mom said, shaking her head.

"I just can't...drop everything and go. I'm happy now. Maybe you can move in with me and Adam."

"No. I want to leave, Killian. I need to leave. I have to get away from him. Do you see what he did to me?" She pointed to her face.

"Did you call the police?"

She snorted angrily, stood up, and began to pace just as I had been earlier. Her motions were disjointed and jerky. "He has the whole police department in his back pocket. It's good-old-boys politics in this town and that means you don't mess with one of their own. Believe me, your father has made sure he's on the inside, way inside. Everyone in this county owes him a favor, most more than one, and he's not afraid to call them in."

"I still don't want to go. Isn't there some way you can stay?"

"Sure, I can stay here and wind up dead. Is that what you want, Killian? It's just as dangerous for you to stay. You may feel safe here with Adam, but what if your father decides you're getting in the way or becoming too embarrassing for him, hurting his precious campaign? He'll be able to get to you. Don't think for a second you're out of reach."

I stared at her, my mouth open and my eyes wide. She stared back, her eyes flashing with anger and, I realized, fear. Then suddenly her eyes changed. The fear remained, but all the anger drained out, just like someone had pulled a plug. It was replaced with weariness. For a moment I thought she was going to collapse as she swayed in the center of the room. I moved to jump up to catch her if the need arose, but before I could get up she backed up a few steps and dropped into a nearby chair, wincing as her ribs were jarred.

"I'm sorry, Killian," she said softly. "I didn't mean to scare you. You're right. There's no sense in dragging you out of school and away from your friends. You're as safe here with Adam as you'd be anywhere. If it's ok with Adam, you can stay here till school is out, then come up with Kathy and me." She rubbed at her good eye and sagged back farther into the chair.

"It's fine with me," Adam said from the doorway, making us both jump. "I'm sorry, I didn't mean to scare you. Or eavesdrop, for that matter, but I came in and I guess you didn't hear me. I couldn't help hearing you."

Mom looked at him silently, then turned and looked at me. I nodded. She sighed again, then stood up.

"Then it's settled. Killian, you'll stay with Adam. We'll take care of whatever legal matters need to be attended to."

"Mom..." I started.

"Killian, it's ok. Really. Now that I think about it, it makes a lot more sense this way. Kathy has enough kids in the house without adding yet another. You'd be in a new place with no friends. Adam's proven he's responsible and he's been good to you, better than your own father."

"Meg, I said it was ok with me and it is; I've grown to think of Killian as just like one of my sons. But I want to make sure that you are sure about this," Adam said.

"I don't have time to be sure," she said. "I have to go. I'm driving to my sister's tonight and I'm emotionally and physically drained. I want to leave now before I get any more tired."

She turned towards me and held out her arms. I took the few steps between us and wrapped my arms around her, more tenderly this time so as not to hurt her ribs. She felt so frail in my arms, and suddenly I felt tears begin to roll down my cheeks. We stood quietly like that for a few minutes before she gently pulled away.

I looked into her tear-streaked face and realized how much I loved her and how much I would miss her, but I knew I had made the right decision for now. There was a peace inside of me and I could see it reflected in her eyes.

"I love you, Mom," I whispered.

"I love you, too," she told me. "It's not forever, you know. I have to come back in a month for a doctor's appointment, so I'll just stay here for Thanksgiving. I can't be away from my baby on Thanksgiving." Then she turned back to Adam. "Take care of my boy, Mr. Connelly. If anything happens to him, you'll see what I'm capable of." She said that last part with a smile, but I got the feeling that she was deadly serious.

"I will," Adam promised solemnly. "I'll take care of him as if he were my own. And we'll expect you to stay here and have Thanksgiving dinner with us."

Mom nodded and looked at me one more time before she started to leave. I walked her out to the car. Adam followed but only as far as the front door, where he stood watching us. She opened the door to climb in and then paused. She gave me a shaky smile, "Are you sure you won't go?"

"I can't..."

She reached out a hand and rested it on my cheek for just the briefest second, then turned to get into the car.

"Mom..."

She stopped and turned back to me again and I leaned in for one last hug. I kissed her on the cheek before stepping back. She reached up to the spot where I had kissed her and I saw a tear slip out of the corner of her eye before she ducked into the car. She started the engine, backed out onto the street and sat there, staring at me for a moment, then waved one last time before driving off.

I stood there watching until she made the turn at the end of the street and drove out of sight, and even then I stood there staring at nothing. I felt Adam's arm settle around my shoulders as he pulled me back towards the house. Once inside, I turned into his chest and began to cry. He allowed me to cry it out without saying a word. When I was done, we walked into the living room and sat down.

"It's not forever, Killian. She'll be back in a few weeks," he said softly.

"I know; it won't even be that much different from the way it's been the last few weeks. It's just weird to know your whole family is out of reach in one way or another. You're the only family I have now."

"Like I told your mother, I consider you one of my sons."

"Well, then I guess I have a brother now, too...Kane."

"Speaking of Kane, I spoke to Ilana today. She said that things are going well, that Eve's lawyer has been very cooperative so far, although they have in no way even suggested that I even get visitation rights, let alone custody."

"When will you know more?" I asked.

"I don't know; these things are complicated. Without Eve's cooperation this could be a long, drawn out process. With Seth it was easy—she didn't want him. He was too much like me, in all the wrong ways."

My eyes widened and I had trouble controlling the smile that was fighting to spread across my face. If I were a cartoon character a light bulb would have just appeared above my head. There's nothing like a good project to distract you from feeling bad, and it looked like I had just found a new project.

Adam could tell something was up. "What?" he asked me suspiciously.

"Nothing, I just remembered I have homework." I lied.

"I've never seen you get excited about homework before," he commented dryly.

"First time for everything," I said cheerily, as I jumped up and started out of the room.

"You'd better not be up to something, Killian," Adam called after me.

"Who, me?" I called back as I grabbed my backpack and then bounded down the hall to my room.

Once in my room I shut the door and booted up the computer. After I was online I shot off a quick e-mail to Kane outlining my idea. That done, I turned to my homework, since I really did have quite a bit.

Later that night after the dinner dishes were done and all my homework was finished, I was in my room reading when Jake called.

"Hey, Killian," he said when I'd answered. "I've decided to tell you about the other person that I saw talking to Seth. I haven't talked to them yet, but I will before tomorrow afternoon, so how about if you come over to my house tomorrow around 3:00 if you don't already have plans? I mean, I know it's a Saturday and all..."

"I'll can be there at three," I told him.

"Great, I'll see you then," he said quickly and hung up.

Now my mind was going a hundred miles an hour trying to figure out who Jake was protecting. It had to be someone he liked or he wouldn't care. I didn't really know Jake all that well, but I knew who he hung out with in general—Zack's crowd, the soccer jocks, even though Jake didn't play soccer. Could the person in question be part of that group? He didn't mind telling me about his own cousins, Asher and Marcus.

The more I thought about all this, the more muddled it all became. In movies and books they always make lists when they are trying to figure stuff out, so I decided to give it a try. I pulled a notebook out of my backpack and made a heading at the top of the page: People Who Talked To Seth. Under that I listed Asher, Zack, Jesse, Becky, Marcus. That was all I had so far. I looked at the list and sighed. It wasn't very much. I added a check next to Marcus' name since I'd talked to him, for all the good that did me.

I stared at the page for a few more minutes, even turning it around a few times, but for the life of me I couldn't see anything else useful. It sure didn't make the killer pop off the page the way they always did in the movies. In frustration I threw the notebook across the room and turned the computer back on.

I was barely online before Kane sent me an instant message.

I LOVE YOUR IDEA! he typed. *Do you really think it'll work?*

i don't know but it's worth a try, I answered.

i don't know why I didn't think of it

i got the idea today while i was talking to your dad

i've got to find the right time to do it. does my dad know about this new plan?

no, i didn't tell him, i was afraid he'd think it was too risky

he'd probably be right, but it doesn't matter, i'm doing it anyway...if it works it'll be worth it

but what if it doesn't work?

don't think like that, it WILL work! Do you have any ideas about who killed my brother yet?

I told him about what Jake had told me and about the frustrating list. Then he said, *well, at least you have some people to talk to now...who knows what you might find out when you talk to them*

i guess

hey, i hafta go...mom just got home and if she catches me on here, she'll kill me

ok, bye

bye, Killian, thanks again...i can't thank you enough...i love you

By the time I got over my surprise and typed and sent *i love you too* back to him he was already gone. I felt a little better about the list after talking to Kane, but now I was worried about my plan. What if it backfires? And to add the confusion, Kane had said I love you to me. What did he mean by that, just brotherly love? Or was it more? I was too tired to think about it now. I swept everything off my bed, got undressed and crawled under the covers. I'd think more about it in the morning.

I was watching a group of people from a slight distance away. I could see them clearly, but none of them seemed to notice me, almost as if there were one-way glass between us. I looked closely and realized that I knew almost everyone in the group. There was Zack and Jesse, Asher, Marcus, Jake, Kane, Becky Rosinski, and someone else who I couldn't quite make out. Seth stood off to one side, not included in their little huddle. They were talking casually among themselves when suddenly the shadows around them began to undulate and swirl as if they were coming to life. Several wisps of darkness separated themselves and formed into a familiar person, the faceless man.

No one else seemed to notice him as he drew closer to the group. I wanted to scream and warn them, but I couldn't seem to make any sound. He paused a few feet away from Seth and turned his head in my direction. Even though I couldn't see his face, I knew he was looking right at me. I felt as if he was smiling at my inability to cry out to him.

Without warning he reached out and grabbed Seth. There was a knife in his other hand and with one smooth, effortless motion, Seth crumpled to the ground dead. I tried to scream out again, but once again, nothing came out. The faceless man looked at me again and I could hear his cold laughter ringing in my ears. Why couldn't anyone else hear it? No one even noticed that Seth was dead. The killer moved forward again, closer to the others. I tried to throw myself forward to stop him but I couldn't move. I was helpless to do anything but watch in horror as he leaped into the circle and raised his knife to kill once again.

"Killian!" someone screamed my name, but I didn't answer. I had to stop the faceless man. "KILLIAN!" he screamed again, louder this time. I turned to see who it was.

I found myself looking up at Adam leaning over my bed, one hand on my shoulder. I was still shaking from the dream; residual images still skated around the edges of my consciousness.

"Are you ok? Were you having another nightmare?" he asked.

"It was awful," I told him groggily.

"It sounded like it," he said with a concerned look on his face. "I talked to a counselor, but I had to get back to him with your medical and insurance stuff and I'm afraid I forgot it with all the legal stuff with Kane. I'll call him again tomorrow."

I nodded; I was only half listening since my mind was still on the dream.

"Do you think you can go back to sleep?" he asked me.

I nodded again and he bent down and kissed me lightly on the forehead. Even with the nightmare fresh in my mind, I was asleep again in minutes. If I had any more dreams the rest of the night, I don't remember them.

The next morning was busy; after I got up, showered, ate, and watched a few Saturday morning cartoons, I cleaned my room. While I was cleaning I came across the notebook I had thrown the night before. I sat down on my bed and looked at the list again. Maybe if I tried to talk to everyone on the list I would find out something more. I'd already talked to Marcus and all I'd gotten from him was that crack about Asher, which I'd almost convinced myself was just Marcus being a jerk. At any rate, I wasn't quite ready to talk to Asher, so I moved to the next names on the list, Zack and Jesse. Let me think about that one; did I want to call Zack and Jesse and ask about Seth? Um...no! I'd have to find someone else to ask them about that, maybe Gilly. Next on the list was Becky. I didn't know her number but I thought Gilly might, so I called her.

Gilly answered the phone and gave me Becky's number after I explained to her why I needed it. She also agreed to try and talk to Zack and Jesse without raising too much suspicion.

After we chatted for a few more minutes I hung up and called Becky. She couldn't figure out who I was at first, but once I mentioned Gilly she was able to place me. What an ego boost. I was now relegated to accessory status, just what I'd always wanted. Oh well, if it meant I had an in with the people I needed to talk to, I could stand it.

"I have a kind of weird question," I told her.

"Ok," she said uncertainly. Actually she said, "OooooKay." If you've ever watched the cartoon Daria and you remember the character Sandy, that's who Becky always reminds me of, just not as exaggerated.

"Did you ever talk to Seth?"

"Seth was, like, that guy who was gay, right?"

"Yeah," I said and held my breath.

"Yeah, I used to talk to him all the time; he was in my art class. He was really cool. That was really sad what happened to him."

"Did you ever talk to him outside of class?"

"Maybe, but probably just about art stuff. He was helping with a project. I got an A on it. It was really awesome. It was this painting of..."

"That's great, Becky," I interrupted, and then tried to steer her back to the conversation at hand. Becky was always a little hard to keep on track. "Did you ever see him talking to anyone else?"

She thought for a minute, or at least I assumed she was thinking. She got quiet, but maybe she was just filing her nails or whatever. Finally she came back with, "You know, I did see him talking to some guy a couple times, but I can't remember his name."

I immediately thought of Asher. "What did he look like?" I

asked her.

I heard someone talking to her in the background and then her voice answering, kind of muffled, as if she had her hand over the receiver.

"I don't know, I have to go," she finally said to me.

"Wait, what did the guy look like? You have to have some idea."

"Why is it so important? Were you hot for him or something? Geez! He's like a surfer dude or something, maybe a skater. Who gives a damn? I have to go, my boyfriend is waiting." And with that, she hung up.

Everything I tried seemed to turn out to be a dead end.

I glanced at my watch. It was only a little after 2:00 and I wasn't supposed to be at Jake's until 3:00, but I decided to go a little early. I was tired of sitting around my house moping and besides, maybe this person Jake was going to tell me about would be the big break I needed. I giggled to myself as I got into the car. Big break...I sounded like a cheesy detective novel.

By the time I arrived at the Sheridan's house it was 2:30 so I was only half an hour early. Not too bad I guess. I knocked on the door and Todd answered.

"Are you here for Gilly or Jake?" he asked, then before I could answer. "Cuz Gilly's gone shopping and Jake went surfing, although he might be back by now. He took the boat out. You can check out back by the creek." He walked away leaving the door open.

I shrugged and pulled the door to, and then walked around to the back of the house. Gilly had shown me the old boat house and dock the night I'd had dinner here, so I knew generally where it was. I had to walk through a small copse of trees to get there, so it was somewhat shielded from the house and I couldn't really see the boathouse until I cleared the trees.

Just as I was about to step out of the trees I saw Jake coming out of the boathouse, and for some reason I stopped. He hadn't seen me yet. His hair was wet and tousled and he was wearing a full wet suit.

He paused outside the boathouse and rummaged through a backpack that I hadn't noticed before, since I'd been so busy watching Jake. He pulled out a big towel and hung it over the door handle. He then proceeded to unzip his wet suit and peel it down. I caught my breath at the sight of him naked to his waist. I felt a stirring down below as I watched him grab the towel and dry off his upper torso. He wasn't overly buff but he was well defined, as most surfers are. And tan all over, at least what I could see. He reached back into the bag and pulled out a T-shirt, which he slipped over his head.

Then he unzipped the wet suit the rest of the way and pulled it down and off. I almost passed out. I had a completely unobstructed view of Jake's perfect butt. I took an involuntary step backwards and bumped into something warm and solid. I let out a yelp and spun around. It was Todd, and he was watching me with narrowed eyes.

"Like what you see?" he said in a low, dangerous sounding voice.

"Todd," I gasped. I would have gasped even if he hadn't just scared two years off of my life. I was still having trouble breathing from seeing Jake naked.

"Killian? Is that you?" I heard Jake call, still down by the boathouse.

"Yeah," I called back, without taking my eyes off Todd.

"Come on down, I'm just getting everything put away; I went surfing this afternoon. The waves were awesome but it was a little chilly."

"Be right there," I yelled.

"Go," Todd said, still in a low voice, "but talk to me before you leave. And if you hurt my brother...or my sister...I'll come after you."

I turned and walked down to the boathouse without looking back, my heart racing.

Jake was now fully clothed and was bent over locking the boathouse door. "Hey, Killer," he said as I approached.

I froze in my tracks. "What did you say?" My voice came out sharper than I'd meant for it to—so much for the subtle approach.

He looked up at me with a confused expression. "I just said hey."

"No, what did you call me?"

"Killer? I'm sorry, you don't like that?" He straightened up and left the lock hanging open in the hasp.

"No, it's ok. It just surprised me. Seth called me that. No one else ever has."

"Really? You'd think it would be a natural nickname for Killian. Especially with that killer smile of yours." He added that last part with that incredible grin of his that got me every time.

I laughed, the tension of the moment forgotten. He turned around and bent to pick up his backpack and I couldn't help but think about his bare butt, and once again the appropriate body part responded. I must have had a funny look on my face when he turned around, because he gave me an odd look then said, "Are you ok?"

"Yeah, I'm fine." I managed to say.

"You don't look it." He glanced meaningfully at my crotch and then gave me a lopsided smile. "So how long were you in the trees?"

Chapter
17

My mouth was moving but nothing was coming out. How was I going to explain this? Jake would find out I watched him change and he'd be mad at me, maybe even stop talking to me.

"Killian, I'm kidding," he said, grinning. "I knew you were there the whole time. Did you enjoy the show?"

"You...you knew?" I couldn't believe what I'd just heard.

"I saw your reflection in the window. Do you think I always change out in the middle of the yard?" he laughed. "I wanted to see how far I could go before you said something."

I blushed and he laughed even harder. Suddenly, he stepped in close to me and kissed me softly on the lips, then stepped quickly around me and walked away down the path towards the house. I stood where I was until I'd calmed down enough to follow him. I caught up to him near the back door.

"By the way," he said when I came up alongside of him. He didn't sound quite so pleased with himself now. "Don't expect a repeat performance anytime soon."

"I-I-I d-don't," I stuttered and he giggled again.

"Oh, and one more thing," he said with his hand on the doorknob, "don't worry about Todd." I opened my mouth to say something, but he gave me a look that effectively said 'shut up' and then went inside.

I followed him in, wondering the whole time where the nervous, self-conscious kid from the other day had gone. This confi-

dent tease was another whole side of Jake that I hadn't even
known existed. Obviously, I still had a lot to learn about my new
friend.

"Come on up to my room," he said, so I followed him up to
his room, which he apparently shared with Todd. He sat on one
of the beds and I decided it might be wise to keep a little distance, at least until I'd figured him out a little more, so I sat on
the chair at the small desk that was positioned between the two
beds.

We both sat there for a few seconds in an awkward silence.
Jake suddenly wasn't looking so sure of himself. The seconds
stretched into minutes with neither of us saying anything and
Jake began to squirm and even had the grace to look a little
queasy. I was enjoying the sudden shift in power until I realized
how sleazy that was and then I just felt guilty. So I decided to
break the silence, at the exact same second Jake spoke up.

"So, you wanted to talk about..." I started as he blurted out,
"Killian, I'm so sorry!"

"Sorry?" I repeated stupidly.

"For that whole thing down by the boathouse. I can't
believe I did that," he was almost in tears and his hands had
started shaking. "That was so not like me."

"It's...ok," I said feeling very lame. "Let's just forget about
it." Oh yeah, like I could forget what I had seen, forget how
beautiful his body was.

He looked up at me through these incredibly thick, black
lashes and I felt as if he were looking into my soul. Our eyes
locked for several seconds before I started blushing again and
looked away.

"Why are you blushing?" he asked me.

"Let's talk about something else," I suggested, ever so subtle as usual.

"Why are you always avoiding my questions?" he asked me.

"Why are you always asking such personal questions?" I
countered.

We stared at each other for a few seconds before I cracked
and smiled. He quickly followed suit and in no time things were
relaxed and we were comfortable with each other again.

"So," I thought I'd try again, "you said you wanted to talk
to me about the other person that you saw talking to Seth."

"Well...yeah...about that..."

"Jake, don't tell me you're backing out on me now."

"Not backing out so much as offering a rain check," he said with an apologetic, lopsided smile. He was the undisputed king of lopsided smiles. I found that I couldn't even be upset with him.

I sighed. Might as well give in with dignity, I thought. "So what is it now?"

"Well, the person in question asked me to hold off for now so they can talk to you themselves."

"They? How many people are we talking about here?"

"Just one, I'm trying to keep things gender neutral," he grinned at me.

"You weren't trying to keep things gender neutral outside," I teased. I was surprised when he blushed a fetching shade of red.

"I thought we were gonna forget about that," he mumbled.

"Sorry," I said, but I didn't even sound convincing to myself. Jake shot me a dirty look. "Look, if you saw me naked would you be able to just forget about it?" I asked.

His eyes immediately lit up with that mischievous look he'd had outside and I knew I'd goofed up. "Hmm...I don't know...there's only one way to find out." In one smooth motion he leapt up and pounced on me like a cat. The swivel chair I was on spun around and dumped us both onto the floor, where Jake began to tickle me.

"Hehehehe...stop!" I managed to gasp out. I tried to push him off and we ended up wrestling for several minutes before I managed to pin him to the floor. My body was pressed against the length of his and our faces were only inches apart. A feeling of déjà vu swept over me. Last time we were in this position, he'd pulled away and the moment had been lost. I decided to not let that happen again. I moved slowly closer, our eyes never losing contact until the last second, when he closed his eyes and lifted his head to meet my lips.

And then we kissed for the second time that day, but this time I kissed back. At first it was just a soft kiss, but then, as I let go of his wrists and I felt his arms wrap around my back, we began to kiss harder. I felt his tongue brush against my lips and they parted instinctively. I felt myself getting hard and apparently Jake felt it too, which wouldn't be too difficult considering my erection was pressing into his crotch. He immediately responded by getting hard, too. He began to grind up into me; my breath rushed out of me, leaving me limp in his arms.

Jake rolled me over, maneuvering so that he was now on
top. He started kissing down my neck and I found it harder and
harder to breathe. When he resumed the grinding I thought I was
going to die right there. He sat up, straddling me, and pulled up
my shirt, running his hands up my chest in the process. Then he
bent down and kissed my chest.

"I can feel your heart beating," he whispered.

I reached up and stroked his cheek, then slipped my hand
behind his head and pulled him up for another kiss. He broke
away again and trailed kisses down my chest, sliding his body
down as he went. He hesitated when he reached my pants.

Just then I heard footsteps coming. Obviously Jake heard
them as well, because he looked up with a slightly panicked look
on his face, leapt to his feet. He stood there a moment with a
what-do-I-do? look on his face, then he grabbed my hand and
yanked me up, too.

We had just gotten our clothing straightened out and our
erections hidden as well as we could when the door swung open.
I almost jumped out of my skin. It was just Todd. He looked at
me and then at Jake, taking in our flushed faces, and his eyebrows drew together in a frown.

"Don't look at me like that, Todd," Jake snapped. "We
weren't doing anything. We were just wrestling."

"Oh yeah, right, Jake," Todd snapped. "What? Do you think
I'm stupid?" He pointed at me. "What kind of a jerk are you?
Gilly's right downstairs while you're up here screwing around
with her kid brother. And you!" He wheeled towards Jake. "I saw
what happened down by the boathouse. You're going after him.
You're both pathetic. You both deserve each other; a couple of
little fags. If it weren't for Gilly I'd kick both of your asses. Get
out, Killian; I'll deal with you later. Right now, me and Jake are
gonna have a little talk."

"Todd..." I tried, but he quickly cut me off.

"Out!"

I cast one last look at Jake, who looked like he could burst
into tears at any second, then dropped my head and walked out of
the room.

Gilly met me at the foot of the stairs. "Killian, I didn't even
know you were here," she said, "but I'm glad you are. I was
going to call you later tonight. We're throwing a big Halloween
costume ball here next weekend, Saturday night. You'll come
right? You'll be my date?"

"Yeah. Yeah, I'll come," I said slowly.

"What's wrong?" she asked. I heard a noise at the top of the stairs and turned to look. It was Jake. Our eyes locked and, for a moment, everything else faded away. Then Gilly's voice broke back through and brought me back.

"Killian? Are you ok?"

I forced my eyes back to Gilly. "Oh yeah, sorry, Gilly. I'm fine and of course I'll be your date, but I hafta go right now."

Gilly looked from me up to Jake and back at me. Her eyes narrowed and for a moment I thought she was going to make a connection, but then her face cleared and she took a step back to allow me to walk next to her to the front door. "Ok, Killian," she said as we walked. "I'll call you later to discuss our costumes."

"Ok," I said as I backed out the door. I looked up at Jake one more time, before spinning on my heel and jogging off to the car. Todd had been standing behind him, glaring at me with eyes full of disgust.

I had a lot to think about on my ride home. How did I feel about Jake? Obviously I was attracted to him and he was attracted to me, but was it more than physical attraction? I hadn't even known him that long. We definitely would have gone farther if Todd hadn't come in when he had. I wasn't sure how I felt about that. Part of me wanted to so badly, but another part of me wanted to be sure before I went that far.

And what about Gilly? Would it hurt her if I ended up with her little brother? She knew I was gay from the beginning, but that doesn't mean she wouldn't be hurt. I don't even pretend to understand how a girl's mind works. There was that kiss on the back porch that night and now she's all excited that we're going as dates to this costume ball.

Then there was Todd. Where did he fit into all this? He'd seemed to have it in for me from that first night. Why? Was he just the typical protective older brother? That was probably all it was, but it still made me uneasy. Now that he knew that Jake and I were gay, where would that lead?

To top it all off, I still wasn't any closer to finding out who had killed Seth. I had to come up with a plan soon.

When I arrived home, an extremely happy Adam greeted me at the door.

"Guess what?" he shouted before I even had the door closed.

"What?"

"Ilana called...Eve's lawyer called her today, on a Saturday. He told her that Eve has decided not to contest my request for custody. Once the paperwork has been signed, Kane will be moving in with us!" He grabbed me up in a huge bear hug and swung me around the hallway. He stumbled over the rug and almost dropped me before setting me back down. We laughed together as we headed for the living room.

"Steve's on his way over; we're gonna celebrate! Oh! I almost forgot. Kane called soon after Ilana and said to tell you that the plan worked, but he wouldn't explain what that meant. Does this have anything to do with your sudden interest in homework last night?"

"Maybe, maybe not," I said with a grin.

"Are you going to explain?"

"No."

"Fine, then, I won't tell you my last piece of good news."

"What?! You have to tell me!"

"Not until you tell me what this secret plan of yours and Kane's is."

"I'll tell you when Kane gets here, I promise, now please tell me the other good news. Ple-e-e-ease?"

Adam gave a huge mock-sigh and then broke into a grin again. He was just too excited to even pretend to be upset. "Ok, well, Asher called in the middle of all this excitement and wanted to talk to you so I invited him to the celebration dinner. He should be here in about half an hour."

I felt my expression freeze, and then slowly melt away.

"What's wrong?" Adam asked. "Did I screw up? I thought you'd be happy. You guys have hardly talked in weeks."

"Asher...hasn't been very...happy about Gilly and I," I told him slowly.

"You haven't told him that it's just a cover?"

"Well, I tried, but he made me so mad, I kinda said some stuff I shouldn't have and I probably hurt him pretty bad."

"Well, then you can apologize tonight and explain things to him and patch things up."

"Well, there's one other problem..." I said, thinking about Jake.

"What's that?"

"Well, it's hard to explain," I started. I felt myself start to blush.

"Does this have anything to do with that boy you brought home the other day? Gilly's little brother?"

It always amazed me how Adam could read me so easily.

"Yeah, his name's Jake."

"And you like this Jake?"

I blushed again. Adam leaned in towards me and gave me a sharp look.

"Just what exactly is going on with you and Jake?" he asked.

"Um...well...it's kinda hard to explain."

"Well, let's try, huh?"

So I haltingly began to tell him all about me and Jake, from our first conversation in the lunchroom to the flirtation to our interrupted lovemaking. When I finished, Adam sat for a moment without saying anything.

"Killian, you'd better be very thankful that Todd came in when he did. He stopped you from making what could have been a very big mistake."

"What do you mean?"

"Do you love Jake?"

"I don't know, no...I guess not. I think I could love him."

"But you don't love him now?"

"No."

"Then all you were experiencing today was lust. Look, Killian, you're young and it's easy to be carried away by lust; but take it from someone who's been there, lust hurts. It uses people. It's no replacement for love. Not even close. Wait for true love, and you'll know it when you find it. Trust me on this though: it's worth it. Maybe it'll be with Jake, or maybe not. Maybe it'll be with Asher, maybe not. Maybe it'll be with someone you've never met, years down the road when you're an old guy like me."

As if on cue, we heard the front door open, quickly followed by Steve's voice, "Adam?"

I watched Adam's face as it lit up. You could see the love he'd just been talking about reflected in his eyes. That was what I wanted. I wanted that love. "We'll finish this later," Adam said as he practically flew out of the room.

I followed as Adam met Steve just inside the door. He flew into his arms and they just seemed to melt into each other.

"I'm so happy for you, babe!" Steve mumbled into Adam's

shoulder.

They hugged for a few more seconds, and then stepped back.

"Let's get dinner started. The other guests will be here soon." Adam said as he grabbed Steve's hand and headed for the kitchen.

"Who else is coming besides Asher?" I asked, trailing behind the two of them.

"Ilana and her husband, and my long-time friend, Bryant and his current beau. Ilana said something about bringing some guests that were in town, so I guess we'll see."

The next 20 minutes were spent cooking pasta and making the garlic and clam sauce that would go over it. When the doorbell rang, Adam went to get it. Once he was gone, I asked Steve a question that had been bubbling in the back of my mind since he got here.

"Why don't you live here with Adam?"

Steve carefully set the pan he was holding down carefully on the counter and turned to face me. He leaned back against the counter and crossed his arms over his chest. "You picked a good time to bring up a very complicated question," he said, "but the short answer is, we didn't think it would be a good idea at the time; between Seth moving in with Adam and my job being in another town, plus things were still up in the air with whether or not Adam would have visitation rights with Kane. Of course, he didn't get them, but we didn't know that when we were making these decisions."

"Why didn't you move in once Seth was moved in and you knew he was gay and that Adam wasn't going to get to see Kane?"

"Well, all that didn't happen over-night. The whole court case with Kane took months; by the time it was all settled, we were settled. It didn't come up again until Adam and Seth moved down here. We were talking about it then, but when Seth was murdered, it didn't seem like the best time to press the issue."

I nodded, but our conversation was over; we could hear voices coming towards the kitchen. Steve turned back to the stove just as the whole party came bursting through the doorway. Apparently everyone had gotten here at the same time.

Adam introduced me to everyone. First there was Ilana, a tall, elegant woman with bronze skin, golden brown eyes, and straight glossy brown hair that she wore cut just below her shoulders. Her husband, Lysander, looked to be somewhat older than her. He was a very handsome black man with close-cropped hair and a pencil mustache. They had different last names, although I missed his, so she must have kept hers for professional reasons.

Ilana's guests turned out to be Lysander's daughter from a previous marriage, Nila, and her partner, Heather. They'd been together for 4 years, since they were both 18 and met as freshmen in college. Heather looked like the quintessential college student; long curly brown hair pulled up into a ponytail, baggy sweater over a white turtleneck with jeans, and glasses. Nila, on the other hand, had the exotic beauty of an actress or a model. She wore her long straight black hair parted in the middle and hanging on either side of her face like a curtain. This only served to accentuate her high cheekbones, straight nose, and pouty lips. Her dark skin seemed to glow in the kitchen lighting. She was quite stunning.

Then there was Bryant and his boyfriend, Calvin. Bryant had wavy brown hair that he didn't seem to wear in any particular style. He looked pretty buff under his Gap sweater and khaki slacks. Calvin had bleached blonde hair and several earrings in both ears; I later noticed that this was not the extent of his piercings. He was very thin and wore oversized baggy clothes.

Last but not least, a few steps behind everyone else was Asher, looking as innocent and hurt as ever with his rosy cheeks and shiny black curls. He was wearing jeans and a sweater over a black turtleneck. I gave him a small smile to let him know I didn't mind that he was there, and he offered back a halfhearted smile of his own.

After all the introductions were made, most of the group headed for the living room. Steve and I stayed behind to finish up the food preparation and set the table, and Asher sat down at the table. We all made small talk, but it seemed forced and more than a little uncomfortable, for me at least, and Asher seemed to be just as uncomfortable.

Dinner was a festive event; everyone was very excited about Kane moving in—everyone except Asher. Since he didn't know Kane it was hard for him to show much enthusiasm, especially since it was obvious that he had something on his mind. Once everyone was settled back into the living room, Asher asked me if we could talk. We excused ourselves and walked upstairs to the room that I would soon be sharing with Kane.

"Killian," he said when we were upstairs, "we need to talk."

"I know, Asher," I said. "I need to explain some things to you."

"I need to explain some things to you, too."

"I'll start," I offered and quickly rushed on before he could say anything. "I'm not really going out with Gilly. It's just a cover so that I wouldn't get harassed. I need to find out who killed Seth and I can't do that if everyone knows I'm gay. Or maybe I could, it seems like not as many people care as I thought. It's just that those that did care were very vocal about it. So anyway, I'm still just as gay as I was before. I wanted to tell you all this right away, but well...I guess I have a bad temper."

"Yeah, me too," Asher said quietly. "I provoked you that day in the lunchroom. I was jealous and hurt and I just said a bunch of stuff that I shouldn't have. I want to ask you to forgive me for all that stuff I said, and ask if maybe we can start over or something...maybe?"

"I'll forgive you if you'll forgive me, but what do you mean by start over?"

"I don't mean as like boyfriends or anything, at least not yet, but I'd hate to lose the best friend I've ever had over something like this."

Who could resist that? I got up from where I was sitting, walked over to Asher and wrapped my arms around him in a big hug. Just then, the phone rang.

I grabbed up the phone and was surprised to hear Kane's voice on the line.

"*Killian*!" he screamed into my ear. "Did you hear?"

"Yeah, Kane, I heard," I laughed, "and it's a good thing I heard before you called, cuz I think I'm deaf in that ear now."

Kane laughed, too. "Your plan worked. I told Mom I wanted to live with Dad and when she asked why I said cuz I related more to him because I was gay, too."

"What did she say?"

"Well, she just sat there for a minute, then she walked out of the room. A little later she came to my bedroom and said she'd called the lawyers and it was being taken care of." Kane's voice changed at this point from super-charged excitement to uncertainty. "She seemed really sad, Killian. Like I had let her down."

"I'm sorry, Kane. Maybe it wasn't such a good idea after all. I mean, it was kinda lying. You don't even know for sure if you are at all."

"No, even if I'm not sure, it was right cuz it means I get to come live with you guys now! Hey, I better go. I don't want Mom getting mad at me at this point. I just had to call you. Thanks, big bro! I love you!"

"You're welcome, Kane. I love you, too. And yeah, you're right; you don't wanna get in trouble now. Bye, Kane."

"Bye, Killian."

I hung up and turned to find Asher had slipped out of the room while I was on the phone. I started to go look for him when the phone rang again. This time it was Gilly calling as she'd promised about our costumes.

I agreed with whatever she said just so I could get off the phone quicker, so I wasn't entirely sure what I had agreed to wear. I figured I'd find out sooner or later. It turned out to be sooner, since I didn't make it out of the room before the phone rang yet again. I answered, expecting Gilly again, but this time is was Jake.

"Hey, Killian," he said as soon as I answered. "I'm really sorry about what happened today. I mean about everything, the boathouse, in my room, with Todd. I don't know what was going on with me. I'd blame it on the moon or something, but I don't know whether it's full or what. Anyway, I'm just really sorry about everything."

"Jake, it's ok. Don't worry about it."

"Just forget about it, huh? Like before?" I could hear the smile in his voice and I could just picture the lopsided grin that I was growing so fond of. "You know, Killer, I really like you a lot."

I started a little when he called me Killer, but I quickly recovered. "I like you too, Jake."

"No, I like you a lot, Killian. I want to spend more time with you, but I don't know how with Gilly and Todd and all."

"Hey, we're friends right? Friends spend time with each other."

"Yeah, I guess you're right. Do you think maybe we could be more than friends?"

"Maybe, but let's take things one step at a time for now. I think we were moving a bit too fast today. It's probably a good thing Todd walked in when he did."

"Yeah, I guess you're right. Well, I probably won't see you really before the costume ball, but I know what you are wearing so I'll look for you."

"At least one of us does. What am I wearing?"

He laughed again. "Gilly wants you to dress up in some costume she found in a thrift store. I saw it and I guess it's pretty cool. It's like this long black hooded cloak that goes over this tunic thing and tights with a fake sword and all. It looks kinda creepy, but cool. Gilly bought this cloak of her own, so I guess you guys are going as a medieval couple or Shakespeare in love...I dunno."

"Did you say tights?"

"I haven't decided what I'm wearing, so I guess you'll be surprised."

"Tights?"

"Hey, Killian, I have to go. I shouldn't have stayed on here this long. I just wanted to apologize and all. I'll talk to you later, ok?"

"I have to wear tights?"

"Yes!" he laughed. "And I, for one, am looking forward to seeing it! Bye, Killer."

His calling me Killer snapped me out of my horror at the thought of wearing tights, "Bye, Jake."

I hung up and turned around to find Asher sitting on the edge of my bed looking like he might cry at any second. "So was that my cousin Jake?" he asked.

Chapter 18

My mind raced as I decided the best way to answer Asher's seemingly simple question. How much had he heard? If he'd been there for more than a few minutes then he'd heard me tell Jake that I liked him. There was no point in lying either way.

"Yeah," I said simply.

Asher closed his eyes for a second and then opened them again. Pain flashed out of them like the beam from a lighthouse.

"Asher," I started, not sure where I was going with it but feeling as if I had to say something.

"You don't have to explain anything to me, Killian," he said quietly. "You don't owe me anything. You said you wanted us to be friends and that's all we are."

"Asher," I tried again, still not sure what I wanted to say.

"Killian, look, I heard you tell Jake that you liked him. You also told him that you wanted to take things slow, so that means you want to pursue something with him. I didn't even know he was gay, or bi, or whatever he is, but it's obvious where that leaves me." I opened my mouth again, but he kept right on. "Don't say anything, please. It'll only make it worse. I'll be ok, if that's what you're worried about. I've lived without you just fine so far and I'll survive again. Yes, I care about you a lot; maybe I'm even in love with you. I don't know because I've never been in love with anyone before, so I don't know what to compare it to. I do want to be friends with you at least. Just...I think I'll need some time for a while. I'll let you know when I'm ready. I'd better go now before I do something that would embarrass us both."

With that, he stood up and walked toward the door.

"Asher, wait," I yelled, louder than I intended, but it had the desired effect. He stopped in his tracks, but kept his back turned towards me. "Yes, I like Jake. He is gay and I'm attracted to him and yeah, maybe it could develop into something more, but for now, we are just friends—same as you and me. I never stopped liking you, but I don't think I'm in love with anyone, you or Jake. I just need time to figure all this out. In the meantime, I hope you don't think I'm being too selfish because I want to stay friends with you."

Asher slowly turned and faced me again and I could see the glistening tracks left by a few tears that had managed to squeeze through.

"I don't think you are selfish and I don't want to be either, so if being with Jake is what makes you happy, then I want you to be with Jake. But I don't want to lose our friendship either; it's the best thing in my life."

We both moved towards each other at the same time and hugged tightly. Asher started to cry quietly on my shoulder and I pulled him closer as I rubbed his back.

"No matter what, we'll always be friends," I whispered into his hair.

He pulled back a little, keeping his arms around my neck, then leaned in for a quick peck on the lips. "I really do have to go, Kill," he said softly.

"Ok, Asher," I said, stepping back. He turned and walked out, pausing in the doorway before continuing out of sight.

The next week passed quickly, with preparations for Kane's arrival and the costume ball. Adam bought a set of twin beds to replace the double bed in our room and another dresser was moved in from the guest room. I tried on my costume, which I had to admit looked really awesome. I was over at Gilly and Jake's several times that week helping them decorate, but Jake and I kept our distances under the watchful eye of Todd. Their mom was always around somewhere, but I never saw their dad. I talked to Asher a few times but we didn't really hang out or anything. Before I knew it, Friday had arrived and that meant that Kane was supposed to be at the house by the time I got home from school.

I was excited as I drove home at what was probably an unsafe speed. It was like I was officially gaining a brother today. I pulled up beside Eve's car and ran inside. Kane was just coming down the stairs and he leaped the last few steps and threw himself at me with a feral howl, flinging his arms around my neck in a huge bear hug that I thought would break my spine. For a little guy, he had surprising strength.

When he finally let me go and I had caught my breath enough to speak, I panted, "Kane! I can't believe you're actually moving in!"

"I know! It all happened so fast. One day I'm wishing I could live here and the next I'm here. And I owe it all to you, big bro!" With that, he launched himself at me again. If this kept up I'd need a neck brace before long.

"Well isn't this touching?" a caustic voice said from above. I looked up to see Eve standing at the top of the stairs in all her fairy splendor. She was wearing a long white, airy dress with a scarf that almost seemed to float around her. It created an eerie effect of wings. As she walked down the stairs, the dress and scarf swirled around her in a mesmerizing ethereal display that made it seem almost as if she was floating. When she reached the bottom of the stairs she broke the spell by speaking once again, "Is this your boyfriend, Kane?"

"Mom, this is Killian. He lives here with Dad. He's like my brother."

"We've met," she said as she shot a withering glance in my direction before fixing Kane with a piercing glare. "And you only had one brother; his name was Seth. In case you've forgotten already, he was murdered because he was gay."

My mouth dropped open at the coldness in her voice, and I winced when I saw the raw pain in Kane's eyes.

"Well, Kane, you know how to get in touch with me if you change your mind about all this. I've got to go. Tell your father I said good-bye."

With that she swept past us—her scarf actually dragged across my face as she blew by. When she reached the door she stopped. At first I thought it was for dramatic effect, but suddenly she spun around and ran quickly to Kane and enveloped him in a tight hug. I was surprised by the sudden display of emotion; I hadn't thought she possessed any. It was over as quickly as it had begun, and she was out the door before Kane could even react, leaving him stunned and more than a little confused.

He stood still for a moment, too overwhelmed to even know what to do. He looked over at me and suddenly burst into tears. My arms were around him in a moment as he cried on my shoulder.

"I never knew she loved me, Killian," he gasped after a few minutes. "I never knew and now she's gone."

"She isn't gone forever, Kane," I whispered as I tightened my arms around him.

"Yes, she is. She walked out and I'll never see her again. I just know it."

"Kane, calm down. Where's Adam? Where's your dad?"

"He went for a walk, he said he couldn't take Mom anymore."

"Ok, well listen to me, Kane. If your mom loves you, then she isn't gone forever. She'll want to see you again."

"You don't know my mom. When she found out that Seth was gay, he moved in with Dad and she never saw him again. She never even mentioned him; it was like he was dead before he even died. And now he is dead and I never even got to say goodbye to him."

He started sobbing again and I led him over to the couch, where we sat down. I realized as we sat there with Kane crying on my shoulder that I had never really grieved Seth's death myself. I'd gone from stunned numbness right into throwing myself into finding out who killed him, but I hadn't really fully grieved his death. Of course, I'd only known him for two weeks. Still, we were already friends and we would have been even better friends if we had been given the chance.

It all seemed so surreal, now that I thought about it. I mean, I hadn't really known Seth that well, and here I was living in his house, with his dad, in his room, with his brother. I was living the life that was meant for him. It was unsettling thought. I felt like I was in an episode of *The Twilight Zone* or *The X-Files*.

I heard the front door open, followed by footsteps.

"Adam?" I called.

"Yeah?"

"We're in the living room," I told him.

He stopped short when he saw Kane's tear-streaked face.

"What happened?" he said, suddenly hoarse. He was at

Kane's side in a second and Kane transferred from my shoulder to his.

"He's afraid he'll never see his mom again," I explained.

"She loves me, Dad, and now I'll never see her again," Kane said in a tear-filled voice.

"Of course she loves you, Kane," Adam said, his voice filling up as well. "It's just...your mother hasn't had an easy life. She's been hurt by a lot of people. That makes one very wary about showing their emotions. It isn't that she hasn't any feelings, it's just that she's always had a hard time showing it. I'm absolutely sure you'll see her again."

I left them to talk alone and went up to my room—our room now. They'd already moved his stuff into the room, but he hadn't had a chance to put anything away yet. I decided to try to start putting some stuff away for him. I hadn't made much progress a half-hour later when Adam and Kane joined me. Kane's eyes were still red and he was still sniffling a little, but he seemed much better. We worked together for a few hours until we had his clothes and stuff put away. By then it was past time for dinner so we all went out to a nice restaurant to celebrate.

During dinner, the subject of the costume ball came up and we decided that Kane should go so he could meet everyone at once. I would call Gilly to be sure it was ok, but I was pretty sure it would be; it was a pretty big affair. The only thing left was to find a costume for Kane, so after dinner we headed to Wal-Mart. Pretty much everything was gone, but we managed to come up with a fairly decent vampire costume. Not entirely original, but pretty good for last minute.

After that, we went back to the house and spent the rest of the night just talking and relaxing. It felt natural and right, as if Kane had always lived here. Before we knew it, it was late and we knew we had all better get to bed, we still had some running around to do the next day before Kane and I went to the party.

After all the bedtime rituals were over and done with and Kane and I were settled in our respective beds and the lights had been turned out, silence descended. It wasn't long, though, before I heard sniffling sounds from Kane's side of the room.

"Are you ok, Kane?" I asked softly, barely more than a whisper.

"Yeah," he whispered back, "I guess so. It's just...there's so much going on right now and I'm so confused...and it's kinda weird being here for the first night. Do you think I could sleep with you like I did last time?"

"Well, the bed's not as big as before, but I guess so."

The words had barely left my mouth before he was sliding under the covers next to me. He wiggled around for a few seconds, then rolled over and finally settled with his back to me. I laid there for a while, watching him breathe, then I slipped my arm over him and started to drift off to sleep. Just before I passed the threshold between wakefulness and sleep, I heard Kane's barely audible voice.

"Tell me again how you knew you were gay."

I thought for a moment about how to answer that. I'd already told him once and I knew he was trying to figure things out for himself, so I decided to go into more detail than last time.

"Well, like I told you before, Seth told me that he thought I was and then kissed me. It really freaked me out then, but later, I got thinking about it and realized that he was right. I knew he was right because I wasn't interested in girls—at all. And it wasn't just that I wasn't interested in girls, I *was* interested in guys. At first I didn't want to believe it, but the more I thought about it, the more I realized that I was. I was really scared and felt really guilty, but I went and talked to a guy at my church and he helped me feel better about myself. Then later, I talked a lot to your dad. He's really smart you know; he helped me a lot. Now I know that there's nothing wrong with me and it's nothing to be ashamed of, it's just the way I am. When I'm ready, I'll come out. There's no big rush, I'll do it when the time seems right."

"Killian," he said when I stopped to take a breath. "Do you think I'm gay?"

"I don't know, Kane. That's kinda something that you have to know for yourself. I can't decide for you."

"Would you be mad at me if I wasn't?"

I sat up and he rolled onto his back so he could look up at me in the little bit of light that the moon was providing through the window.

"Why would you think I would be mad at you?"

"I just don't want to disappoint you. Right now, you're not just my only friend here, you're my brother. I want you to like me." With that he started sniffling again, and I knew he was about to cry. I reached out and stroked his hair.

"Kane, there's nothing you can do to make me not like you. You're such a sweet kid. I'm really glad you're my brother. I love you already. Of course I won't be mad at you if you aren't gay. I want you to be who you are and that's it. Don't let anybody else try to make you something you're not."

He sat up and threw his arms around my neck, squeezing so hard I could barely breathe.

"Thank you, Killian," he whispered fiercely in my ear.

We lay back down with my arm around him again, and just as I was once again about to doze off, Kane spoke again.

"I don't think I'm gay. I like girls."

I stifled a giggle and squeezed him gently, pulling him tighter against my chest. "That's ok, Kane."

"Good."

And soon we were asleep.

Chapter 19

The next day passed quickly and fairly uneventfully, and soon enough it was time to get ready for the costume ball at the Sheridans. As I had known she would be, Gilly was thrilled that Kane was coming along. Adam helped me and Kane with our costumes. When we were dressed we looked pretty good, even if I do say so myself. We decided not to use too much make-up on Kane since no one knew him yet and we wanted everyone to see what he really looked like. He wore his usually spiky hair slicked back and had his vampire teeth in.

My costume didn't require any special make-up and the hood pretty much hid my face anyway when it was up. I was still very self-conscious about the tights, but Adam and Kane assured me that they looked great with the tunic, which stopped just above my knees. The cloak was surprisingly heavy once I had it on, and I figured I would be hot for the rest of the night unless Gilly let me take it off. I didn't think she would, though, since it kind of made the costume.

When we were ready, Adam took some pictures, then surprised me by giving me the camera and telling me to be careful with it. After some final instructions about curfew and the usual parental warnings, we were off in my car.

By the time we arrived at Gilly's at what I thought was early, the yard was already full of cars and we had to park on the road outside the gate.

"Wow, there's a lot of people here," Kane said nervously.

"You'll be fine," I told him. "Just be yourself."

He took a deep breath and we got out and started for the front door. Before we got there, however, the welcoming committee, namely Zack and Jesse, met us. Zack was dressed as the killer from Scream; he held his mask in his hand. Jesse was dressed as a bloody corpse.

"Well, well, well," Zack started in right away in his smarmy voice. "What do we have here? Who's your friend? Don't tell me this is your boyfriend? What will Gilly think?"

"Hi, Zack," I said evenly, being careful not to let any emotion show. "This is Kane. He just moved here. He's Seth's brother and he's just like my own brother, so back off and if I see you anywhere near him for the rest of the night, I'll make sure you regret it."

Zack's eyes widened and Jesse took a step closer. Zack reached out a hand and stopped him without really touching him.

"Is that a threat?" he asked in a tight voice.

"Yes," I said in the same even tone.

"Don't start something you can't finish, Killian."

"Who said he can't finish it?" said a new voice.

I turned to see who had spoken. To my surprise, I found Asher and Marcus both standing behind Kane. Kane looked somewhat scared, Asher and Marcus just looked plain angry.

Zack and Jesse looked at the four of us as we squared off, then Zack threw me one last dirty look before turning away. As he walked away with Jesse tagging along behind, he said loud enough for us to hear, "Come on, Jesse, they aren't worth it."

I turned back to Marcus and Asher.

"Thanks, guys," I said sincerely.

"No prob. I've known Zack for years. He's just a big coward really," Marcus said. "Hey, Killian, I'm sorry I was kind of rude the other day when you were asking me about Seth. I was having a bad day but I still shouldn't have been like that."

"It's ok," I told him. "Marcus and Asher, this is Kane, Seth's little brother. He moved in with us today. Kane, this is my best friend Asher and his brother, Marcus."

Asher's face lit up when I called him my best friend. Everyone shook hands and together we walked towards the house once more.

When we walked inside even I was surprised at what we saw, and I'd helped decorate. The enormous entry hall had been decorated to look like a haunted house. Cobwebs were draped everywhere and candles burned eerily in silver candlesticks and sconces. Madonna's dance music thumped from speakers in every room, and people in costume were milling around all over.

Suddenly someone was at my elbow propelling me forward. I flinched away thinking it was Zack or Jesse, but it turned out to be Gilly.

"Hey," I exclaimed.

"Killian, can I talk to you for a second?" she said, her voice filled with tension.

"Yeah, but hold on," I said. "This is Kane, Seth's brother."

She looked at him without seeing him, then started pulling me away again. "Yeah, great, hi," she mumbled.

I shrugged towards Kane, Asher, and Marcus and allowed myself to be dragged off towards the kitchen.

As soon as the kitchen door swung shut, Gilly dropped my arm and faced me.

"What's going on with you and Jake?"

"What?" I gasped.

"Todd said that something is going on with you and Jake and I wouldn't have believed him but I saw how you looked at him the other day."

"Gilly..." I started, but she cut me off, which was just as well since I hadn't decided what to say or how to handle this yet.

"Killian, you know I like you. I can't believe you would go after my own brother."

"Gilly, you knew from the beginning that I'm gay. We're not even really going out. It's just a cover. And I'm not going after your brother."

"Oh yeah, I guess he's going after you then? Is that it?"

"Yeah, that is it, actually," said Jake as he walked into the room. "You guys might want to keep it down. I could hear you coming down the hall."

We both stared at him for a moment before we reacted, Gilly glaring and me surprised, then we both reacted at once.

"Jake, you don't have to..." I started.

"I hate you!" Gilly screamed.

Now it was our turn to stare at Gilly, both of us in shock this time.

"Don't look at me like that," she seethed. "You, Jake! You knew how much I liked Killian and you just stand there and calmly tell me that you went after him? And you, Killian Kendall! You think you can just play with my emotions, then throw me away when you find someone else?"

"Gilly, it's not like that and you know it," I said angrily. "You said from the beginning that you understood that I didn't and couldn't have any feelings for you beyond friendship. You said that pretending to date me would be ok with you. You said that you just wanted to be friends, that this was something you could do for me as a friend. If that's not what you felt then you should have said so up front, and I never would have played this stupid game."

I watched her deflate right in front of me and I immediately regretted my angry words. Once again, I'd hurt someone I cared about because of my temper.

"Oh, I didn't realize that this was all just a game. I'm sorry, Killian. You're right. I was stupid to think that you could love me. Why would anybody love me?" She started crying.

"Gilly, I didn't say that," I said awkwardly.

"You didn't have to."

Jake shifted from foot to foot, obviously uncomfortable.

"Look," I said, "there's a party going on out there that you guys are supposed to be hosting, so why don't you go get your costumes on and let's try to have fun...ok?"

"Screw you," Gilly said, and stormed off out the back door of the kitchen.

"Sorry about that," Jake said. "Welcome to our dysfunctional family. We may look like the Walton's from the outside, but trust me, all is not well on the inside. Maybe I should have stayed out of it."

I shrugged, "Maybe, you never know though at the time. You did what you thought was best."

He walked over to me and wrapped his arms around me for a brief hug.

"I'll go get my costume on and meet you on the dance floor," he said as he backed out the way he'd come.

"Which is where?" I asked him before he could get away.

"Set up in the back yard. Just go out the back door...you'll see."

I went back to the front hallway to look for Kane, Asher, and Marcus, but an obnoxious bunch of giggling girls had replaced them. I decided to head out to the back yard to see if they were there.

The music gradually got louder as I walked through the

house, so that by the time I reached the back door it was almost deafening. When I opened the door it was like walking into a wall; an almost physical wave of vibration and sound washed over me.

I stood in the doorway and gaped. A raised platform had been set up in the backyard and it filled the entire open space. Lights had been strung through the trees and dozens of spotlights were flashing different colored lights onto the dance floor. Dance music pumped out of huge speakers set up in strategic locations and people writhed, wiggled, bumped, and grinded everywhere. My, what one could do with a little money. I stepped out into the mass of bodies and started my futile search for someone I knew. I hadn't really taken the time to see what Asher and Marcus were wearing, but vampires were everywhere. So were Scream masks and ghouls. I felt a hand on my shoulder and turned to see Zorro, who on closer inspection turned out to be Asher.

"Great costume!" I yelled over the music. And it was. It was all black, with leather boots and mask and a long flowing cape. He wore tight black pants and a loose blousy black shirt that was open halfway down his chest. I wondered how I had missed it earlier. I decided that he couldn't have been wearing the whole ensemble at the time.

"Yours too," he screamed back.

"Gilly found it."

"I know, I heard you talking about it on the phone with Jake."

Time to change the subject, "Where's Kane?"

Asher pointed behind me and I turned around to search the crowd. It took me a minute, but finally I spotted him and Marcus talking to a group of girls dressed as three fairies in three different color dresses. He was definitely straight, too, judging by the way he was ogling the shortest fairy's generous cleavage. Marcus wasn't wearing a costume.

"Where's Marcus's costume?" I asked.

"He didn't want to wear one. I said that was dumb since it was a costume ball, but he told me to shut up so I did."

I felt another hand on my back. This time when I turned around I didn't know who it was. Well, I knew it was Batman, but who was under the mask and skin-tight costume I couldn't tell. It was obvious, however, that he was in very good shape and I couldn't help but wonder if that was a codpiece in there...

He motioned to me to follow him. I looked at Asher who just shrugged, some help he was.

I decided to follow the caped crusader and see what happened. There were hundreds of people here; I couldn't see how he could hurt me with so many people around, so I figured I was safe. He led away from the lights and crowds and into the shadows of some nearby trees. Once there, he reached up to remove the mask, but before he could, the music stopped. We both turned towards the DJ stage that was set up at one end of the dance floor.

Standing in the spotlight, microphone in hand, was Gilly in a totally different costume than what she had shown me. She was dressed in an elaborate gown that looked like something out of the movie *Elizabeth* or maybe *Shakespeare in Love.* Her hair was piled up on top of her head and her cheeks were bright red. I couldn't tell if it was from anger or if it was blush.

"Hello, everyone," she said into the microphone. "I hope everyone is having a good time so far." An enormous roar greeted her, "Please remember that no drugs or alcohol are allowed at my parties and if you are caught with either, you will be asked to leave." Scattered boos met this statement. Gilly ignored them and plowed on. "Before we turn the music back on I have an important announcement to make."

I noticed someone moving quickly towards the stage, but I couldn't quite tell who it was.

"It's time you all found out the truth about someone you all know," Gilly went on. I felt as if someone had dumped cold water all over me. The person was pushing through even faster towards the stage now. I felt myself take a few steps forward myself...as if I could somehow stop her.

"That person is..."

Before she could finish the person who had been rushing toward her dived onto the stage with a spectacular belly flop, grabbed the microphone cord and yanked it out of her hand. They scrambled to their feet where it became obvious that it was a male in a pirate costume, although I still couldn't see who or if I even knew him. The unknown male and Gilly then had a heated discussion, complete with angry hand gestures, which was picked up somewhat by the fallen microphone.

"What the hell do you think you're doing?" Gilly hissed.

"What do *you* think you're doing? You can't do that. Not here," the other person shot back. It was Jake's voice.

They both seemed to realize at the same time that they were being broadcast and quickly moved away from the center stage. Jake motioned for the music to start up again and soon everyone had gone back to dancing, forgetting the little drama that had just transpired before them. It wasn't so easy for me.

I turned back to Batman, but he was gone. I looked around, trying to find him but he was nowhere to be seen. I thought for a minute, my mind still on the whole scene with Gilly, then dove back into the sea of flesh. I shoved and darted my way in the general direction I had come from hoping to catch a glimpse of Kane or Asher or anyone I knew for that matter.

I was getting more and more frustrated as I searched the crowds to no avail. Then I saw something that totally took my breath away. In the middle of a circle of enthralled spectators, someone was dancing. Not just dancing like everyone else, but dancing with wild abandon, pure joy personified. I was drawn to the dancer, almost against my will. As I drew closer I could see it was a boy, someone I didn't know. He was wearing a black body suit onto which were sewn brightly colored strips of material, every color of the rainbow, all different materials and textures. The effect was dizzying and mesmerizing. He was graceful and thin, his height hard to estimate since he was twirling and leaping about, but I guessed about 5'9", and 135 pounds. He was crowned with a full head of golden curls that almost seemed to flash in the lights.

"Who is that?" I asked someone beside me.

"I don't know. I've never seen him before."

Someone else leaned towards me, "No one knows who he is," she said. "I've been trying to find out for the last 20 minutes."

I stood and watched him. All thoughts of finding Kane and Asher were gone. He continued to dance as if no one was there, in a world of his own. And what a beautiful world it must have been, too. His face radiated peace and contentment. He wasn't stunningly gorgeous, but he was simply beautiful. He made me happy just to watch him. I suddenly found myself crying and I didn't know why. I wasn't sad or hurt or angry. There were just suddenly tears rolling down my cheeks, one after the other.

And suddenly he stopped. The music kept on, but then I suspected he was dancing to his own music anyway, not the notes we heard. He stood there for a moment and then turned and walked right over to me and stood in front of me. I could now see his eyes. They were an odd shade that seemed to shift as he moved, now they were blue, now gray, now blue again. He reached out and softly brushed a tear from my cheek.

"I'm Dashel. You can call me Dash," he said softly.

"I'm..."

"Killian," he interrupted. "I know who you are. I also know that you are hurting. I can feel it. Come on, walk over here so we can talk."

I looked over my shoulder, looking again for Kane or Asher.

"Don't worry about your friends. They went inside. They're fine," Dash said, then he led me back towards the trees where I'd been just a few minutes before.

He looked around and then suddenly just dropped to the ground Indian style. I looked down at him in surprise. He just grinned up at me and patted the ground next to him. "Pull up some dirt," he said cheekily.

I sat down next to him, pulling the cloak tighter around me since it was getting a little chilly.

"Why are you carrying so much pain around inside you?" he asked me. He didn't beat around the bush.

I thought about it for a minute before I answered. Was I carrying around pain? I didn't think so. I thought I was doing pretty well, actually. I opened my mouth to tell him that, but what came out surprised me. "What else is there to do with it?" I asked.

He smiled again, "Give it away."

I could see myself reflected in those amazing eyes; I could see the confusion on my face. "What? How do you give away pain? Who would want it?"

"Most people wouldn't want it. But I'm not talking about giving it away to just any person."

"What?" Now I was really confused.

"There is only one who can take your pain and replace it with peace."

"Who?" Even I was taken aback by the desperation in my voice. Why? I hadn't I been able to see the pain before, but now it seemed as if it would overwhelm me at any moment. All the hurt and fear from Seth's murder and my attack, my dad's rejection and beating, my mom moving away...everything just suddenly bubbled to the top. I hadn't even realized how much I had been stuffing it away, ignoring it and hoping it would just go away. Obviously it hadn't. I gasped with the sudden surge of emotion.

"The only one who can take away your pain is God."

I was quiet for a moment. "God?" I whispered quietly at last.

He nodded solemnly. "Have you forgotten about Him? He hasn't forgotten about you." He broke into that infectious grin of his, then quickly became serious once again. "Dude, you have got to let go of all that stuff, it's going to eat you up inside. How can you be happy when you are carrying around so much negative stuff?"

"I...I don't know how to give it to Him."

"It's easy. Like this..." He threw his head back, squeezed his eyes shut and just sat there. Slowly, a smile spread its way across his face. Suddenly his eyes snapped open and he looked at me again. "Now you try it."

"What did you do?"

"I gave it to Him."

"Huh?"

"First I feel Him. I always feel Him there all the time, a constant presence everywhere, but when I *need* Him I...call, kinda, with my need, reach out, and He's there. And I feel His arms around me and I cry into them, and picture all my problems coming out in my tears. They aren't real tears, but...well...you get the idea."

"It's that easy?"

"Yup. Now you try it."

I looked around nervously.

"No one's watching you. Besides, who cares? Just let it go."

He was right. No one was paying any attention to us. It was like we were invisible. I looked at Dash for a few more seconds then took a deep breath and closed my eyes. Slowly I tipped my head back until my face was pointed towards the sky. I thought about all my pain, all the hurt and sadness. And I waited for God. At first I thought nothing was going to happen. Then I noticed a pinpoint of light appear above me. It began to grow, slowly at first, then faster and faster. Then, with a brilliant flash of pure white light that I could actually see through my closed eyelids, I felt myself enfolded in unseen arms. And I was crying, real tears along with my symbolic tears. And slowly, slowly, I felt it all drain away.

I opened my eyes, blinking rapidly to make the spots go away. I heard Dashel laughing before I could see him. It was a clear, joy-filled laugh that made me want to join in.

"All gone?" he said.

I nodded, at a loss for words.

"Yosh major, dude!" he crowed gleefully. He jumped up and did a little dance right where he stood.

I grinned even though I had no idea what he had just said. He stopped dancing and reached down to pull me up. As I took his hand I felt a sensation like electricity course out of him and into me. I was standing before I knew what hit me. Dash threw his arms around me in a tight hug, then stepped back with his hands on my shoulders.

"Dance with me," he commanded.

"What? I can't dance!" I laughed.

"You just felt God's arms around you and you say you can't dance? Open up your heart and just...dance!" And with that he spun off in a leaping twirl.

I stood awkwardly, not sure what to do. Then I threw up my hands and gave in. At first, I simply tried to imitate Dash's movements, but soon I was lost in the feeling and was hardly even aware of his presence. I don't know how long I danced, but next thing I knew I was bone tired. I stopped dancing and collapsed to the ground again. Dash plopped down next to me and then flopped onto his back. I lay back too, our arms touching.

"Feels good, huh?" he said.

"Very." I agreed.

"You caught on fast."

"Guess I had a good teacher."

"The best, but it wasn't me."

"Are you always so cryptic?"

He laughed. "Pretty much. I don't mean to be."

"I've never met anyone like you before."

He sat up. "I'm pretty unique." He studied me for a minute. "I'm getting ready to split. But before I go I have a message for you."

I sat up as well. "A message? From who?"

"Don't you know?" he asked with a grin. Then he frowned. "You are in danger. You were almost killed in this very spot earlier tonight." My mouth flew open, but he raised his hand and continued, "In your effort to avoid the pain caused by Seth's death, you have forgotten what you started out to do. You have to finish that now. Find Seth's killer. It's up to you to bring closure to this horrible thing that has happened. But please be careful. If you take foolish risks, you will have to pay the price." Then, as suddenly as the serious mood and the frown had appeared, they were gone. Everything was sudden about Dash. His movements, his moods, even his speech. The grin was back and Dash was on his feet again.

"Dude, it's been so radiotopically unbelievably awesome, but now I have to go."

"Why? Where are you going?"

He shrugged. "I did what I was sent here to do." He started off into the crowd.

"Wait, Dash! Will I see you again?"

He shrugged. "Who knows, dude? It's not really up to me. I hope so."

"Killian," a voice called from behind me. I spun around and saw Kane pushing through the crowd with Asher right behind him. "Where have you been? We've been looking all over for you. We were getting worried."

I spun back around, but it was too late. He was gone, swallowed up by the crowd.

"Killian?" Asher said.

I glanced back at him, then continued my futile search for Dash.

"Are you ok? Who are you looking for?" Kane asked me.

I turned back to them. "I'm great. I haven't been this good in weeks and weeks. It was amazing!"

"What was?" Asher said, obviously confused.

"There was this guy named Dash, and he was dancing and I started crying, and he came over to me and talked to me and he helped me give my pain to God and then we danced and now he's gone."

"Whoa, dude," Asher laughed while Kane stared at me as if I'd gone crazy. "Slow down. Who is this guy? I've never heard of any Dash, does he go to our school?"

"I don't know. No one seems to know him. He didn't even tell me his last name. But he told me I had to find Seth's killer."

Kane snapped to attention at that. "He said what?"

"He said that I had to find Seth's killer, and I had to be careful because I was in danger."

"This guy sounds really creepy," Asher said.

"No, he wasn't. He wasn't like anyone I've ever met."

"Well, it sounds like he was the man of your dreams, huh?" Asher said, sounding more than a little jealous. "I thought that was Jake."

"You thought what was me?" Jake asked as he appeared at my side.

I shot Asher a dirty look before turning to face Jake. He was wearing a pirate costume, complete with hook, open tattered shirt, and a plastic parrot on his shoulder.

"Nice dive earlier," I said.

Jake grimaced. "Thanks, I think I got a splinter in my nipple."

"So what was that all about, anyway?" Asher asked.

Jake's eyes shifted away and he shrugged. "Who knows? You know how women are. I just grabbed for the mike cord and hoped for the best."

"That was you that jumped on stage earlier?" Kane asked, jumping into the conversation for the first time.

"Oh, I'm sorry," I said realizing that I hadn't made any introductions. "Jake, this is my new little brother, Kane. Kane, this is my friend, Jake. He's Gilly's brother."

Kane smiled and extended his hand. Jake answered his smile with one of his patented lopsided grins.

"So since this is one of your parties, maybe you know who this guy I met was," I started.

"Whoa, don't pin this shindig on me. This is Todd and Gilly's baby all the way. I just help decorate and do impromptu stunt dives, you know...the normal stuff."

We all laughed. "Well anyway," I continued, "maybe you know him anyway. His name was Dash. He's about Asher's height with curly blonde hair?"

"Dash?" he said. "No, I'm pretty sure I don't know anyone named Dash. Why, what was so special about this guy?"

"Killian has a crush on him," Asher volunteered, with just a hint of satisfaction in his voice.

"I do not. I just met him tonight. It was just that he was..."

"Different from anyone you've ever met before?" Asher finished.

"Yeah, something like that," I muttered. "Just forget about it."

"Yeah, forget about him," Jake agreed. "Let's dance!"

The rest of the night was just plain fun. I hung out with Asher, Kane, and Jake all night and everyone seemed to get along. Marcus came and went with some of his friends. Jake and Kane hit it off and it was obvious that they were going to be good friends. There was no more drama with Gilly; in fact, I didn't even see her anymore. I never saw Dash again either. I caught a glimpse of Zack and Jesse a few times, but they kept their distance.

The party started winding down around 1:00 am and Adam wanted us home by 1:30 anyway, so Kane and I decided to go. We said our good-byes and started back out towards our car. It got darker and darker the closer we got to the gate. It seemed the security light had burned out or something. By the time we got to my car the only light came from a sliver of moon that hung low in the sky, but it was enough light to see that all my windows had been smashed.

Chapter 20

"Oh shit!" I gasped.

"What happened?" Kane asked. He sounded scared. I knew how he felt.

"Someone smashed my windows."

"What are we going to do?"

"We're gonna go back to the house and call the police." I said, backing away from the car. Then I remembered the camera Adam had given to me before we left. It had hung from my belt all night, forgotten. I grabbed it now and took several pictures of the car. I didn't know why, exactly; it just seemed like the thing to do.

We ran into Jake as we were walking back to the house.

"I thought you guys were leaving," he said when he saw us.

"So did we," I said.

"Someone smashed out all the windows in Killian's car," Kane told him.

"*What*?" Jake gasped.

"Yeah, I need to call the police—and Adam, so he'll know where we are and can come pick us up."

"You can stay here tonight if you want."

"Thanks, Jake," I said. "We might end up doing that."

The police got there about a half hour later, just after Adam arrived. He had insisted on coming to get us, saying he wanted us home. Soon the whole area out by the road was lit up brighter than the back yard dance floor. They worked, while Adam, Kane, Jake, and I watched from a distance. Asher and Marcus joined us after a little bit. Everyone who was still here was being kept in the back yard until the police knew more. The whole thing was being treated a little more seriously because of my stabbing back in September.

One of the cops disengaged himself eventually and came over to us. "Mr. Kendall?" he asked Adam.

"No, I'm Mr. Connelly. Adam Connelly. Killian is staying with me while his mother is out of town."

"Connelly?" the cop asked with raised eyebrows. "Any relation to the Connelly kid..."

"He was my son," Adam said quietly.

"I'm sorry," the cop said quickly. "That was insensitive. I'm Officer Hoetz."

"It's ok, Officer Hoetz. You couldn't know."

He nodded, "Well, here's what we've concluded so far. In light of what happened last month and how it involved Killian here, we took this more seriously than we normally would have. I mean, windows smashed at a party might be upsetting, but it isn't an earth-shattering event. But under the circumstances...well, as you can see, we took precautions. We searched the car and the surrounding area and we kept everyone that was still here on the premises. It paid off. We found a scrap of material caught on a piece of glass and we may be able to match it up with one of the people still here. We're trying to do that now. We are also taking names and releasing people as we can. We don't want to keep everyone here all night, but things took a nasty turn when we found this in the front seat of the car." He held up a plastic zip-lock bag with a folded piece of paper inside. "Someone threw it in after the windows were smashed, because it was on top of the broken glass."

"What is it?" I asked.

"It's a note."

"What does it say?" Adam asked.

Officer Hoetz thought a moment, then nodded and reached into his pocket. He pulled out a pair of rubber gloves and slipped them on. Then he opened the bag and drew out the note, opened it, and read it.

"Killian," he read, "you'd think after last time, you'd learn. This is just a warning. Next time you won't be so lucky."

We all stood stunned as Officer Hoetz folded the note again

and sealed it back in the bag. Adam snapped out of it first.

"That proves that Seth's death was murder, and now the killer is after Killian."

"Mr. Connelly, calm down," Officer Hoetz said soothingly. "It doesn't mean anything of the sort, necessarily. It just means that someone is unhappy with Killian and is trying to scare him. Maybe he stole someone's girlfriend or something."

Adam snorted, "Here we go again, huh? My son was murdered and no one wants to do anything about it."

"Mr. Connelly, I understand your grief, but there was no proof..."

"No. You *do not* understand my grief. And there's plenty of proof, but no one will even look at it. How was that note written?"

"It was computer generated. Simple red ink on white paper."

"That's exactly like the threatening notes Seth was getting before he was murdered."

Officer Hoetz pulled out a notebook and jotted something on it, flipped it closed and stuck it back in his pocket. "We'll look into it, Mr. Connelly."

"I hope so," Adam said angrily.

Another officer approached Hoetz and asked if he could speak to him for a minute. He excused himself and they walked off to one side and spoke quietly with their heads together.

"This is a nightmare. It's like Seth all over again," Adam mumbled as he rubbed his forehead.

Kane turned into Adam's shoulder and started to cry softly.

"Oh, damn, I'm sorry, Kane. I didn't mean to upset you any more," Adam said wearily.

"I'm just scared something's gonna happen to Killian," he sniffled.

"Nothing is going to happen to Killian," he soothed. "Not if I can help it," he added under his breath.

I had been listening to all this as if from a distance, not really taking it in. I felt a pair of arms slide around me from behind and twisted awkwardly to find it was Asher. I turned rest of the way into him and returned the hug. I needed that right now.

The rest of the night was spent in routine police work, or so

Officer Hoetz told us. They couldn't match the fabric sample at first glance, but that was inconclusive anyway since so many people had left before the cops got there. As he said wryly, it's not like we lacked for suspects...a couple hundreds' worth. Of course, I had my own list of suspects, with Zack and Jesse at the top of the list.

I stayed up the rest of the night thinking, since I was too unnerved to get any sleep anyway and I had so much on my mind. I had gone in several different directions, but I seemed to make breakthroughs in every area. I decided that I was ready to come out at school, for one thing. It was obvious that Gilly and I were through, and it might help goad the killer into making a move. If he got caught, it would be worth any danger to me. Or at least that's what I reasoned at four in the morning.

I also decided to confront Zack once and for all. I was feeling very reckless and angry by this point, ready for action.

Last, but not least, I decided to give Asher another chance. Not that I was ruling out Jake, but it seemed like Asher was always there for me, no matter what. He was definitely a true friend, and isn't that what you want in a boyfriend?

With that last thought still playing through my mind, I fell asleep just as the first rays of light broke over the horizon.

Adam let me sleep in the next morning, for which I was very grateful. I didn't get up until 1:00 in the afternoon and I was still very tired, but there were things I wanted to do that day that I didn't want to put off.

Kane was already downstairs when I came down, but then he'd fallen asleep as soon as we got home last night.

"Hey, you didn't sleep much last night, did you?" he asked me as soon as he saw me.

"No, but you didn't seem to have any trouble," I said as I ruffled his hair.

"I was really worn out, I guess," he explained.

"No kidding."

I wandered into the kitchen, grabbed a pack of cookies out of the cabinet and poured myself a glass of milk before sitting down at the table. Kane followed me in and sat down across from me, snagging a few cookies in the process and dipping them in my milk.

"Hey, get your own," I protested. "Where's Adam?"

"He went down to the police station to see about your car. They impounded it last night."

"Oh."

"Asher called this morning and so did Jake."

"Oh," I said again. "You and Jake seemed to hit it off."

Kane shot me a funny look and I quickly explained. "I meant as friends."

"Oh, yeah," he smiled. "He's really funny. So what was on your mind last night that you couldn't sleep? Upset about the whole car thing?"

"Partly, but I also made a lot of decisions last night."

"Like what?"

"Well, like that guy Dash last night made me realize I had been avoiding a lot of stuff, and it's time I faced it instead of pretending it doesn't exist or whatever."

"What are you talking about?"

"Well, I decided to come out at school."

"Whoa! That's a big deal, isn't it? I mean, won't that be really hard?"

"Oh yeah. I'm scared, but I'm also tired of pretending to be something I'm not. I mean, I'm not, like, gonna get on stage at an assembly and announce it, but I'm gonna stop pretending."

"I'm also going to confront Zack. I want to do that today, before I lose my nerve."

"Is that the jerk from last night? The guy in the Scream costume?"

"Yeah, that's him."

"Confront him how?"

"Just tell him to leave me alone once and for all, and all my friends. And find out why he hates me so much. We used to be friends...kinda."

Kane shook his head. "I think you need some more sleep," he said.

"Wait, I'm not even done yet," I told him.

He raised his eyebrows just like Adam does and I almost started laughing. "I'm going to give Asher another chance. I mean, he's always there for me when I need him and he's a true friend."

"What about Jake? I can tell he really likes you, too."

"I don't know what to do about Jake. I mean I like him, but...it's different with Asher and me. We have a history, you know? I just met Jake."

Kane smiled. "Follow your heart, Killian. You'll know what's right."

"How'd you get so smart?" I asked fondly.

"I dunno, good genes I guess."

I laughed and got up to call Zack's house. I wanted to make sure he was home before I drove to his house. I talked to his mom for a few minutes then hung up, leaving my hand on the receiver while I was lost in thought.

"What?" Kane asked after a moment.

"Zack never came home last night. They've called Jesse, and Jesse says he left him at the party. They split when the cops arrived."

"What's that mean?"

"I don't know." Just then the phone rang, startling me and causing me to jump. The receiver was still in my hand and it clattered to the floor. I scooped it up and said hello quickly.

"Killian?" It was Adam. "Is everything ok?"

"Yeah, I just dropped the phone."

"Killian, listen, is Kane there with you?"

"Yes," I said.

"Good. After we hang up, lock all the doors and check the windows and don't go anywhere until I get home."

"Why? What's going on? Adam, you're scaring me."

"I'm sorry, Killian, they just found Zachary Phillips's body floating in the creek behind the Sheridan house."

The phone suddenly became heavy and my arm slowly dropped down until I was holding the phone at my side. I could still hear Adam's voice squawking but I could no longer understand individual words. I couldn't seem to find words to say either. My mind had become a total blank.

I heard Kane asking me what was wrong, then I felt him come up behind and me and gently take the phone from my hand. I heard him talking to Adam, asking him what was going on, asking when he'd be home. I heard the phone hang up and then Kane was standing in front of me.

"Killian, snap out of it. I need your help," he said.

I forced myself to focus on him.

"Why are you acting like this?" he asked. "You weren't close to that guy, were you? Wasn't he the jerk?"

I shook my head to clear it. "We used to be friends. I've known him since we were little kids. We grew up together. Now he's gone. The killer got him, too. And he's not going to stop till he gets me." I was getting more and more hysterical with every passing second.

Kane grabbed my shoulders and shook me. "Killian, listen to me," he said urgently. "No one knows if Zack was murdered yet. All they know is that he was dead in the creek. Maybe he got drunk and fell in. Don't jump to conclusions yet. Dad said they are sending his body up to Baltimore for an autopsy; it's a rush because of everything that's been going on. Besides, why would anyone want to kill Zack?"

"I don't know. I just know that this is bad. Very bad. It's too much to be a coincidence."

"Well, of course it's bad. It's always bad when someone dies. But you need to calm down right now. Dad wants us to lock all the doors and windows. Help me do that."

We went around the house locking and checking all the doors and windows on the first floor, then after some thought, the windows on the second floor as well. We'd watched too many movies, though, and by the time we were finished we'd thoroughly spooked ourselves. Kane had brought a bat with him, which we retrieved from the closet, and I armed myself with a large kitchen knife. Then we barricaded ourselves into the living room to wait for Adam to get back.

As we were sitting there, it suddenly occurred to me that we were acting like little kids. It was broad daylight and here we were hiding in our living room. The more I thought about it, the more ridiculous it became, until I was laughing out loud.

"What's so funny?" Kane asked, sounding a little insulted.

"Just that here we are, you're 14 and I'm 16, and we're acting like a couple of babies scared of our own shadows. It's broad daylight. I'm not going to live my life in fear. I had plans for today and I'm sticking to them."

"But Adam wanted us to wait for him here," Kane protested.

"I'll leave a note. Do you wanna come with me or do you wanna stay here?"

"I'm not staying here alone!"

"Ok, then lemme go shower and get dressed and we'll go see Asher and maybe go see Jake if we have time." I became quickly sober again, "He must be really shaken up. I mean, having a dead body in your back yard has got to be horrible. I wonder who found him?"

"Dad didn't say," Kane said.

I shrugged and sighed as I stood up. I returned the knife to the kitchen before heading up for my shower. Adam was home by the time I showered and dressed. He and Kane were talking quietly in the living room when I came downstairs; the bat was still resting across Kane's lap.

They both looked up and fell silent as I came in.

"What?" I demanded.

"What do you mean?" Adam asked innocently.

"You stopped talking when I walked in the room. You must have been talking about me."

Adam and Kane exchanged glances, then looked back at me.

"Sit down, Killian," Adam said.

This wasn't going to be good. No conversation that started with the words "sit down" was ever good. I crossed the room and sat down on the couch next to Kane.

"Does this have to do with Zack?" I asked.

"Yes. I couldn't go into it over the phone, or rather I could, but I didn't want to. I wanted to be here to tell you in person."

"Why? Tell me what? What's going on?"

"Killian, I told Kane that they were taking Zack to Baltimore for an autopsy, and they are, but what I didn't tell him is that they don't really need to determine the cause of death. They pretty much know that already."

"What are you saying?"

Adam swallowed and took a deep breath. "Killian, Zack was murdered just like Seth. His throat was cut. He was most likely dead before he was thrown into the creek."

I sat stunned for several moments. "I don't understand," I said finally.

"Well, without the autopsy and all the forensic examinations, nothing is positive, but it's a little much. I mean, no one likes coincidences, and it's a little much to believe that we have two killers running around our little town. Zack's throat was cut, just like Seth's. The police don't understand what the connection could be yet. They are still looking into it. They do think that it was Zack that either broke your windows or left the note, or maybe both. The fabric fragment that the police found matched a tear in Zack's costume."

"But that doesn't make sense. If Zack is the killer, who killed him? And if he isn't, why would he leave that note?"

"Like I said, the police are working on that. Now that they are taking this case seriously, it's not up to us to figure it out anymore. As of right now I want you out of this, completely and totally. I want to know where you are at all times and I don't want you going anywhere alone. You are to come directly home after school and nowhere after dark until this killer is caught."

"But I..."

"But nothing, Killian. I want you out of this. And I mean out. I must have been crazy with grief when I agreed to let you get involved with this in the first place."

"I'm already involved, Adam," I argued.

"This is a cold-blooded killer we're talking about. He's already killed two boys, one of whom was my son. Killian, I have come to love you as if you were my own. You and Kane are all I have left. I don't think I could bear to lose either of you at this point. I couldn't bear it, Killian. Do you understand what I'm saying?" His voice was so thick he could barely even speak, and tears had begun to roll down his cheeks. I sat stunned for a second as the impact of what Adam had just said sunk in. Then almost without thinking, I was off the couch, on my knees in front on Adam with my arms around his waist as I sobbed into his chest. I felt Adam gently wrap his arms around me, and after a few beats, I felt Kane slide in next to me to complete the group hug.

"We're a real family now, aren't we?" I heard Kane whisper.

"Yes. Yes, we are," Adam answered.

After I got myself back together, I called Jake to see how he was doing. Todd answered the phone and said that everyone was pretty shook up right then and that I should call back later.

A sudden disturbing suspicion shot through my mind. "Todd," I called as he went to hang up.

"Yeah?" he said.

"I didn't see you last night. Were you there?"

He was quiet for a moment. "I was upstairs in my room. Costume parties aren't really my thing." And he hung up.

I sat staring at the phone until the operator came on and told me that if I wanted to make a call, I needed to please hang up and try again. I hung up for a second then picked up again and called Asher.

Asher wanted me to come right over, but Adam didn't want me to go anywhere and couldn't take me anyway, and my car, while having been released from impound, was now at the shop getting the glass replaced. We settled for talking on the phone for several hours. We talked about everything from the beginning till now, all the misunderstandings, the hurt feelings...and our true feelings for each other. As we talked things began to fall into place for me, like seeing a puzzle come together before my eyes. I knew now that it was Asher I truly loved. By the time we hung up, I had my first official boyfriend.

Chapter
21

It was two days before I got my car back and several more before Adam would let me go anywhere except school. Meanwhile, Adam called the police twice a day to check on the case progress, which was minimal. All they would tell him was that they were pretty sure it was someone at the party—Well, duh! I was pretty sure of that, too. Give me a detective badge and get me on the force!—and that they were still examining evidence. They did give us one piece of information that lifted a huge burden from my shoulders; they told Adam that the medical examiner had placed the estimated time of death at or around midnight.

I felt guilty for even still having it in the back of my mind, but I had never been able to completely shake the idea that Asher had something to do with the murders. When I found out about the time of death, I was finally able to put that nagging doubt to rest. I had been with Asher, Kane, and Jake all night except for the brief time I was with Dash, and they were with each other that whole time.

Suddenly, I couldn't wait any longer to see Asher. Of course, Adam didn't want me to go anywhere by myself, but it didn't take too much whining before he agreed to let me drive directly to his house as long as I called as soon as I got there. I was out the door before he could change his mind.

Marcus answered the door. "Killian, hey! Come on in.

Dude, did you hear about Zack? Well, I mean, sure you have. Wasn't that awful? He died while we were at the party! I mean, we were right there! It could have been any of us!"

"Not really," I said without thinking. I picked up the phone and called Adam and assured him I was safe and sound at the Davis'.

"What do you mean?" Marcus asked as soon as I hung up.

"Well, just that...if the murderer killed Zack, he must have had a reason. I don't think it was just a random murder any more than I think Seth was killed in a random mugging."

"Whoa! Zack was murdered? And you think it was connected to Seth's murder?"

Oops. I had forgotten that the police hadn't yet released the information that Zack was murdered; just that he was found dead in the creek. I had already said way too much and didn't know what I should say now, so I settled for, "Yeah, I do. It just makes sense, you know? I mean, I don't know that he was killed, I just assumed..." Smooth, real smooth, Killian.

"You know more than you're saying, don't you?"

"Hey, is Asher here?" I tried desperately to change the subject.

"He's upstairs in his room. Have you talked to the police?"

"Something like that," I called over my shoulder as I loped up the stairs. Marcus went as far as to follow me to the base of the stairs, and for a moment I thought he was going to follow me up, but then he just shrugged and wandered off. I breathed a sigh of relief and walked down the hall to Asher's door. I stood in front of it for a few seconds before taking a deep breath and knocking. I watched in amusement mixed with apprehension as Asher opened the door and his eyes widened in surprise. What if he wasn't happy to see me? I hadn't called first or anything.

"Hi," I said, suddenly shy. This was the first time I had seen Asher since we'd become boyfriends, and I was surprised at how nervous I was. I'd known Asher almost all my life; why should I be nervous?

It wasn't long before my nerves were calmed, though, as Asher broke into a huge smile and opened the door wider.

"Hi, come on in," he said softly.

I stepped into the room and he shut the door behind me. As he turned to face me, that strange phenomenon that always seems to happen to me at key moments in my life went into effect— time slowed to a stop. Nothing else existed as I looked into his beautiful blue-gray eyes; it was just Asher and me. It was as if we melted into one another as we embraced in a tender hug. Moving as a single unit, we pulled back slightly only to move back in again—this time for the softest, most gentle love-filled kiss I had ever experienced. In that moment, in that utterly perfect moment that would be burned into my memory for the rest of my life, I knew I had made the right choice. I knew that I was meant to be with Asher, now and forever. He completed me. We stood there with our arms around each other and my head on his shoulder, moving to the silent sounds of music that can only be heard with the heart. The notes of an old song that Mom had listened to over and over when I was little began to float through my mind. Soon, the words followed, and I began to softly sing them:

"Someday, when I am old, and the world is cold, I will feel a glow just thinking of you and the way you look tonight. Oh but you're lovely, with your smile so warm, and your cheek so soft, there is nothing for me but to love you just the way you look tonight."

I was very self-conscious about my voice—not that I couldn't sing, I'd been told I had a very good voice. In fact, I had been in chorus all the way through middle school, often getting solos. When my voice had changed it had become low and husky, which I now found perfectly suited to the old Billie Holiday ballad.

"With each word your tenderness grows, tearing my fear apart, and that laugh that wrinkles your nose touches my foolish heart. Lovely, never, never change. Keep that breathless charm; won't you please arrange it 'cause I love you just the way you look tonight..."

Asher cut off my serenade with another one of those wonderful, tender kisses. This one quickly escalated to a deeper level of passion. Suddenly, Asher pulled back. His eyes locked on mine as if he were searching them for something.

"Stay with me tonight," he said softly.

I stood there for a long time. Too long I guess, because before I could say anything I saw the fear and uncertainty flicker through his eyes.

"Killian?" he asked with fear in his voice.

"Asher, I want to. I want to so bad."

"Then what's stopping you?" he asked, pulling me closer and running his hands up my back under my shirt.

"I can't," I felt his hands freeze on my back and I rushed on, "Asher, I want to do this right. More than anything, I want this to work. I don't want to miss anything along the way; I don't want to skip any steps. I don't want to do anything that would ruin what we have."

His arms dropped and he took a few steps back, away from me. Pain was written all over his face and I knew that I had goofed once again. Why couldn't I ever get anything right?

"So...let me see if I've got this right," Asher said slowly, on the verge of tears. "You are saying that sleeping with me would ruin our relationship?"

"Asher, that's not what I meant...well, actually, in a way it is, but not in the way you mean."

"Please explain it to me, then," he pleaded in a desperate voice.

"I used to think that love was this unstoppable force and that it just picked you up and took you along with it, like a fast-moving river or a tidal wave...but now I know that what I thought was love was just lust. Real love develops over time, more like how a tiny trickle of water from a spring carves a canyon over time. Adam has helped me to see how important sex is; it's a beautiful and powerful thing, and Asher, I do want to share that with you. But I want it to be right. I want it to be perfect. I don't want to rush into something this important, something that has such a huge potential to change everything." I closed the distance between us again. "Asher, I realized something when we talked on the phone the other night and it was confirmed so strongly just now when I was in your arms...I love you—I love you, Asher!"

Tears spilled over and ran down his cheeks, but he just ignored them. He reached out a trembling hand and touched me softly on the cheek, just for a second and then it was gone, almost leaving me wondering if it had even happened.

"Killian, I've loved you for years. I was so jealous when I saw you with Seth. I wanted so badly to tell you how I felt, but I was scared. And then when you got hurt and I thought I might lose you...I was terrified. When I finally told you I thought everything would be perfect, but nothing went right. I was still scared at first and then there was Gilly. When you said that she was just a cover I thought that maybe I still had a chance but then I heard you talking to Jake and it was like I had lost you again. And now after all that...here you are, standing here telling me you love me. I want so much to believe that—to believe that you do love me—but I'm scared of losing you again. Maybe tomorrow it'll be someone else, maybe Jake again or that guy Dash or someone new. Maybe I'm not enough for you. Killian, I love you with all my heart. When I'm with you, it's the happiest I ever feel, and when I'm not with you it's like a part of me is missing. You're all I ever think about. But as much as I love you I don't think I could take getting dumped on again. Why am I never enough for you?"

I reached out and gently wiped the tears from his soft cheeks.

"Because I was stupid and confused; I didn't see what was right in front of my eyes. I won't be gone tomorrow or the day after that, the day after that, or ever again. There won't be anyone else. What I'm trying to say is...you are enough. You are all I want—now and forever. You complete me."

Asher let out a muffled sob as he collapsed into my arms. I felt my knees buckle as well. I felt physically drained, as if I'd run a marathon. I steered us over to his bed and lowered us onto it. We wrapped ourselves around each other and I held him until he fell asleep. Once I was sure he was in a deep enough sleep, I slipped out from under him and with a soft kiss on the lips, I left him for the night. I had a lot on my mind on the drive home.

For Asher and me, the next month passed by in a haze that only those who have experienced those first few intoxicating weeks of a new love could understand. Nothing else seemed to matter or if it did, it was only in the abstract, as if everything was far removed from us. Oh, I kept up with the developments on Seth and Zack's murders, but that was about it. And even though the police were now taking both killings very seriously, those developments seemed to be few and far between. They insisted that they were still examining the evidence and that they were confident that they would find the killer.

Jake hadn't talked to me much since I'd told him about Asher and me. After a lot of talking and consideration, Asher and I decided to come out at school. We didn't make a big production or really change how we acted, but we told our close friends and let the word spread from there. For the most part, no one really seemed to care. In fact, several people who I would have never expected to had gone out of their way to let us know that they supported us. Gilly was still pretending I didn't exist, but two of her closest friends made a point of showing that they were behind Asher and me 100%. Not that everything was a fairy tale—no pun intended. There were still a few jerks that would make crude comments under their breath every time one of us walked by, and more than a few incidents of name calling, but as Adam said, what doesn't kill us only makes us stronger. And as time went on and it became obvious that our supporters outnumbered our detractors, those incidents became more and more infrequent.

All in all, I felt worse for Jesse than for Asher and me. I had seen him a few times wondering through the halls, looking as if he was lost. I felt myself actually feeling sorry for him. I know Zack was the real brains behind their dynamic duo—what little brains there were—and I was sure that Jesse must have really been missing him. I didn't let myself dwell on it too much, though; after all, he had made my life a living hell and had beaten the crap out of Asher. And besides, I had more important things to worry about, like how much I loved Asher...and seeing my mom again.

Thanksgiving was only a week away, and I was beginning to get very excited. Mom was planning on coming down for a big Thanksgiving feast that Adam and Steve had been planning for weeks already. Besides those of us who lived in the house and Mom, we were also expecting a few other couples who didn't have families or whose families were either too far away or not exactly welcoming.

It was the Saturday before Thanksgiving and after much begging and nagging, Adam had finally agreed to let Asher and me drive to Rehoboth Beach and do a little early Christmas shopping. The outlets there have all the best stores: Gap, Old Navy, Pacific Sunwear, and hundreds more. The only stipulation was that we had to be home before dark.

We had a great day of goofing off and we even did a little shopping. We would have made it home in plenty of time, too, if Asher hadn't suddenly had one of his brainstorm ideas.

"Hey, let's go home the back way!" he suggested out of the blue.

"I don't know the way," I argued.

"I do, and besides, it'll give us more time to spend together. We've got plenty of time."

So of course I agreed. Two hours later, we were hopelessly lost, I was tired and cranky, my gas gauge was riding dangerously close to empty, and the sun was riding dangerously close to the horizon. My teeth were gritted so hard my jaw was beginning to ache, and it had been a while since Asher had tried to say anything.

Suddenly I started to recognize our surroundings.

"I think this is near where Jake and Gilly live. I'm going to try to find their house and call Adam from there."

"I dunno, Kill," Asher said uneasily. "You and I aren't exactly their favorite people right now. It may not be such a good idea to just show up on their doorstep."

"We don't really have much choice. I'm not sure I can make it to the gas station, and it's almost dark. If we run out of gas somewhere, I want Adam to know where we are, and if I don't call him and it gets dark before we get home we won't be allowed to go anywhere alone again until we're 18."

"I'm sorry," he said weakly.

"Let's go the back way," I snapped in agitation.

"Geez." Asher pouted. "I said I was sorry. I thought I knew the way. You don't have to get nasty. You could have said no, you know."

I pulled into the Sheridans' driveway with my jaw set again. I threw the car into park and jumped out, slamming the door behind me. Asher stayed in the car, staring straight ahead with his arms crossed over his chest. I stalked up to the door and knocked.

Of course, Todd answered.

"I thought we'd gotten rid of you, fag," he snarled when he saw who it was.

I tried not to, but I couldn't help but flinch. "Nice to see you again, too, Todd." I quipped, hoping to seem as if he hadn't got to me. "Look, I'm sorry to bother you but can I please use your phone?" I hated to have to ask him anything and almost just went back to the car, but I could feel Asher watching me and I was damned if I was going to go running back like a puppy with its tail between its legs.

"You want to use our phone?" he said incredulously.

"I'm almost out of gas and I need to call Adam."

"Who is it, Todd?" Mrs. Sheridan called from down the hall.

"It's Killian," Todd said, as if he was telling her there was a dead rat on the front step.

"Well, for goodness' sake," she said as she came into view, "Come on in, Killian. It's good to see you."

"It's good to see you, too, Mrs. Sheridan," I said truthfully. "I need to use your phone for a minute, if that's ok."

"Of course it's ok. Come on, I'll show you where it is."

I edged past Todd, who still stood in the center of the doorway as if he didn't want to let me in, and followed Mrs. Sheridan down the hall to the kitchen. Out of the corner of my eye I thought I caught a glimpse of movement at the top of the stairs, but when I looked again there was nothing there. I wondered if it had been my imagination or if Gilly or Jake had been there a second ago.

In the kitchen, Jamie was perched on a stool stirring something in a big pot on the stove.

"Hi, Killian," he chirped. "Are you staying for dinner again? I'm making pasghetti sauce."

"Yes, Killian, why don't you?" Mrs. Sheridan added. Obviously she was either blind as to how her three oldest children felt about me or she just didn't care.

"Thank you for the invitation, but I have a friend in the car and I really need to get home. Actually, that's why I'm calling Adam now."

"Well, the offer stands anytime," she said, and then turned to the counter where she was chopping vegetables for a salad.

I made a quick call to Adam, which he was very appreciative of, thanked Mrs. Sheridan again, and beat a hasty retreat— or tried to, at any rate. I almost made it out the door when Gilly called my name. I turned around to see her coming down the stairs looking for all the world like a modern day Scarlett O'Hara from Gone With The Wind—that is if Scarlett had blonde hair and wore tight jeans. I almost expected her to swoon and say, "Whatever shall I do? Wherever shall I go?"

Instead she had me caught in a glare that would have left me dead on the spot if looks could kill. "This may be the last time I ever have the chance to say this while we're alone and I'm not going to miss it," she hissed venomously. "I just want to say that you are the lowest scum I have ever met. I can't believe I ever had a crush on you. You are such a sleaze. You not only cheated on me—with my own brother—but then you turned around and dumped him. God, I hate you. I wish I had told everyone at that damn party just what an asshole you are. You are so lucky that Jake stopped me. Although now I bet he wishes he hadn't."

"Gilly," I said as soon as she took a breath, "there is so much wrong with that bunch of shit that I don't even know where to start. So I'm not even going to try. Good-bye, Gilly. I'm sorry you got hurt, but we both knew there was nothing between us from the beginning."

"What about me?" Jake asked from the top of the staircase. "Are you sorry I got hurt? Was there ever anything between us?"

I looked up at him and I could see the raw pain in his eyes. "Yes," I said much more gently than I had been with Gilly. "Yes, I am very sorry you got hurt and, yes, there was something between us. It just didn't work out. I hope we can be friends again someday."

"Oh please. Give it up, Killian," Todd snarled as he came up behind Gilly. "Your goody-two-shoes act is getting really stale around here. We've seen what you're really like. Now get out and don't come back again. You aren't welcome here anymore. I don't care if your damn car is on fire."

I looked up at Jake one last time before I turned to let myself out, but he was gone. The image of his tear-stained face followed me all the way to the car.

I slumped into the driver's seat and rested my head on the steering wheel.

"Didn't go well?" Asher asked.

"Don't start," I said warningly.

"I'm not trying to. Honest. I'm sorry, Killian."

I sighed. "I'm sorry, too. And no, it didn't go well. At all. To say the least."

"What happened?"

"Let's just say that I had to go through hostile confrontations with almost every member of the family except Jamie."

"I'm sorry, baby," Asher reached over and took my hand.

"Yeah, me too," I said with a squeeze back. I sat up, started the car, and drove away without looking back.

Chapter
22

Thanksgiving had finally arrived and it was none too soon for me. I woke up early, too excited to stay in bed any longer. I couldn't wait to see Mom for the first time since she'd moved to Pennsylvania to live with my Aunt Kathy. She had called the night before to make sure it was ok with Adam if she brought one of my cousins for the ride. I'd never even met this particular cousin; Aunt Kathy never liked Dad so we didn't see her very often, and when she did come down she always left the kids at home. Mom had said they expected to be here a little after noon.

The time flew by quickly as Steve kept us all busy with preparations for the meal. Altogether we were now expecting 13 people; Adam jokingly called it our very own coven, and Steve commented that he hoped it wouldn't be our last supper. I lived with a bunch of would-be comedians. We had put all the leaves in the dining table and set up a couple of card tables with table-cloths. Adam and Steve had been cooking since daybreak and the whole house was filled with the aroma of roasting turkey and sage.

We were so busy with our preparations that no one even noticed Mom pull up until we heard the knock on the door. I almost broke my neck trying to answer it. I threw open the door and then threw myself into Mom's arms. After a long hug I stepped back to get a better look at her. She looked fabulous, better than I had ever seen her. Her hair was a little longer than it had been the last time I'd seen her, and she'd had it styled. She was wearing just a hint of make-up—the first I had ever seen her wear—just enough to accentuate her natural beauty. She looked so young and pretty.

"You look incredible!" I gasped.

"You don't have to sound so surprised, you know. I was young when I had you. And you look pretty good yourself there, sport."

"True love must agree with him," Adam said with a grin as he came up behind me. "Hello, Meg. It's great to see you. I'm so glad you were able to come."

"I wouldn't miss it for the world, Adam." Then, with a raised eyebrow she turned her attention back to me. "And what's this about true love? I know my baby can't be in love."

I felt a blush creep up my neck as a new voice entered the conversation, "He doesn't look like a baby to me, Aunt Meg," said someone who could only be my mystery cousin. I couldn't even remember his name.

Mom stepped aside and I caught my first glimpse of whatever-his-name-is. He looked nice. He had wavy blondish hair and bright green eyes that reminded me of cat eyes. He was older than me by a few years at least and also taller, maybe 5'10". He had a look about him that made me think he smiled a lot—as he was doing now. He had a great smile.

"Killian, this is your cousin, Aidan," Mom said. "He's thinking about transferring to the college down here for next year."

I waved a greeting and he responded by waggling one of the suitcases in his hands.

"Oh, excuse my rudeness," Adam exclaimed. "Let me help you with those. Come on in and I'll show you where you'll be sleeping. I hope you don't mind sharing a room with Killian and my son, Kane."

"Sounds like fun," Aidan said with a laugh as he followed Adam in. Mom and I trailed behind.

"Aidan, this is Adam," Mom said a bit belatedly. "He's taken Killian in and I guess you could say he's been his surrogate father."

Kane was in the hallway so our little entourage paused long enough for another round of introductions, which was repeated again a few seconds later as Steve wandered in to see what all

the commotion was about. Once we had things settled in their
rooms, Steve assigned everyone a last minute task. We all
worked busily until the first of the guests began arriving. Ilana
and Lysander were the first on the scene, arriving with a bottle
of wine in hand. Then Asher rolled in. He'd begged off from
their big family dinner since things would have probably been a
little tense with all the Sheridan clan being there. Everyone else
arrived at the same time, which made me wonder if they had
come together. They were the two couples from our celebration
dinner a few months back, Bryant and Calvin and Heather and
Nila.

They hadn't changed much except Calvin seemed to have
paled even more; his hair was pale blonde with almost white eyebrows and almost colorless blue eyes. He looked as if he had
faded out and in fact, most of the time he did seem to fade into
the background. Bryant was definitely the dominant force in
their relationship. Heather was also quiet, though not to the
extent that Calvin was. Her long brown hair was pulled back into
a braid that hung to her waist, and her brown eyes peered out
uncertainly from behind her glasses. She was wearing a white
shirt and a plaid skirt that made her look like a Catholic school-
girl. With a little more confidence I thought she could be beautiful, but she would always pale in comparison with Nila, her
partner. Tonight she looked like a Nubian princess, Aida maybe.
Her dark bronze skin glowed with health and her exotic good
looks made it hard to look away from her. She was wearing her
hair in many tiny braids with gold beads at the end of each one.
The beads complimented the other gold jewelry that she wore—
multiple ear piercings, a nose ring, a necklace with a stylized
African animal I thought might be a lion, bracelets on both
wrists, one arm cuff, and several rings. With her ankle-length
form-fitting white dress, she made a stunning entrance.

Dinner was fantastic, as I knew it would be. Afterwards, the
dishes were left to sit as we all gathered in the living room
accompanied by various moans and groans about having eaten
too much.

"Let's go around the room and each of us say one thing
we're thankful for," Aidan suggested once we were all settled
and in various states of unconsciousness.

"Let's not and say we did," Mom joked. "I think I'm going
to fall asleep."

"Come on, it's Thanksgiving," I said, backing Aidan up.

"Just one thing?" Bryant asked mischievously. He threw a lascivious grin at Calvin, who giggled.

"Yes, just one thing," Adam said, "and please remember that this is a family show."

We all laughed.

"Who wants to go first?" Kane asked.

"Why doesn't Aidan go first since it was his idea?" Steve suggested.

"Ok. I have mine already anyway," Aidan said. "I'm thankful that I have already made so many good friends down here, and I haven't even moved yet."

"Awwwww," we all said in unison and then burst out laughing again.

Aidan looked to his left. "Nila?"

"Hmmm, let me think," she said in her heavy Jamaican accent. "I am thankful for all of you also. It's hard to be so far away from my mother at holiday time, but it's nice to be here with my father and such good people. And I am always thankful for Heather."

"Hey, that's two things!" Bryant yelled as Heather turned bright red.

"Judges?" Kane asked Adam and Steve.

They exchanged a look. "We're allowing it," Adam said. "Heather, you're next."

"I'm thankful for having met Nila," she said quickly and turned to Bryant.

"Oh, it's my turn already?" he said in mock surprise, "Hmm...let me see...where to begin?"

"You're gonna lose your turn if you don't begin soon," Adam said threateningly as everyone laughed.

"Ok, ok...geez," he pretended to pout for a second then turned serious. "I'm thankful for people like Adam and Steve who do selfless things like take in kids who need a place to stay and invite their friends to Thanksgiving dinner when their own families tell them they aren't welcome. The world is a better place because of you." He raised his wine glass in a salute.

Everyone sat silently for a moment, batting their eyes furiously.

"And I'm thankful for Calvin. Ha! That's two!"

Everyone laughed and the moment was gone. We all looked to Calvin expectantly. He blinked as if surprised to suddenly be the center of attention. He cleared his throat nervously, then began to speak so softly that I had to lean in to hear him.

"I'm thankful for the support and encouragement that Bryant gives me. I don't know what I'd do without him. If it wasn't for him I wouldn't even be alive." It was the most I'd heard him say all evening, and I wasn't surprised to see tears suddenly appear in Bryant's eyes. He reached over and took Calvin's hand while swiping at his eyes with his other hand. I knew there must be more to this story than met the eye and wondered what it was. I knew it was really none of my business but I couldn't help but be curious.

"I'm thankful to have this beautiful woman as my wife," Lysander said into the silence that followed Calvin's little speech. "And honey, why don't you tell them what else we have to be thankful for."

Ilana positively beamed. "I'm pregnant," she said.

The room erupted into a cacophony of congratulations, back slapping, hugs, and how-far-alongs. Eventually everyone settled back into their seats.

"My turn?" Steve asked.

"Yup," we all chorused.

"Well, I'm thankful that Adam and I have decided that it's time for me to move in here."

Another round of excited chatter followed this announcement, and then it was Adam's turn.

"I'm thankful for so many things, it's hard to choose just one," he said.

"It was your rule!" Bryant said.

"Rule over-ruled," Adam said with a grin. "Seriously though, I am very thankful this year. More so than years past. Losing Seth made me appreciate what I do have so much more. And even though I lost one son, I regained a son I thought I had lost forever and gained another son altogether. I love both of you boys so much. You are truly my greatest blessing in life."

I felt a lump form in my throat, and from the look on Kane's face I knew he was as touched as I was.

"Wow, I have to follow that, huh?" Kane said a little shakily. I noticed several people dabbing at their eyes. "I'm thankful for my family—my whole family; Steve, Dad and Killian. Your turn, Asher."

Asher turned and looked at me for a moment before turning back to the room and saying, "I'm thankful that sometimes true love does conquer all."

This was met with another chorus of awws and I knew I was blushing again. I regained my composure and took my turn.

"I'm thankful that for the first time in my life I feel completely loved and accepted by everyone who is important in my life."

I heard several more sniffles from around the room. It seemed like almost everyone was crying by now. When Mom began to speak her voice was thick with emotion.

"As I sit here and look at my son, happy, healthy, safe...in love and loved by so many people, I can't help but be so very thankful that God spared his life. I know what a gift that truly is, and my heart aches for you, Adam." I looked at Adam to see his shoulders shaking with barely repressed sobs. "You've lost so much," she continued, "and yet you've given so much. I can't even begin to tell you how thankful I am for the way you've taken Killian in, even to the point of loving him like your own son."

She stood up and crossed the room to hug Adam as he seemed to collapse under his grief. I had been so caught up in my own pain and life that I had never even stopped to consider how much Adam must have been hurting. Without even thinking I moved to hug him as well, and it wasn't long before I felt Kane at my side. When I went back to my seat everyone in the room was crying openly. Once we got ourselves back together, a concerted effort was made to lighten the mood. We played Guesstures and Taboo and after Bryant and Calvin, Heather and Nila, and Ilana and Lysander left, the rest of us played a round of Balderdash.

Soon it was time to go to bed, though, and it was decided after a call home that Asher would spend the night. That meant that there were four of us staying in Kane's and my room.

"Reminds me of summer camp," Aidan commented as we went upstairs.

Once there, sleeping arrangements were hashed out. Kane ended up giving up his bed for Aidan and sleeping on the floor in a sleeping bag, while Asher and I were sharing my bed. With two other people in the room there wasn't much chance of anything happening.

After the lights were out we cuddled into each other and we were almost asleep when Aidan's voice snapped me back from the brink.

"So...uh...no one said as much, but you guys are, like, a

couple, huh?"

No one spoke at first, and when the silence began to stretch a little thin I spoke up. "Yeah, I guess we just figured you knew. I thought Mom might have said something. Does it bother you?"

"No, not at all. I'm pretty open about stuff like that. If it bothered me I don't think I would have been able to stand being here tonight. I think I was the only straight person here besides Aunt Meg."

"I'm straight," Kane piped up from the floor.

"Sorry, and Kane."

"And Ilana and Lysander," Kane added.

"Ok, ok...I was exaggerating to make a point. I won't do it again, I promise."

"I guess there were a lot of gay people here tonight," Asher said thoughtfully, or maybe he was just tired. It was hard to tell in the dark. "You were definitely in the minority. That's weird."

"Not really," Aidan said. "If you think about it, it kinda makes sense. You know that old saying 'Birds of a feather flock together?' I think in a way it's true. I mean, you're going to naturally want to be around people that accept you for who you are and who are the most like you. That's probably the real reason Aunt Meg invited me to come down here."

"What do you mean?" I asked.

"Well, she said she thought I'd like to see the area before I moved down here next year, but I've been down here before and I've already put in for the transfer, so it's not like I'm going to change my mind at this point. I think she knew that it was going to be mostly gay people here and this is her way of telling me it's ok with her if I'm gay."

"Why would she think you're gay?" Kane asked.

"Kane!" I said in exasperation.

Aidan just laughed. "It's ok. He's just being up-front about it. I respect that. And to answer your question as honestly as I know how, Kane...it's probably because I'm not real sure myself."

"You said you were straight earlier," Kane insisted.

"I know, but I think it's just from habit. Sometimes I'm not so sure. I guess you could say I'm still trying to figure things out."

"Oh," Kane said.

"In a way I envy you two, Killian and Asher, I mean. You've got everything all figured out and you have each other and you seem so happy together."

"It's not been easy," I said.

Asher snorted, "That's putting it mildly."

"My brother was killed because he was gay," Kane said, his voice filled with pain.

"I know," Aidan said simply. "I'm sorry."

"Killian almost died, too," Kane continued.

"I knew that too, but I've never heard the whole story about what happened exactly."

Between the three of us we told him the whole story, from the first day I met Seth to the present.

"Wow," he said when we were finished. "You guys have really been through hell and back."

"Tell us something we don't know," Asher mumbled. He seemed to be getting very tired. He buried his face in my chest and his hair tickled my chin.

"But it's awesome how you've each come out stronger because of it. And in a way it forced you to deal with issues that you probably would have let sit unresolved until you were completely confused...like me."

"I guess," I said slowly, "but for me, it wasn't that I really thought I was straight, it was just that I'd never really thought about it either way. And when I did, I knew...it was just a matter of admitting it...to myself. I mean, you have to know whether you are attracted to guys or not. If you are then you're at least bi, right?"

"Geez, Killian, and you yelled at me," Kane grumbled.

"No, it's ok. He's right," Aidan said quickly. "I should know by now. It's something I need to figure out. I can't just keep going along, like, in this limbo."

"I think it'll wait till tomorrow. Go to sleep," Asher's voice came out muffled from where his face was still on my chest, but his annoyance came through loud and clear.

"It is late," Kane said.

"It is," Aidan agreed. "And Asher's right; it's waited this long, it can wait till tomorrow. Can I talk to you some more tomorrow before I leave, Killian?"

"Sure, but I don't know what I can tell you. It's not like I'm an expert on this stuff."

"More of an expert than I am—at least you've been through it. Good night."

"Good night," I said through a yawn.

"G'night," Kane said, and Asher mumbled something that may have been good night, but it was really anyone's guess.

Chapter
23

The next thing I knew it was morning and Adam was bang-
ing on our door telling us we'd slept late enough. I felt like I had
just fallen asleep and my arm was numb from Asher sleeping on
it all night. I pulled it out from under him and he blinked sleepily up at me. There was an imprint on his face from my shirt, and
with his hair all mussed up and his eyes all bleary he looked so
cute that I couldn't resist leaning in for a slow lingering good-
morning kiss.

"Bleah!" Kane yelled. "Not before breakfast, please!"

We all laughed and Asher and I tumbled out of the bed onto
the floor, where an impromptu wrestling match ensued. Aidan sat
on the bed watching us with an amused smile on his lips and a
thoughtful look in his eye. I had a feeling that he wasn't thinking
about the scene before him at all.

The morning flew by as everyone pitched in to clean up the
mess from the previous evening. Before I knew it, it was time for
Mom and Aidan to leave for home. I realized that Aidan and I
hadn't had time for our talk, but then I still didn't know what I
could say anyway, so it was just as well.

The good-byes weren't too drawn out since Mom would be
back in a few weeks for Christmas and there was a chance Aidan
would be coming with her again.

As they were getting in the car, Aidan paused and turned to

me. "Oh, Killian, about our talk last night. I've been thinking about it all day and I think I've got it all figured out—it's guys. Thanks." And he ducked into the car.

Mom and Adam gave me quizzical glances but I just grinned and gave Aidan a thumbs-up. I'd let him tell in his own time.

That night Asher and I were home alone watching *The Matrix* for about the twenty-third time. Adam and Steve had dragged Kane off to Steve's apartment to start packing up his stuff. We were at the helicopter scene when the phone started ringing.

"Pause it," I yelled as I ran for the phone.

I picked up the phone but before I could even speak a strangled voice cried out my name.

"Killian! Is Killian there?"

"May I ask who's calling?" I said cautiously as Asher came up behind me.

"Killian, is that you? This is Jake. Please come over now."

"What? Come over where? Why?"

"Please just come over," he sounded like he was crying. "Gilly and I were home alone and the lights went out. Gilly went to check the breaker but that was, like, half an hour ago and she hasn't come back and I've been calling her and she hasn't answered and I'm scared."

"Maybe she's just playing a joke on you."

"I thought of that. That's why I called you instead of 911. But now I'm getting really scared."

"What's going on?" Asher asked.

I shrugged. "Look Jake, I don't think it's a good idea for me to come over there after the last time. If you're really scared then hang up and call 911."

"Ok, I..." he broke off suddenly. It was deathly quiet on the other end.

"Jake?"

Still nothing. Then, "Who's there?" His voice was hoarse with raw fear.

"Jake?" I said again.

"*Who's there?*" he was screaming now. "Gilly, is that you? This isn't funny."

"Jake, call 911," I said urgently.

"Oh my God," he moaned.

"Jake? What's going on?"

"Please don't—" His voice sounded farther away now.

I heard a short muffled scream followed by a dull thud, then the clattering of the phone as it hit the floor.

"Jake?" I screamed. "Jake, are you there?"

"Hello, Killian," a new voice barely more than a hoarse whisper said into the phone. "I think you know who I am."

At first I thought I was dreaming, that this was all some sort of horrible nightmare and I would wake up in a few minutes still on the couch with Asher just in time for the big morphing finale. I spun around to face Asher. My hands were shaking now and I was having trouble holding onto the phone. I had to hold it with both hands.

"It's nice to talk to you again," the voice continued. "It's been awhile. What's it been? I've seen you since the park, haven't I? Oh yes, at the party. Holy smashed windshield, Batman." He chuckled softly at his own joke.

My whole body seemed to be alternating between extreme hot to extreme cold. I felt myself break out in a cold sweat.

"You know, you're like a bad penny—you just keep showing up. But I think things might be turning around for me tonight. This is an added perk. I didn't even think about Jake calling anyone; I'm getting careless. But since he did, I might as well take advantage of it, no? And he did call just the right person."

"What did you do to Jake?"

"He's still alive, for now. Whether or not he stays that way is up to you."

"What's going on?" Asher said.

"Is that Asher?" the killer crowed. "This just keeps getting better and better. Listen closely. If you want Jake to live, then you and Asher make haste and get over here right away. If you get here in 20 minutes, I'll let Jakie-poo here live. For every minute over that I cut off one body part, starting with the toes."

"I'm calling the police."

"Now that would be a very bad idea. Jake'll be dead before you even dial 9. I'll be long gone before they ever get here. I've gotten away with everything so far, so you know I can do it. Do you want Jake's blood on your hands? Just like Seth's?"

"Oh my God," I whimpered.

"That's right. You know what to do. Be here in 20 minutes or Jake's dead. Oh, and don't even think about calling the police when you hang up. If anyone other than you pulls into this yard, I'll rip Jake's heart out. That reminds me, park under the security light and stand by the car before you come in so I know it's just you and Asher. You can let yourself in."

I heard the click of the receiver being hung up and felt as if everything I had was draining out through the soles of my feet. The phone slipped from my hands.

"Killian, what's going on?" Asher said in a scared voice.

"The killer has Jake."

"What? Call the police!"

"He said if I do he'll kill him before they get there. He said he wants us to come there in 20 minutes or Jake dies."

"We're not going!"

"We have to or Jake will die."

"Killian, think! We have to call the police. They are professionals; they'll deal with this. If we go, we might as well kill ourselves. Besides, how do you know it's not just some sort of sick joke that Gilly and Jake are playing on you?"

"It was him, Asher...the voice..." And suddenly I was in the park, lying on the ground looking up at that dark figure looming over me. There was an excruciating pain shooting through my side and fear that I could taste in the back of my throat. Everything slowly faded to black and just as suddenly the figure above me seemed to morph into Asher.

"Are you ok?" he asked in a panicky voice.

"What happened?"

"I don't know, you just passed out or something."

I sat up. "We have to go."

"Killian, no, we can't! Call the police, they have guns and training..."

"I can get a gun!" I said.

"What? Are you crazy?"

"My dad has a gun."

"No way, Killian! No fucking way!"

I stood up and opened the front door, then turned to face Asher. "You can stay if you want. I'm going and I don't have time to argue." And with that I was gone, running towards my car. I was in it with the engine running when Asher slid into the passenger seat.

"This is totally crazy, but there is no way I am letting you go there alone."

I practically flew to my old house and was very relieved to

see that no one was there. It would make breaking and entering so much easier. I jumped out of the car, leaving it running, and ran to the front door. Without even pausing, I grabbed the brick we kept there to use as a doorstop and smashed in the door window. I reached through and unlocked the door. I raced up the stairs two at a time and into my parents' old bedroom. I yanked open the bedside table drawer and breathed a sigh of relief when I saw the gun was still there. I took it out and looked at it carefully. It was loaded, just as I'd hoped. My dad had made me take shooting lessons the year before in the futile hope that it would make me manlier, and I was very grateful for them now.

I passed Asher on the front step in my race for the car and was already moving as he jumped in. We peeled out of the driveway with screeching tires and tore off down the road at very unsafe speeds. Asher held onto the dashboard with white knuckles and clenched teeth, but he knew better than to say anything. We got to the Sheridan house just before our 20-minute deadline.

I parked under the security light as instructed. I picked up the gun and checked to make sure the safety was off before tucking it into the waistband of my jeans.

"Oh my God! Ohmygod! Ohmagod!" Asher whispered, "Please, please don't do this."

"You don't have to go inside. Just get out of the car and walk up to the house. You can stay outside. It'll be safer that way anyway."

Asher started to cry. "I have never been so scared in my entire life," he managed to say. "But if you think I am going to let you go into that house alone, Killian Travers Kendall, then you don't know me very well."

A cold fury had taken over me that was made me feel detached from everything, as if it was happening to someone else and I was only watching from a distance. Not even Asher's heartfelt outburst seemed to penetrate it. I was filled with hatred for this person who had killed Seth and made my life a living hell in the months since. I wanted that person dead, and I wanted to be the one that killed them.

"Let's go," I said in a deceptively calm voice.

I stepped out of the car and stood for a moment, staring defiantly at the house. I couldn't see anyone, but I knew the killer was watching us from one of those blank windows even as I stood there. I began to stride purposefully towards the house with Asher right at my heels muttering "Oh God! Oh God! Oh

God!" with every step. There wasn't a single light visible in the entire house except for an odd, dim flickering in the window of the door.

The door was unlocked when we reached it, and it swung soundlessly open when I turned the knob. There wasn't even an ominous creaking hinge. The source of the flickering light turned out to be a small oil lamp sitting in the center of the floor. I stepped cautiously inside and looked around but couldn't see anything outside of the small circle of light cast by the lamp.

Asher grabbed my arm, making me jump slightly. "There's something under the lamp," he whispered. I looked closer and saw a scrap of paper tucked under the base. As I leaned down to pick them both up, the security light we had parked under suddenly went out, so that the only source of light we had was in my hand. The meager illumination that it provided suddenly seemed to be less than adequate. I felt a little of my bravado slip away, and a tendril of fear begin to creep into the space left by its departure.

I looked down at the slip of paper and the three words written on it, "HIDE-AND-SEEK."

"What does that mean?" Asher whispered.

"It means the bastard is playing games with us. He wants us to find him." The fury rushed back in with a vengeance. This little game might have been meant to scare us, but it only served to make me more determined to see the killer die before the night was over. I patted the gun and thought that the game should have been tag...and I was it.

"Let's call the police," Asher hissed.

"No," I said loudly, my voice sounding unnaturally loud in the complete silence that surrounded us. "No, let's find him."

I tried to picture the house from the few times I had been in it as we began to search the downstairs, but everything took on a different perspective in the dark. Doors I thought were close by seemed so far away when I searched for them in inky blackness. It was a nerve-wracking process made worse by the fact that the oil lamp kept threatening to gutter out and leave us in total darkness. The not knowing of every game of hide-and-seek in the dark was intensified by the life and death situation at hand.

With the exception of the kitchen, which we couldn't get into because the door seemed to be blocked, we finished the downstairs with nothing more than jangled nerves and then it was time for the second floor. We climbed the stairs cautiously to find every door along the upstairs hallway closed tight. The game of hide-and-seek suddenly took on a sinister feel of the old game show Let's Make A Deal, except we'd be losing much more than money if we chose the wrong door.

I was trying to gather up enough courage to open the first door when Asher grabbed my arm again. He pointed to the crack at the bottom of one of the doors. A very dim light shone through.

As I stood there looking at that sliver of light, I felt all my courage drain away. All I wanted to do was get out of that house, more than anything I'd ever wanted in my life. Such a sense of horror and fear washed over me that my knees actually buckled. It took every ounce of strength that I had not to run screaming out of the house. I took a deep, shaky breath and tried to summon some of the courage I'd had just moments before. I handed the lamp to Asher, whose eyes widened even more than they already were. His shaking hands caused the light to jump and bounce eerily around the hall.

I drew myself up as straight as I could, threw back my shoulders, and drawing another deep breath, stepped forward and threw open the door. It took a moment for my eyes to adjust to the lighting in the room, but when they did I couldn't hold back the cry that escaped from my throat.

All the furniture had been pushed to the outer walls, clearing a sizable space in the center of the room. In the center of that space sat Jake, bound and gagged and tied to a chair, lit only by the single candle at his feet. His chin rested on his chest and his eyes were closed as if he were asleep. A thin trickle of dried blood ran down from a cut above his eye. I couldn't tell if he was breathing or not in the uncertain flickering of the candlelight.

"He's not dead, at least not yet," said a voice from the shadows, almost as if it had read my mind. When he stepped forward, the weak light from the candle revealed a familiar figure from my dreams. He was dressed all in black, just as he had been the first time I saw him, even to the ski mask. The sudden flash of silver in the candlelight brought back an even more vivid memory. The last time I had seen such a flash had been right before I was stabbed. I wondered if it was the same knife; I'd read once that people who killed with knives often use the same one over and over, as a kind of lucky talisman.

"This really must be my night," he rasped with an evil-sounding chuckle. "I had planned on killing Jake, but I must have been a very good boy if Santa's brought me my Christmas presents this early. You two are just an added bonus."

"You said you'd let Jake go if I came," I said, trying my best to keep my voice steady.

"I lied. I do that a lot. Never trust someone who's tried to kill you, Killian."

"Look, you can have me. Just let Asher and Jake go."

"I can have you? Oh how generous. Here's a newsflash for you; I already have you. And Asher. And Jake. It's just a matter of who wants to go first? Let's see, I have so many options. You first while Asher watches in horror, Jake first just because it's the easiest, Asher and Jake first while you watch it all...ooh, I like that last one. Don't you?"

"You're insane," I whispered.

"Probably, but I've always thought that sanity was highly overrated."

"Why? Why are you doing this? If I've hurt you in some way, I'm sorry." I was trying to stall more than anything—it's not like I really cared at this point, I was beyond caring—but I couldn't shoot him because so far he'd kept Jake in between the two of us, and I wasn't a good enough shot to risk hitting my friend.

"Why? It's really very simple, even for your little mind. You're an abomination in the eyes of God. You deserve to die. You and everyone like you. You deserve to be wiped off the face of the earth. You see, Killian, I did everyone a favor by killing Seth, and I'm about to do them an even bigger favor by killing the three of you."

The more he spoke the less disguised his voice became and the more familiar it seemed to me. I had to keep him talking.

"Then why Zack? He wasn't gay. He hated us as much as you."

"I killed Zack because he was an idiot, and idiots are dangerous. He saw me smash your windshield and leave the note, which he read after I left. The stupid fool actually had the nerve to try to tell me what he'd seen and demand that I pay him to stay quiet. He's quiet now, isn't he?" He laughed that cold laugh again and I felt a chill run down my spine.

"It all started when Seth moved here. He was like a virus, spreading to those who were weak, like you. I tried to stop it but it was too late—he'd already corrupted you, and you spread it to Asher and my brother, like a disease. I should have killed you when I had the chance."

His words rang in my ears over and over: my brother. Everything he said after that was lost in the impact of those words. I knew who it was. I knew who the killer was.

I drew a deep breath and steeled myself to make my voice as calm as possible. "So this is all a holy war? A vendetta on God's behalf? How noble of you, to take it upon yourself to purify the world like this. I never thought of you as a particularly religious person...Todd."

His body tensed at the mention of his name, and then he reached up and pulled the mask off, revealing his beautiful face. He was grinning broadly now, delighted that I'd figured out who he was. I'd read somewhere once that Lucifer was God's most beautiful creation, and standing here now looking at Todd I could believe that evil could wear the mask of beauty very easily.

"Very good," he said, as if to a particularly slow pupil who had finally figured out a math equation. "You finally figured it out. I admit it ruins a little of the fun of the situation, but in some ways I like this even better. Now you know who is going to kill you."

"You're going to kill your own brother?"

"He's not really my brother, you know?" he looked down at the still-unconscious Jake. "Not my whole brother anyway. I hate him. I found out the truth about him a few years ago. I overheard my parents fighting. They do that a lot, you know. Usually about Jake. Never about what they should have been fighting about."

I tried to maneuver myself so that I could get a clear shot at him. He didn't seem to notice, he was so caught up in his narrative.

"Everyone thinks we're such a perfect family. They don't know the real story, what goes on behind closed doors. Dad's a deacon at church, Mom volunteers at every church function. No one knows how Dad beats the shit out of us every time we sin. No one knows how my father is an adulterer. No one knows that Jake here is the fruit of his adultery. No one knows how my father has raped Gilly so many times she doesn't even fight it anymore. It has to stop. They all have to be punished. God has said they must die."

In my horror, I had almost forgotten what was happening, but his last words snapped me out of the trance I had fallen into. "Todd," I said softly, "you're right, they need to be punished, but let the law handle it. You don't have to be the one. The killing has to stop. This has to stop."

"Enough!" Todd screamed. "The killing will stop. It will stop when all the sinners have been punished for their wickedness. I have been anointed to carry out the punishment." And with that he grabbed Jake by the hair, yanked his head back, and quickly raised the knife.

"*No!*" I screamed. I pulled the gun out, aimed, and fired in one smooth motion. Everything went into slow motion, each detail permanently engraved into my memory. The sound of the gunshot was deafening. The bullet struck Todd just as he brought the knife down, but the impact slammed him backwards, causing the knife to rip into Jake's shoulder instead of the tender flesh of his exposed neck. I fired a second shot as I heard the sound of shattering glass from behind me. During the exchange with Todd, I had almost forgotten Asher was behind me. Todd's body jerked as the second bullet ripped through his chest. He stared at me with a look of total disbelief, his mouth open as if screaming but no sound was coming out. I raised the gun slightly and fired off a third shot, right between his eyes. And then it was over. Todd was lying dead on the floor in a growing pool of blood, and my ears were still ringing from the shots. It had all happened in less time than it takes to tell it, and now that it was done, I seemed unable to take it all in. I had just killed another human being...and enjoyed it. I felt an immense sense of satisfaction that I had removed this vile person from this world. And that scared me. I stood there with the gun still in front of me for an immeasurable amount of time. It may have been seconds, it could have been minutes, it could have been hours. Slowly I became aware of a crackling sound from behind me and a steadily increasing heat at my back. I dropped the gun and turned slowly around.

Asher lay on his side in the hall. The oil lamp that he'd been holding had shattered and the oil had caught fire. The flames were only a few inches from Asher's face.

"Asher!" I screamed as I leaped over the flames. I dragged him away from the fire and shook him to wake him up. His eyes fluttered open and he focused on my face. "There's a fire," I said urgently. "We have to get Jake out." I pulled him roughly to his feet. Once I was sure he was steady, I jumped the flames, which were already a little higher, and rushed to Jake's side. I fumbled with the knots for several precious minutes before Asher appeared at my side, holding the bloody knife in his hands.

"Cut them," he said softly.

I looked up at him, then grabbed the knife and quickly sawed through the thick ropes. Jake was slippery with blood from his shoulder wound, and by the time the two of us got him out of the chair and propped between us the flames had completely engulfed the doorway.

"How're we going to get out?" Asher said, a note of panic creeping into his voice.

"The window," I suggested. We dragged Jake to the window and I looked out. There was no way; we were on the second floor and there was nothing below us but a concrete driveway.

"We can't!" Asher wailed. The smoke was growing steadily thicker and it was becoming harder to breathe. "Break the window. I need air," Asher said, before bursting into a fit of coughing. I lowered Jake to the floor where the air was a little clearer, then grabbed the chair he had been in and smashed the window outward. Cool air rushed in, allowing us a few precious breaths. Then, with a deafening whoosh, the fire behind us suddenly burst into a raging inferno fed by this new source of oxygen. Asher screamed and shielded his face as a blast of superheated air washed over us. We both dropped to the floor next to Jake.

For a minute all I could think about was the pain. Slowly my mind began to function again. So we die anyway, I thought. Please, God, don't let us die.

"Killian, do you hear something?" Asher asked me, interrupting my prayer.

I listened intently and thought that maybe, just maybe, I heard a voice calling over the roar of the fire.

"Is there someone there?" I screamed.

"Killian?" There was definitely someone there.

"Please, help us!" I called back. "It's me, Asher, and Jake. We can't get through the fire."

"Is the bed on fire?"

I looked over at the bed. It was against the same wall we were and the flames hadn't yet reached it.

"No."

"Get the comforter and wrap it around yourselves, then run through the fire as quickly as you can."

"Are you sure?"

There was a pause. "There's no other choice."

Asher already had pulled the heavy quilt off and crawled

back to me and Jake. We got into crouching position and draped
Jake between our shoulders. Then we draped the quilt over our
head and wrapped the loose ends tightly around our bodies. The
heat was almost unbearable by now, and the light from the fire
even penetrated through the think material of the quilt so that I
could see Asher's face quite clearly.

"Asher, I love you," I sobbed. "If we don't live..."

"We will," he cried.

"But if we don't, I want you to know that I'll always love
you and I'll see you in heaven."

"I love you too, Killian. Always and forever."

"Let's go!" I screamed.

I squeezed my eyes shut and ran as fast as I could in the
direction of the door. It was like running in a three-legged race
with dead weight between us. The heat was like nothing I had
ever felt before. Every nerve in my body seemed to be screaming
in agony, and every breath seared my lungs and throat. I stumbled on the quilt as it unwound from around us, and would have
fallen, but I crashed into what I could only assume was the door
frame with a bone-crunching thud, the full weight of Jake's body
adding to the impact. I ricocheted off and the momentum actually carried us through the door and into the hall.

"This way!" someone screamed from off to our right.

We ran blindly in that direction and didn't stop until we ran
into something soft.

"Oof!" our obstacle grunted from the impact. We went down
in a tangle of smoldering quilt, arms and legs; there seemed to be
too many for the number of people present. When the quilt was
ripped off of us and I saw our rescuers, I understood why...there
were two of them: Judy...and Dash.

"Hurry!" Judy screamed. "We need to get out of here
quickly. That fire is spreading faster than a black snake on a hot
road. This old house is gonna go up like dry tinder."

"Jake is unconscious," I gasped, greedily gulping the relatively cool air. "He's lost a lot of blood."

"Then we'll have to carry him. Dashel and Asher, get his
legs. Killian, you and I will take his arms. Hurry!"

We lifted Jake and careened down the stairs as quickly as
we could without falling. We took a short breather at the bottom
of the stairs while Judy opened the front door.

"You go," I said suddenly. "I'm calling 911." I was gone
before anyone had a chance to say anything. I took off down the

dark hallway and ran into the kitchen door at full speed, bouncing off of it like a rubber ball. The door had only given about an inch before it had hit something. I placed my full weight against it and pain shot down my arm where I'd hit the doorframe earlier, but I did manage to shove the door and its burden a few more inches. It was just enough room for me to squeeze in. I popped through and promptly fell on top of whatever was blocking the door. It didn't take long to realize that it was a person, and from the way it felt...a very dead person.

I didn't even have to time for that to fully register before the second story windows over the kitchen exploded from the heat. The flames leapt out the window, illuminating the kitchen with their ghastly orange glow. I instinctively ducked my head to shield my face and found myself staring into Gilly's wide, vacant eyes. For a moment it wasn't Gilly's face I was seeing, but another young person with the same type of wound.

"I'm so sorry, Seth," I sobbed. "I'm sorry I didn't get there sooner...didn't stop Todd sooner. Oh God, Seth, please..."

Another loud crash from upstairs made me look up, and when I looked back down again Seth was gone and Gilly lay in his place. I clawed my way up the counter and grabbed the phone. Dead! Just like Seth. Just like Zack. Just like Gilly. Just like Todd. So much death. Suddenly it was too much; it was more than I could handle, and huge wracking sobs washed over me as I slid to the floor, wedged between Gilly's lifeless body and the cabinet. Just then the door swung open with a thwack as it slammed into Gilly.

"Killian? Are you in there?" It was Dash.

"Yes," I sobbed.

"We have to get out. The whole second floor is on fire. Mom already called 911 from the car phone. Come on!"

"I...I can't."

"Yes, you can. Why can't I get the door open?"

"It's Gilly."

"She's in there?"

"Yes."

"Is she ok?"

"She's dead."

There was a pause, and then, "There's nothing we can do, then. We need to get out of here, now!" He squeezed his way through the door and looked down at Gilly. "Oh my God!" He gasped when he saw her. He forced himself to look away, then reached down and yanked me roughly to my feet. Still holding my hand, he half-dragged me through the door and into the hall-way. We hadn't gone more than two feet before yet another huge crash boomed above our heads. It was followed by an ominous creaking of wooden beams that stopped us dead in our tracks just seconds before a large section of the ceiling crashed down right in front of us, showering us with sparks and burning debris.

"Is there a back door?" Dash screamed.

I yanked him back towards the kitchen and we raced to the back door. We burst into the cool air of the backyard.

"They're in front, by your car." Dash panted.

We ran around the corner of the house and were about half-way across the front yard when an enormous explosion ripped through the night. We were thrown to the ground as a massive fireball rolled into the sky.

For a moment I just lay there, grateful just to be still and breathing. Finally I forced myself up on the elbow that wasn't throbbing with pain, and then rolled onto my side. I looked back at the house, now completely engulfed in flames, and thought about how close I had come to dying—several times over—in that house that night. But the evil had died with the house and now maybe, just maybe, I could finally begin to heal.

Asher dropped to my side and threw his arms around my neck, sobbing into my shoulder. I wrapped my good arm around him, my injured arm cradled between us, and we rocked back and forth on the lawn. I watched the house burn over Asher's shoul-der. Every square inch of my body was in pain; God only knew how much worse it would get as the adrenaline wore off, but I was alive. And the boy I loved was alive, and for the moment, that was all that mattered.

Epilogue

Christmas that year had a special significance; we were celebrating the gift of life with a new understanding. So much had happened in the last few months that when I look back it seems almost as if I had lived a whole lifetime in that short period. I know I felt as if I had. All of the survivors of the fire gathered on Christmas morning and had a special private time together. We had all been treated to lengthy stays at the local hospital, where we'd been treated for various cuts, bruises, and abrasions, varying degrees of burns, one dislocated shoulder (mine), and smoke inhalation. Some of us required longer stays than others, with Judy and Dash having been the shortest. Jake was the last to be released, only having been discharged a few days before Christmas. His arm was still in a sling and he had to go to rehab daily. He looked much older than he had before, but who could blame him after all he had been through? His long hair was gone now, as was Judy's. What hadn't burned off had been chopped off at the hospital to make it easier to treat their cuts. Judy had gone back to her natural blonde, and for the first time I could see the family resemblance. I was amazed that I hadn't seen it in Dash from the first.

So much information that had been hidden for years came out in the month after the fire that at times I felt like I was just waiting for Jerry Springer to call and say we were booked for the show. I was sure that if I was still confused and shocked, Jake's poor head had to be absolutely spinning.

It had turned out that Judy was Dash's mother. She'd become pregnant when she was very young and the father had promptly abandoned her. Her family had been scandalized and wanted her to have an abortion, but she'd refused and ran off to California, where she had the baby and raised him herself while working as a waitress and going to school at night.

When Dash was two years old, Judy got a call from her sister, Janice, who was pregnant and wanted Judy to come back and help with her two other children, Todd and Gilly, until she had the baby. All her pregnancies had been difficult and she'd lost a baby in between Gilly and this pregnancy. Judy agreed and flew back, bringing Dashel with her. While she was there Tom, Janice's husband, raped Judy. She immediately told Janice, who begged her not to report it. Judy agreed for Janice's sake but left on the next flight. It wasn't long before she realized she was pregnant. She called Janice and told her. A month later Janice showed up on her doorstep. She had lost her baby and now she had an offer for Judy. She wanted to take Judy's baby and raise it as her own. The baby was Tom's anyway, Janice had argued, and besides, they could give him so much more than a single mother with a waitress income. Judy reluctantly agreed, and Janice stayed with her until the baby was born. Janice named him Jacob, and when she took him home she told everyone that she had given birth to him while she was in California staying with her sister.

Judy kept a close eye on things, dropping in unexpectedly and calling often. She had begun to culture her psychic image, purposefully exaggerating when she was around Tom to scare him into believing she was more powerful than she was. It must have worked because he never laid a finger on Jake, even though he routinely abused Todd and Gilly, sexually and physically. Eventually Janice had Jamie and after waiting so long for another child of her own, she became fiercely protective of him, protecting him from Tom's abuse.

In the aftermath of the devastating fire and the even more devastating revelations, Tom committed suicide by shooting himself. Two days later, Janice took an overdose of a prescription sleeping medicine and died in her sleep. Asher's parents took in Jamie, and Jake was given into Judy's custody since she was his birth mother. In the space of just a few days, Jake had lost one entire family and gained a new one. The transition had not been a smooth one, and he had been spending as much time with a psychiatric therapist as his physical therapist. We'd all been in counseling since that night. It turned out that I was suffering from post-traumatic stress disorder; I was having flashbacks that would literally cripple me with fear until they had passed. As I went for twice-weekly counseling sessions, though, these episodes came farther and farther apart.

We were all hailed as heroes by the local media, and the story even made it to the national level. Dan Rather interviewed us all for a special episode of 60 Minutes. It was almost more excitement than I could handle, and I was very relieved when the hoopla died down and things began to return to some semblance of normalcy. I was thankful for the president's latest gaffe, since it diverted the media's attention elsewhere. Bad news sells better than good news, it seems.

All the attention from the press did, however, serve one very positive purpose: it spawned a special investigation into the police department and its alleged mishandling of Seth's murder case. Charges of misconduct and homosexual prejudice sprung up from militant gay rights activists all over the country. In the process, a level of corruption was discovered that led directly to—surprise—dear old dad. He was forced to resign amid flying accusations as all his underlings scrambled to drop the whole ball of wax in his lap, and he was now facing more charges than his lawyer could keep up with. I was ashamed to admit that I felt a certain amount of grim satisfaction at all of this. I had more than a few conversations on the subject with my counselor.

On a happier note, Steve did move in with Adam, Kane, and me; that was one transition that came off without a hitch. Mom decided to stay in Pennsylvania with Aunt Kathy, but she agreed that I could stay with Adam and Asher at least until I graduated.

After Christmas Judy, Dash, and Jake planned to fly back to California. Jake told me that while part of him didn't want to leave, he was looking forward to starting over in a new place where there weren't ghosts from his old life waiting around every corner.

Perhaps the happiest note of all, at least as far as I was concerned, was that Asher and I were closer than ever. It seems that facing death together brings people together in a way nothing else can. I was beginning to think that maybe Asher was right, and true love does conquer all. I was definitely sure that we could conquer anything that life could throw in front of us...as long as we faced it together.

Adam parked the car, and he, Kane and I climbed out. We walked side-by-side across the emerald green grass; daffodils waved their cheery heads, and robins hopped out of our way as we went. Spring had exploded full force upon the Shore the way it always did—without warning. Last week, temperatures had been in the low 30s and now we walked comfortably in short-sleeved shirts. It was an idyllic scene, except for one thing—we were in a cemetery. We'd come to plant a flower on Seth's grave.

Wordlessly, we knelt down in a small semi-circle in front of Seth's simple granite headstone and Adam dug into the soft earth. Then he shook the plant out of its pot and placed it lovingly into the hole, filling it in and watering it with the small jar of water we'd brought.

It was a bleeding heart. It wasn't blooming yet, but it would in time, just as we would heal in time.

Still without speaking a word, we stood up and started to leave. I paused and turned back to the grave as Adam and Kane went on.

"I chose the right path, didn't I, Seth?" I whispered, and then turned and walked away.

Available soon from
Renaissance Alliance

Jacob's Fire
By Nan DeVincent Hayes

Jacob, a university professor/scientist has found a formula to cure AIDS—a formula that causes mass destruction if improperly used. The government and a private pharmaceutical firm want Jacob's formula, and go to brutal, vicious, murderous means to get it. But Isleen, the pharmaceutical rep who is assigned to cajole him into selling the formula to her firm, refuses to exert unethical means, and, instead, she and Jacob eventually become friends and allies who try to fight "Big Government." Isleen tries convincing Jacob that world events are following biblical prophecy, the end time is near, and that he should reconsider his staunch Judaic position. She wants him to believe that the Second Coming of Christ is at hand.

Mystery, intrigue and suspense intertwine with secret societies and politics while the global leaders attempt to form a "New World Order" on the political, religious, and economic levels. Jacob innocently gets caught up in this web of shadow organizations and soon finds himself trying to find an antidote for the plague that has been unleashed on the world, all the while watching as the prophecies Isleen told him about continue to unfold. In the end, Jacob must make a decision on the Truth before it is too late.

Other titles from
RENAISSANCE ALLIANCE

Darkness Before the Dawn
By Belle Reily

Chasing Shadows
By C Paradee

Forces of Evil
By Trish Kocialski

Out of Darkness
By Mary D. Brooks

Glass Houses
By Ciarán Llachlan Leavitt

Retribution
By Susanne M. Beck

Storm Front
By Belle Reilly

Coming Home
By Lois Cloarec Hart

And Those Who Trespass Against Us
By H. M. Macpherson

You Must Remember This
By Mary D. Brooks

Restitution
By Susanne M. Beck

Available at booksellers everywhere.

Josh Aterovis is a twenty-four year old starving artist and author from the Eastern Shore of Maryland. He lives with his partner, their cat and one fish in a small house complete with white picket fence. *Bleeding Hearts* is his first novel. He is currently putting the finishing touches on the second book in the series and working on the third. Aterovis is a pseudonym which means Black Sheep in Latin.

Printed in the United States
2251